THREADS

OF

DECEPTION

To Mark,
Happy Reading!
♡

THREADS

OF

DECEPTION

A SUDDENLY FRENCH MYSTERY

ELLE JAUFFRET

LEVEL
BEST BOOKS

Jauffret

First published by Level Best Books 2024

This novel is entirely a work of fiction. The names, characters and incidents portrayed in it are the work of the author's imagination. Any resemblance to actual persons, living or dead, events or localities is entirely coincidental.

Elle Jauffret asserts the moral right to be identified as the author of this work.

First edition

ISBN: 978-1-68512-751-0

Cover art by Ebook Launch

This book was professionally typeset on Reedsy.
Find out more at reedsy.com

To Aiden and Neil,
And to people with accents—you are music to the world.

Praise for Threads of Deception

"Elle Jauffret spins a powerful, complex, and compelling mystery! *Threads Of Deception* dives deep into the human experience and does so with elegance and insight. Highly recommended!" Jonathan Maberry, *New York Times* bestselling author of *NecroTek* and *The Dragon in Winter*

"A charming traditional mystery with a unique French twist—and a captivating mix of fashion, food, and fascinating characters! Elle Jauffret is a smart and fresh new voice, and this chic, cinematic, and unpredictable story, revealed in a gorgeous setting, will keep you turning the pages as fast as you can."—Hank Phillippi Ryan, *USA Today* bestselling author of *One Wrong Word*

"*Threads of Deception* is a fast-paced mystery with unique characters, refreshing humor, and unexpected adventures that will keep you turning pages. Jauffret's use of an unusual medical condition, fascinating backstory, and vivid setting add to the intrigue and interest, but her descriptions of scrumptious food will have you planning a visit to the nearest French bakery. By the last page, she's left just enough breadcrumbs to draw you forward into what will no doubt be a delightful series you'll enjoy with a book in one hand and *pain au chocolat* in the other."—Annette Lyon, *USA Today* bestselling author of *Just One More*

"Elle Jauffret's *Threads of Deception* is a delectable debut novel in which Jauffret stitches together a mouth-watering mystery that will leave readers hungry for more!"—Daphne Silver, Agatha Award-winning author of *Crime and Parchment*

"With a charming and confident heroine, a sexy police detective, and dripping with Hollywood intrigue, *Threads of Deception* is a must-read for mystery lovers, a fierce debut for author Elle Jauffret!"—Gretchen McNeil, author of *Ten* and the #murdertrending series

"When it comes to serving up an intriguing, unique and satisfying mystery, Jauffret is the crème de la crème."—Wendy Toliver, bestselling author of *Regina Rising* and *Red's Untold Tale*

"Death and deception in the cut-throat world of fashion? Yes, please! *Threads of Deception* was such a delicious ride. Claire Fontaine is a smart and likeable protagonist in the vein of Finlay Donovan and Aurora Teagarden. Highly recommend!"—Lorien Lawrence, author of the Fright Watch series and *The Many Hauntings of the Manning Family*

A Note from the Author

Dear Readers,

Three quotes have inspired this book:

- "An accent can be an entry into a character." —Toni Colette
- "Rather than love, than money, than fame, give me truth." —Henry David Thoreau
- "Never eat more than you can lift." —Miss Piggy

To schedule a talk with your book club (online or in person), comment or ask a question about my book(s), please, visit https://ellejauffret.com/Contact. I look forward to hearing from you!

Chapter One

The white sand beaches and quaint colonial revival homes of Claire Fontaine's hometown were only thirty miles away. Yet, the coastal town and year-round sunshine felt out of reach, thanks to the overzealous action of a misguided U.S. Customs and Border Protection (CBP) agent. Now, the only view Claire was forced to enjoy was the prison-grey walls of the San Diego Airport Detention Center. The chair on which she sat and the table where her purse rested were both bolted to the concrete floor.

"I'm not going to ask you again. Where's your foreign passport?" Auggie McGraw demanded, pacing the room. He was about 5'2" with tiny shoulders and a big, red face as if he were about to explode. A ripe beefsteak tomato filled with steam. What had triggered his anger was a mystery to Claire. Probably constipation, she thought after noticing several grease stains on his black polo shirt. She wanted to share with him the recipe of her wonderfully laxative and delicious kale-prune smoothie, but it didn't seem like the most opportune moment.

"I've already told you. I don't have a foreign passport. I'm an American. Californian born and raised." Claire spoke slowly, enunciating as much as she could despite her lazy tongue and aching jaw.

She shifted on her chair and winced. Her hips and back had fully healed since "the explosion," but sitting too long on a hard surface put painful pressure on her tailbone. Unlike her work colleagues, Claire was the only one to survive the bombing of her law firm. After days in a coma followed by weeks of physical and speech therapy, Claire was ready to restart her life.

She had taken her doctor's recommendation to "take it easy" seriously, and she had followed the FBI's advice to "relocate and stay low for a little while." Her return to Caper Cove was to accomplish just that. But her return to Southern California didn't start as smoothly as she had hoped.

"Where's my luggage? You have no right or basis to detain me," she said in her most patient voice. As a criminal attorney, she did her best to cooperate with authority figures, but this was getting ridiculous. On top of that, she was starving. She hadn't eaten since the night before and was craving fish tacos and beignets—the comfort food on which she had grown.

"Oh yeah. We've got plenty basis." He pointed at his chest and tapped at his polo's U.S. Department of Homeland Security logo as if the patch and the embroidered *U.S. Customs & Border Protection* underneath were justification enough. "We've reasonable suspicion you're lying."

"Lying?" she frowned, struggling to understand the man's obstinate determination to believe she was foreign. "Lying about what?"

The agent shot her a superior, I'm-smarter-than-you smile. "About the purpose of your presence here in San Diego and why you switched seats with the old grandma on the plane on your way here?"

"I've already told you. I gave the elderly lady my seat because it was her first time on a plane, and she wanted to look out the window," she explained. Obviously, no good deed ever went unpunished. "I'm returning home to Caper Cove. I've spent the last ten years in Washington, D.C., working for the law firm of Beaumont, Farrell, and Volk. Just Google my name; you'll see."

"An American and a lawyer? With that accent?" He scoffed. "Yeah, right."

Claire inhaled slowly through her nose—one, two, three, four—and held her breath.

Here we go again, she thought. She might have physically survived an explosion, but the head trauma she suffered had left her with a speech disorder. Something called Foreign Accent Syndrome (FAS). An accent so strong that she couldn't recognize herself when she spoke. An accent that always made people assume she was a French tourist on vacation.

She exhaled through her mouth, mentally counting to four again, a technique called box breathing, which the Navy SEALS and litigation lawyers like she was, utilize to relieve stress.

"If you're going to keep me here, which is unconstitutional, by the way, let me at least answer my texts. I was supposed to meet my friend an hour ago; it would be rude of me not to inform her of the delay." Suggie was probably worried to death about her. Claire had called her immediately upon landing and was looking forward to spending the next two weeks with her childhood best friend.

The agent snorted. "Your friend? You mean, your accomplice. We've found knives in your bag. All with a gold handle."

"My chef's knives?" The gourmet knives had been a gift from Judge Pike, a federal court judge and her late mentor, to celebrate their common love of cooking when she made partner at her firm. The utensils were the only valuable property Claire owned after having lost everything in the blast. They were not only the tools of her new trade, they were also a daily reminder that life must go on despite grief and loss, that accepting a private chef position in Caper Cove was the best way for her to heal far from the East Coast and move on.

"Yeah, your knives. 'Fess up. You some kind of killer for hire who likes her weapons shiny and sharp?"

Claire exploded in laughs. Did this man really think she was a knife-thrower on a killing mission? Where was she: in a circus, interrogated by a clown? Wait... She looked around the tiny room and paused at the two-way mirror. "Okay, I get it. You've got me. This is one of those hidden camera shows, isn't it?"

She rose from her chair, walked toward the dark window, and flattened her face against the glass, squinting to see on the other side. Wondering what network or production company was behind the glass and on which network it would air.

"Sit down, or I'm going to handcuff you to the table!" the constipated man shouted, jolting her. His warning was specific, his fists were pumping air, and anger tainted his tone—three unequivocal signs of danger.

The agent's threat suddenly registered in Claire's head. This wasn't a joke.

The man in front of her really believed she was a criminal, a menace in a pink silk blouse, designer jeans, and shiny black pumps. And he wasn't ready to let her go, no matter how many times she explained who she was or why she was here. So, she did the first thing that crossed her mind.

She screamed.

Chapter Two

"The lungs you have on you! You could have been an opera singer or freediver. We could hear you from the main terminal," Suggie Oh said between laughs. "Using screaming as a weapon to draw attention was brilliant. But I'm surprised you didn't press charges."

"I'm just happy it's over." Claire reclined in her seat and bit heartily into the crispy Bungeo-ppang Suggie had bought her. The fish-shaped Korean pastry was a welcome tradition Suggie always made to celebrate her friend's return. Claire closed her eyes and let the sweet red bean and the car's gentle vibration melt her tension away.

The warm air rushed through the open windows and ruffled her French bob, reminding Claire how much she had missed San Diego County's temperate weather.

"Aren't you going to file a complaint at least?" Suggie glanced in Claire's direction, her long black curls floating in a ponytail behind her. "I'm surprised that years of criminal litigation haven't made you ruthless. Especially after your firm's bombing."

"To be honest, that surprises me too," Claire said. They both laughed. Growing up, Claire had never left a wrong unaddressed and unrectified. "The agent was so embarrassed he shriveled and almost crawled under the table. I doubt he'll pull a power trip like that anytime soon. His supervisor swore to send him to sensitivity training and maybe relocate him."

Besides, Claire had promised herself to avoid any contentious situations or litigious matters and to focus entirely on her health and her new job as a private chef. And, of course, to get reacquainted with her childhood home.

"If that's what you wish."

As the car swerved left, the small town of Caper Cove, population ten thousand (not counting the thousands of year-round tourists), appeared in the distance. The sight of her childhood home wiped Claire's mind clean of the airport incident. The marina, the pier, and the colorful colonial revival houses hadn't changed since she left. With its miles of shorelines, white sand beaches, and historic lighthouse, it was hard not to fall in love with this small resort town on the spot.

"You sure you don't want to stop by your dad's first and grab a bite to eat?" Suggie asked as she stopped at an intersection. A sign indicated left to Caper Cove Village or right to Golden Peak (also known as *Millionaire Row*).

"I'm sure. Vee's waiting for me, and I don't want to be late my first day on the job. I need to check in with the head of production to get information on the crew members' diet restrictions and allergies. I can't afford to kill someone on my first catering gig. And I really need that paycheck."

When she had accepted the partner position days before the attack on her law firm, Claire had emptied her bank accounts to pay the firm's required capital contribution each new partner had to make. A payment that had turned into smoke and ashes as a criminal explosion eradicated her office. Now, Claire was officially broke with only three hundred dollars left in her bank account. She needed that catering job. Besides lawyering, cooking was her only marketable skill and way to support herself. To say that she was eager to start working and prove herself as a talented private chef was an understatement. She was desperate. The thought of having to financially depend on her father was unbearable.

Suggie threw her an inquisitive stare before turning right toward Caper Cove's highest peak. "The insurance hasn't sent you a check yet?"

"No, they're withholding all payments while they're investigating the bombing. But I consider myself lucky. My health insurance has covered everything from my hospital stay to my physical therapy and will pay for my speech therapy for as long as I need it."

"Personally, I love your new accent. It perfectly fits your French bob hairstyle and northern Mediterranean complexion. Who knew a tragedy could turn a badass attorney into a sexy French chef?"

Claire laughed as she watched the red-bricked public library and blue wooden post office pass by. She should consider herself lucky. She could have been plagued with a German or Russian accent, or even African or Chinese—which would have made it difficult to navigate through life. People tended to hastily judge others based on their elocution, mocking or rejecting those who appeared or sounded different. She had observed how members of the jury harbored skepticism towards witnesses who spoke with certain accents, dismissing or ridiculing them solely on linguistic differences.

"If only I spoke French, that would make my accent more tolerable." Like most thirty-five-year-olds, Claire had forgotten most of what she learned from the French classes she took in high school. The foreign words she recalled the most were Korean words and phrases Suggie had taught her, so she could politely greet Suggie's grandparents.

"Jokes aside, what about your tax return? Didn't it go through after the bombing?"

"Well, that's sort of a surprise." As a newly minted caterer and Suggie's maid of honor, Claire had spent all her money pre-ordering the ingredients for her best friend's upcoming wedding.

"What do you mean a surprise?" Suggie asked as she parked the car on the street in front of 179 Golden View, their destination.

Claire stepped out of the car and paused in front of the mansion that would be her place of work and lodging for the next two weeks. Built atop a cliff overlooking the ocean, the property exuded an aura of exclusivity and tranquility. Behind its wrought iron gate, the sunlit courtyard beckoned with the scent of jasmine.

Suggie gasped. "That's where you'll be staying?"

"Yes. And this is where you'll get married in twelve days. Ta-dah!" Claire said, extending both arms and hands outward, fingers splayed in the opulent residence's direction, like a magician showcasing his magic. "Your mom told me that you'd given up on finding a wedding venue within your budget and devolved into having a city hall ceremony. As your BFF and your maid of honor, I couldn't let you pass on your dream wedding, so I asked Vee to use the house. She agreed."

Suggie's eyebrows shot up. "Here? At your place of work?"

"The film production's only using it for about a week. After that, it's ours for the entire weekend. I've pre-ordered everything to prepare a feast for up to one hundred fifty people."

"You did all this for me?" Suggie's eyes welled up with tears. "With our decision to get married before Daniel's deployment, we didn't think it was possible..."

"Your mom helped. And Vee wrote the villa rental in my employment contract, so everything's guaranteed to work. You're going to have your dream wedding, after all."

"But...you spent all your money."

"Don't worry about it. Working on that TV show is going to give me a lot of exposure. After Vee's social media endorsement posts, I should get a few referrals and be propelled on my new career path. Hashtag Private Chef Claire should gain enough traction for me to get steady employment and be financially stable."

Vee Brooks was a rising fashion designer and the star and favorite finalist of the highly popular Fashion Warriors TV show. She was also the first legal client Claire had defended in a court of law. Vee had only been sixteen years old at the time, and Claire had represented her as part of her pro bono criminal defense clinic while finishing her last year of law school. The not-guilty verdict had been the seed of their friendship and life paths. When Claire found herself unable to return to work as a criminal attorney, it was Vee who offered her the job as a caterer for the show. All the cooking-for-singles classes she attended and the culinary retreats at the French Culinary Institute Claire had taken over the years were finally paying off.

"I'm so excited for you. Catering for the Fashion Warriors finale is *huge*. Having my wedding here, in the same amazing house, is a dream come true." Suggie threw her arms around Claire's neck. "Thank you."

"That's what besties are for." She freed herself from Suggie's embrace and handed her a tissue from the dashboard Kleenex box. "Let's go check out the house and take a peek at Vee's collection."

"Yes!" Suggie whisper-shouted between happy sobs.

Claire pulled her luggage from the car's trunk and led the way to the gate. She pressed the buzzer and waited for the speaker to crackle with Vee's welcoming voice, but no one answered.

"She must be in her creative mode with her earbuds on," Claire explained as she dialed Vee's number on her phone. No one picked up. That was strange. Vee was punctual. She knew Claire would be arriving around twelve noon, right when Vee herself took her daily break to get her insulin shot. "Good thing she gave me the code of the gate and the house."

"Are you sure?" Suggie asked. "She's a celebrity now. Maybe she forgot."

Claire laughed. "It's unlikely. Vee's extremely reliable. But don't worry, she told me to make myself at home if I arrived in her absence. You see the security camera, right over the garage door?" Claire pointed at the black dome camera affixed to the gable. "It'll announce our presence."

After checking her phone to retrieve the gate code Vee had messaged her, Claire punched the four digits into the entry keypad. With Suggie in tow, she unlatched the pedestrian gate, ambled to the villa, passing the Fashion Warriors Productions vans which obstructed the driveway. Claire was about to punch the code on the next keypad when she noticed its green light. The door handle gave in under Claire's pressure and the door creaked open.

"This is weird. The door's unlocked," Claire said as she pushed the large wooden and glass door and stepped on the foyer's white marble floor.

"Not that weird. Caper Cove's always been a really safe town. Away from the resort, most people still leave their doors unlocked."

"Maybe, but Vee and the TV crew are from L.A. and New York. No urban residents in their right mind would leave a door unlocked no matter where they were." Claire parked her rolling suitcases by the door and paused at the base of the double staircase. "Vee? It's me, Claire. I'm with my friend Suggie," she shouted.

No answer.

To the right of the foyer, through double French doors, was a large entertainment/family room, then an office and a state-of-the-art gym at the end. Straight ahead, in the t-shaped portion of the house, was a huge ballroom with crystal chandeliers and bay windows looking out on an emerald-green lawn and the ocean. The bedrooms, each with a door of a different color, were located at the far west corner. The blue one was supposed to be Claire's, but before she could settle in her new home, Claire needed to find Vee.

"The place is gorgeous. I can't believe I'm getting married here!" Suggie's eyes shined bright and wide with excitement. "Where to now? To the left of the foyer, or up the stairs?"

"Let's check the kitchen. Vee always makes blue jasmine tea whenever we get together."

Claire dialed Vee's number again, perking up her ears in an attempt at locating her friend's phone, but to no avail. Beside the sound of chirping birds and brisling foliage, she could hear a whistling kettle.

"This way." Claire strode back, a knot tightening in her chest and stomach, filling her with unease. It wasn't like Vee to fail to lock the front door, or forget her guests' arrival—growing up in an inner-city neighborhood where every building had barred windows teaches you to always latch your door.

"Vee?" Claire called out again.

They wandered farther back, past a formal living room and a formal dining room, before arriving in a huge kitchen. With its commercial stainless-steel appliances, including a refrigerator with transparent doors and its white marble countertops, the room seemed straight out of the pages of Architectural Digest. A bright red kettle whistled on the stove. Claire turned the gas off and swept the room with her gaze. A teapot, three mugs, and a plate of Linzer cookies had been set on a tray on the counter.

Suggie pointed at the wide-open folding patio doors. "She must have gone outside."

Claire nodded and stepped onto the tiled patio. "Vee?"

Grey clouds veiled the sun, turning the initially sunny day into an overcast April afternoon. A manicured lawn spread several yards toward the cliff edge where an infinity pool gleamed. Glass railings delineated the property except to the right, where an opening broke the continuity of the protective fence. Built alongside the ridgeline, an insanely steep wooden staircase led to the beach. The barrier-free parcel of dirt surrounding the landing was blooming with wildflowers up to the precipice. The perfect picture spot for a social media post without a railing obstructing the ocean view. A blanket had been spread near the blossoming daffodils, allium, and anemones. On it rested a tipped-over plastic cup and a plate of sushi. A single red pump lay a few feet away.

"Vee?" Claire approached the picnic setting.

The proximity of the blanket to the cliff's brink was peculiar, especially since Vee suffered from vertigo. She would've never ventured, even less set up her lunch, so close to the edge, Claire thought.

A chilly breeze rushed through the backyard. Claire's scalp began to prickle.

"Vee?" Worry tainted Claire's voice. Her shoulder tensed, and a wave of apprehension hit her as she inched toward the ledge.

"Be careful. We've had a lot of rain lately; the cliff edge might be unstable," Suggie cautioned as she retreated backward to the safety of the patio.

Claire nodded and cautiously ventured to the wooden staircase. Heights didn't faze her, her D.C. apartment had been located on the 27th floor. However, the structural integrity of the staircase seemed precarious. She shook the railing with both hands, making sure that it was solid enough to sustain her weight, and glanced down the hundreds of steps.

Down below, to the right of the staircase, a woman in a yellow dress with a single red shoe was lying with her arms stretched in front of her. Face down in the sand.

A sharp-edged wind slashed against Claire's face.

"Vee!"

The woman didn't react to Claire's screams, and seagulls started to pick at the woman's legs.

"Vee!" Claire shouted again.

Claire flew down the stairs, propelled by a state of panic and overwhelming fear, yelling Vee's name until she reached the sand. She kneeled by the woman, turned her face up, and tried to get a pulse. Her friend looked like a discarded ragdoll. Several bruises and scrapes covered her arms and legs, possibly from the fall. By the unnatural angle of her neck, her blueish skin, and her mangled face, Claire could tell that any reanimation attempt would be futile. As a criminal attorney, Claire had seen her share of dead bodies, but never had it been the one of a close friend.

She pulled her phone from her back pocket and dialed 911.

"What's the nature of your emergency?" a distant voice asked.

"I'm on the beach, straight down the cliff from 179 Golden View," she said, catching her breath, struggling to enunciate clearly despite her stress-induced French accent. "My name's Claire Fontaine. My friend has been killed."

Chapter Three

The forensic photographer hurried to take the required pictures before the high tide washed away any evidence. The EMTs waited patiently with an empty stretcher, nervously bouncing on their feet, wondering whether they would have time to take the body by land before the waves reached the cliff. The lifeguard/rescue truck had already left, knowing the shore would soon be underwater.

Claire was more worried about shielding the corpse from the destructive power of the ocean water on evidence than capturing the scene on film. She had already taken multiple pictures of the body and its surroundings while waiting for the police to show up. Despite her wish to leave murder cases to her past life, the sight of her dead friend had yanked her back into her investigating criminal attorney mode.

"And you're sure it's Vee Brooks?" Detective Torres asked as he jumped sideways to spare his dress pants and high-top sneakers from the salty onslaught of an incoming wave.

"Yes, I'm sure." Though the question annoyed Claire, the detective was right to ask. The fall down the cliff had damaged Vee's face. "She was missing from the house, but she was expecting me. Her other red shoe is on top of the cliff, and that's her tattoo." A wave of grief hit her as she pointed at her friend's wrist, where an inked green leaf stood out against the pale skin.

When Vee had gotten her tattoo, Claire had accompanied her. They were celebrating Vee's release after Claire defended her in juvenile court and obtained a not-guilty verdict. The single laurel leaf symbolized Vee turning a new leaf. It also signified a step toward victory as Vee quit her rebellious life to embrace the right path. Vee had tried to convince Claire to get a matching design, but Claire had been too chicken at the time.

"Done. Body's ready to go!" the photographer shouted.

The EMTs transferred Vee's soaked body to the stretcher and hurried north, where one of the neighbors had offered them to use their funicular—the private cable car that would take them up the cliff.

With a quick head tilt and a nod, the detective invited Claire to join them. She accepted the offer readily and accompanied the three men and Vee's corpse to the lift. The ascension to Golden View would be faster than she would manage climbing back the hundreds of steps of the wooden staircase on her own.

"I'm sorry for your loss, but frankly, I don't know why I was called here. Looks like an accident to me," Detective Torres said as the funicular quickly ascended. "Your friend stepped too close to the edge and fell. Tourists don't realize how unstable the cliffs can be, especially after the rain. I'm sure you get this type of accident in France."

Claire inhaled deeply through her nose and bit her bottom lip. Though she wanted to tell him she wasn't French and that her accent was a speech disorder caused by a recent concussion, she didn't have the time to provide him with a lengthy explanation. She had just found her friend dead and needed to understand what had happened.

"It wasn't an accident."

Detective Torres' eyebrows peaked. "You saw someone push her?"

"No, it just can't be an accident. Vee suffers… suffered from vertigo," she said, fighting her tongue and her brain to focus on her pronunciation. "She would have never ventured close to the edge on her own. Just yesterday, she told me that she only stayed on the terrace and didn't dare approach the wooden staircase leading to the beach."

"So you believe she was pushed?"

Pushed, dragged, baited, purposefully distracted, or maybe even blinded. There were many words and many scenarios that could explain what had happened. But, *accident* wasn't one of them. Claire could feel it in her bones. "I'm not sure, but it's worth inquiring."

Deep lines formed on the detective's brow. "Your friend's death's tragic, but you don't need to complicate things. I don't know how you do this in France, but here, we call a tragic fall what it is."

Claire crinkled up her nose. "I don't know how they do it in France either, but in Washington D.C., and any other American locale with a decent police department, we investigate suspicious deaths." She wanted to say more, but the funicular pinged loudly, and its doors opened as soon as it arrived at the top. She quickly exited the lift and watched the EMTs carry the stretcher to the waiting ambulance outside. Then, she followed Detective Torres back to Vee's villa through a private side gate.

"You okay?" Suggie asked as she hurried to Claire's side.

"I'm not sure. I can't believe Vee's dead." Claire hugged her friend, grounding herself, redirecting her focus from the shock and her racing thoughts to the present moment until her heartbeat retrieved its slower pace. She swallowed hard, burying sadness and anger deep within herself, a silent pact she made as a young death row attorney. Tears were a distraction in the pursuit of truth.

A small crowd had flooded the backyard's lawn. A dozen people in Fashion Warriors Production T-shirts, curious neighbors, and the police officers interviewing them. Some were crying, others holding each other.

"What's going on?" Claire asked.

"They all came back from their lunch at the same time. They said Vee killed herself."

"What? Who's saying that?"

Suggie directed her gaze to a woman in fluorescent pink, strappy cargo pants, and Dolly Parton hair who was flashing her bedazzled phone to Detective Torres. Her name was Cordelia Jones. Claire remembered her from the second season of the show, during which the woman won every pattern-making challenge. "See, look," she said, tapping at her phone screen with pointy manicured nails. "This was no accident. She jumped to her death. She said so in her text!"

"Can I see that, please?" Claire plucked the device from the woman's hand. The woman let it go without resistance, a smile on her face from delivering

15

the scoop.

Claire squinted at the screen in disbelief. The text had been sent from Vee's number, but the message didn't make any sense. It read: *I can't do this anymore. Goodbye.* Vee never used the words *can't* and *goodbye.* She hated these two words!

"When did you get that text?" Claire asked.

"Twenty minutes or so ago. We were all having lunch when my phone pinged." Cordelia gave her an inspective once-over and looked Claire straight in the eyes. "Why? Who are you?"

"Claire Fontaine. I'm the one who found Vee. She was my friend," she stuttered. "This can't be right. I talked to her last night; she was feeling great." There was no way Vee took her own life. Even in the far remote possibility she did, she would have called Claire first, or at least added her as a recipient to her text.

A sixty-something-year-old man, who resembled a tall garden-gnome in a red pinstripe suit and a brown toupee, approached her. Claire recognized his face and his narrow, cold-blue eyes from the pictures Vee had sent her. It was Karl Smith, the Fashion Warriors show creator and producer.

"Personally, I'm not surprised. The stress of the competition might have been too much for her to handle," he said in a matter-of-fact tone. "Design competitions are stressful, creatively, physically, and emotionally. The finalists often push themselves beyond limits. Many participants suffer breakdowns in the wake of the event."

Claire shook her head energetically. "There's no way Vee killed herself. She was confident and upbeat about the competition, and she was the clear favorite."

"Being popular and confident didn't make her less prone to breakdowns," the man added with an ounce of condescension. "Considering her past, that girl was ripe for a mental blowout."

"What do you mean considering her past?" Detective Torres grabbed his pen from his pocket and scribbled on his notepad.

Suggie imitated him and started to take notes on her phone.

Karl Smith shook his head and shrugged as if the answer to the detective's question was obvious. "She was struggling with addiction."

Claire wanted to shout, "Not since she was sixteen," refusing to give credence to the producer's words. Vee had been clean for a decade and had just received her ten-year sobriety medallion. She had been so proud of it she had texted a picture to Claire. But Claire couldn't share that knowledge with the world. As Vee's former attorney, she was required to keep the personal details of Vee's life private. Even in her late friend's defense. She was bound by the attorney-client privilege and the rules of professional conduct. Vee's juvenile record had been sealed and was to remain undiscoverable. She had given Vee her word.

"No, she wasn't," Claire corrected.

Torres turned to Claire. "Can you expand on that?"

"In the ten years I've known her, Vee never drank or consumed drugs. She was a purist in that sense. She wouldn't even drink coffee because she considered it a mood-altering substance."

"Yep. She believed in that crap about the body being a temple and that people shouldn't taint it with anything other than organic, unprocessed food. Because of her, alcohol was barred from the set. We couldn't even have a beer here after work," a camera crewman added.

A low hum of agreement rose from the TV crew.

"Yet, it looks like Sober Vee was enjoying wine on her own," Cordelia said as she pointed at the clear, tipped-over cup. "That's a cocktail to-go cup. I got the same for lunch."

Claire shook her head. No way it was Vee's drink. Vee wouldn't even let her use pure vanilla extract in her cooking since the solution contained thirty-five percent ethyl alcohol—something Vee avoided because of her husband's own struggle with addiction.

"Have you contacted her husband?" Claire asked.

Torres turned to one of his deputies. "Did you call next of kin?"

"No, not yet, Sir. We were waiting for you."

Torres scowled, perplexed. "Waiting for me, what for?"

"Her husband is Clay Poderas, sir. We thought it better if you placed the call yourself."

A deep furrow appeared between Torres' eyebrows. "Clay Poderas, as in the running contender for the governor's office?"

"The one, sir."

"Why didn't you tell me earlier?" Detective Torres beckoned the three police officers closest to him. "You, take a picture of everyone and everything, then clear the scene and seal the perimeter. You," he said, pointing at the second, "I need the names, contact info, and background check on everyone here. And you," he said to the third police officer, "put a priority rush on that autopsy. Tell the coroner this is the wife of a running governor. Go!"

Claire smiled with bitter sadness. The only reason the detective proceeded to secure the scene was because Vee was the wife of a politician, a potentially powerful man. Not because he believed Claire's suspicion of foul play or because he thought Vee's death warranted a thorough investigation.

"You don't believe it was a crime, do you?" she asked him.

"Nope. Just going by the book. It's protocol to consider any injury involving a politician's family a crime." He gave her a once-over and added. "Same with beautiful women and loaded tourists. Like the poor and the uglies don't matter."

Claire paused a second before interjecting and nodded. From years of defending innocents who had been unfairly sentenced, she knew about the justice system's systemic unfairness. Individuals' socio-economic status often dictated the level of attention or diligence their cases received, leaving the poor and under-represented at a distinct disadvantage. "But there're many indicators that a crime was committed here."

"Enough with the theories, lady. This isn't a true crime podcast. Right now, you need to let us do our job and leave the premises. This is officially a crime scene. From now on, the house is under restricted, police-only access."

"You must be joking!" the producer said in a high-pitch, anger-tainted voice. "Until when? I've got a show to shoot."

"Until the case is solved." Detective Torres left on these last words.

Cordelia Jones gasped. "What's going to happen?" she asked as she faced the producer.

Karl Smith's assistant, a frizzy brunette with magnifier-like glasses, approached with a clipboard. "The police are going to contact Vee's family and investigate."

"I mean, what's going to happen to the show finale?" Cordelia snapped.

"Vee's dead, Cordie," a cameraman interjected with a disapproving tone.

"Okay, but we aren't," Cordelia sneered as she shot a contemptuous gaze at the man. "I spent the last eight weeks slaving over my designs. I've got a mind-blowing collection to show the world and a competition to win."

"I understand your disappointment. You may have invested eight weeks of your life, but I've personally spent a year and sunk millions in this show. I'm sure the police will quickly realize Vee's suicide for what it is," the producer lectured as he typed on his phone. "I must warn you: if they don't allow us back in the villa or access to our cameras by the end of the week, the show's off. I can't afford to pay you all to sit on your butts and do nothing. And I'm firing the private chef Vee had hired as we speak." He snapped his fingers at his assistant, who hurried to send a "canceling services" email, which Claire would later read on her phone.

Fazed at first, Suggie shook her head vigorously and rushed after the detective. Claire raced after her.

"Excuse me, Detective. When you said the house is under police-only access, did you mean the whole house?" Suggie asked, worry lines carving her forehead.

"Yes, the entire property. Why? You live here?"

"No, but my wedding's supposed to take place here the weekend after next," Suggie said, her eyes shining with pre-tears.

"But I do. This was supposed to be my home for the next two weeks," Claire added, puzzled that the police would need to seal the entire property, especially since the tragedy took place at the edge of the cliff, away from the house. She had seen her share of yellow-taped buildings before, and the barricade tape had only stayed until the forensic team went through. One to three days tops.

"Well, you'll have to find another place to stay and postpone the wedding. This place is off-limits until the case is closed. If that bothers you, you're welcome to file a complaint when you come down to the station to give your statement." He motioned a police officer to escort them out of the house, as if they were some sort of criminals not to be trusted to follow his simple request to leave. "And don't return to France without giving us notice. We may have a few questions for you," he shouted in Claire's direction.

Claire chewed her bottom lip, refusing to acknowledge his last comment. She grabbed her bags from the entrance and wheeled them back to Suggie's car. She settled on the passenger seat and sighed. *"Until the case is closed. What a jerk! Did you see his smirk? It's like he was challenging me."*

Her eyes on the road, Suggie turned her blinker on and waited for the traffic to clear. A motorized line of curious tourists and a crowd of nosy neighbors clogged the street. "What are you going to do?" she asked.

"It's not like I have a choice. I'm going to solve the case." No TV shoot meant no private chef gig and, hence, no pay. And no wedding meant lost deposits on the food order and no raving reviews about her catering, which meant no new clients. Claire was already broke. Keeping the villa off limits would mean her official ruin. "I'm going to solve this case to make sure Vee's killer is brought to justice and to get that yellow tape removed in time for your wedding. But first, I need to find a new place to sleep."

"You're welcome to stay with me or Umma, if you want." Suggie proposed. Since her fiancé was about to deploy, Suggie had surrendered her apartment and moved back with her mother for the months to come. Without rent to pay, she would save to buy a home upon her soon-to-be-husband's return.

"Thanks, but I promised my dad I would stop by his place if I ever needed a place to stay. It'll be the perfect opportunity for me to reconnect," she said. This wasn't charity, but temporary help to her *and* the police during the investigation. A police-imposed relocation that was out of Claire's control and had nothing to do with her financial independence, she lied to herself.

Claire and her father hadn't talked much since she graduated law ten years ago. Yes, there were always the annual birthday cards and Christmas phone calls, but their own busy lives—her sprouting legal career and his open-year-round taco shop—had kept them apart and a little distant. "You want to grab lunch at The Osprey with me?"

"I'm sorry, I can't. This is my chance to write about what just happened and make my mark as a true journalist. It's not every day that I'm the first reporter on a crime scene." Though the successful accountant of OhLaLa, the resort's luxury spa owned and managed by her mother, Suggie dreamed of becoming a journalist. With that intent, Suggie had created The Caper Cove Whisper, the popular go-to blog for local news, hoping a national news outlet would, one day, pick up one of her stories.

"I completely understand. Just keep my name out of the article, please. I don't want people to associate my name with death. At least, not before I find new catering clients."

"Okey-doke. Your name won't be mentioned." Suggie maneuvered the car out of the parking space, merged into the flow of traffic, and turned right toward the scenic route west.

In front of them, at a distance, the ocean blended with the sky. Pushed by a softening wind, dark bulbous clouds floated away, freeing the sunshine.

"Do you think I could have saved her if we had arrived a few minutes earlier?" Claire asked, recalling the whistling kettle and the teacups and Linzer cookies on a tray, ready to serve. "What if I had taken an earlier flight or if I didn't have that stupid accent and that CBP agent hadn't stopped me... Do you think Vee would still be alive?"

With a swift motion, Suggie released her grip from the steering wheel and reached out to Claire with her right hand. "I'm afraid we'll never know. But it doesn't matter, and it's beyond your control. All you have to remember is that you're not to blame for what happened. Not for Vee's death nor for your firm's bombing."

Claire sighed. Suggie was right. Still, Claire couldn't stop what-if scenarios from assaulting her mind. Too many deaths had occurred around her. She had lost her colleagues and friends in a criminal bombing, which she miraculously survived. And now, someone killed her friend. Though she had complied with the FBI's order to stay away from the D.C. investigation and lay low, she refused to remain passive here, in her hometown. She didn't exactly know how, but she would find out who killed her friend. With or without the help of the police.

"You think it could be a local?" she asked.

Her eyes fixed on the curve of the road, Suggie pondered on the question. "I can't imagine someone from Caper Cove doing this. Nobody knew Vee Brooks was in town."

A warm sunlight enveloped Caper Cove Bay, dispelling the dismal mood as if promising Claire a quick answer to her questions.

"Maybe it's one of the show's finalists." When it came to crimes, Claire knew that the perpetrators were often the ones who had the most to gain financially from the victim's death.

"Or a crazed fan. We've had to hire extra security at the spa whenever we get VIP clients. It's unreal what admirers can do when they find out their favorite celebrities are in town."

Chapter Four

The Osprey, Claire's father's taco shop, was located right on the shore, nestled among the sand and salt and surrounded by bright cabanas. Its extensive taco menu and its large outdoor patio with a thatched roof made it a popular spot during the day. Tourists and locals grabbed one of the signature fish tacos and custom mocktails before relaxing in the sun or after a morning of beach and surf. At night, the bar transformed into a cops' hangout with music, beer, and pool tables.

Pulling her rolling suitcases behind her, Claire proceeded to the outdoor patio. Her father, Francis "Frank" Fontaine, was chatting with customers at the bar, probably sharing the town's folklore with them. Clad in his trademark turquoise surfing shorts, matching T-shirt, and flip-flops, he embodied the spirit of the town. Except for his tanned, shaved head, which used to be full of hair a decade ago, he hadn't changed much. His surfer physique still caught the attention of women and men. Claire didn't have the time to take another step when her father spotted her from behind the counter.

"Claire?" Frank boomed, his voice carrying over the music and chatter of the bar, filling her with warmth. Her father blinked and rushed to hug her. He lifted her off the ground as if she was still a little girl, triggering a surge of emotions—a mix of joy and nostalgia with a tinge of remorse for the lost years.

"I didn't expect you before tonight and with luggage," he said, lowering her back to the ground. "Do you need a place to stay? Is everything alright?"

"I'm fine, Dad. But yes, I need a place to stay if you don't mind."

Her father paused as she spoke and smiled. Since her hospitalization, they had only communicated via texts, and he hadn't heard her speak until now. Yet, he didn't comment on her accent.

"If I mind? Are you kidding me? I'll always have room for you. Follow me." He grabbed a suitcase in each hand, led her to the back of the three-story building and up a stairway to the second floor. "I've revamped the place after buying Craig's share. Turned the right wing into a three-bedroom communal rental, you know, for extra income. I hope you don't mind sharing the bathroom and living space with another tenant. He's one of the boys in blue. He's been helping me with the renovation."

"It's okay. I'm happy to be here. Plus, that'll remind me of my university days with Suggie." The four years of pre-law Claire had spent in New York had been the most eye-opening time and fun she had ever experienced. Discovering urban life and boys had been a highlight in her life, especially since that worry-free/study time had cemented her friendship with her childhood BFF, Suggie. Having a cop as a roommate might also help quell the nightmares that had been plaguing her since her workplace tragedy.

Her father unlocked the front door of the apartment and guided her straight through the open-concept three-bedroom home. The walls were painted a warm, sandy beige, which complemented the light hardwood floors. On the left, a plush, cream-colored sectional sofa dominated the living room. Right above it, an ornate gilt mirror reflected the window daylight while adding a touch of French elegance to the space. On the right, five blue barstools lined the marble counter, which marked the start of a gourmet kitchen. A double oven, stainless steel appliance, and range hood seemed to be screaming at her, "Cook with me now!"

The modern French-Californian style was a nice change from the former Midwestern hunting decor, which made Claire wonder whether the interior design was the result of a feminine input. Her father had remained single since the divorce, but that might have changed.

Frank passed the two bedroom doors on the right, before opening the left one, which had the number "1" etched in gold on its front panel.

"This is yours," he said as he entered the room. He set Claire's luggage between the glass-topped desk and the white French bed.

The room had the same color scheme as the rest of the apartment, with the added glamour of a sparkling crystal chandelier, an apple-green toile de Jouy wallpaper, and a white faux-fur carpet by the bed. A blue womb chair and its matching ottoman stood by the window next to a small shelf filled with books. It was her sister Aurora's dream bedroom—the one her sister had sketched in her diary before she vanished.

Serendipity, Claire thought. It was as if the universe knew the secret reason for her return to Caper Cove—to find out what had happened to her sister two decades ago—and was encouraging her. Assisting her. Any detail about her sister's seventeen-year-old mind, including her choice of furniture and architecture, could yield important clues as to her disappearance. Something she couldn't share with her dad. Or at least not right now. Her father seemed to have found some balance and happiness in his life, and she refused to be the one to destroy it all.

"If it's too girly, let me know. I can change the décor," he said.

"It's perfect, Dad. Thank you." Claire hugged her father. She could only imagine what missing a daughter must have been for him, the past twenty-two years. The stress had cost him his marriage and his youngest daughter. Even if she had visited every summer, Claire felt guilty to have remained so long on the East Coast.

"How's Suggie doing? Is she going to join us for lunch?" Her father drew back the curtains and opened the window, inviting the fresh breeze in.

"She's doing great. She wanted to come but had an urgent article to write about a dead body."

"The fall-suicide on Golden View? A real tragedy."

"How do you…" Claire didn't finish her sentence. Of course, her father knew. As a retired, seasoned cop, he stayed in the police loop. Police officers shared a lot among themselves, and, like any self-respecting cop bar owner, her dad always kept a crackling police scanner in the office. "I'm the one who discovered the body. The victim was a friend of mine."

"I'm sorry to hear that. Are you okay?" Her father grabbed her hand, ready to envelop her in a tight embrace.

"Oddly enough, I am," Claire said, saddened by the fact that she wasn't more distraught by Vee's death. She was heartbroken but hadn't cried. Her years working on felony cases, from drug trafficking to rapes and murders, had desensitized her to trauma and violence and prompted her pragmatic and analytical side to resurface. Right now, she didn't feel like examining and sharing her feelings about the accident. She had had enough mandatory therapy—bi-weekly sessions since the D.C. explosion—to last her a lifetime. "All I want to do is find out what happened."

Her father nodded as if he understood his daughter's compulsion to investigate. "What's your take on it: accidental fall or suicide?"

Claire hesitated. "You may think I'm crazy, but I think it's murder."

"I'd never think you're crazy. If you think something's wrong, something's wrong. But murder? You must have serious evidence to support that claim."

"I do."

Her father wrapped his arm around her shoulders and guided her gently toward the door. "Let's get you a taco plate and you can tell me all about it."

* * *

Minutes later, Claire was seated at the outdoor bar, biting heartily into a *French taco*—a soft wheat tortilla filled with lobster meat and dressed in garlic-parsley butter, the usual dressing for escargots.

"So, what makes you think your friend was murdered?" her father asked as he perched on the stool next to hers, resting one arm on the counter. He leaned forward toward his daughter, his eyes wide with focus, ignoring the bussers and food-carrying waiters who bustled behind them.

"Everything," she said, touched by her dad's attention. Unlike the jurors and courtroom judges, or her therapists, her dad had no professional obligation to listen to her. He did it out of care, without a personal angle—something Claire hadn't enjoyed in years.

After swallowing her last taco bite, Claire went on to explain, in detail, how she discovered her friend's body and what proved it was murder and not an accident like the police assumed.

"The sushi plate might have been hers, but the cocktail couldn't be. Vee would have never ordered alcohol. She celebrated her tenth year of sobriety last week. She was so proud of it she sent me a selfie with the medallion the very same night she got it. Plus, the cup was empty, and there weren't any lipstick smudges on the rim. Vee always wore lipstick even when she ate. It's one of the first things she put on in the morning, and she was still wearing lipstick when I found her."

"I see." Her father bobbed his head. "You think the picnic setting was staged?"

"I'm not sure, but it had to be. Vee would've never ventured so close to the edge on her own, and she wouldn't have jumped. She couldn't have been in a dark mood either; she was wearing yellow, her happy color. The one she always wore when she was in a celebratory mood. Plus, the tea kettle was on when we arrived. She was making tea for us when this happened. Blue jasmine tea, our reunion tea. That doesn't make any sense."

"It sure smells fishy. Do you know of anyone who would want to harm her?"

"That's the thing. Besides the competing designers, I can't think of anyone. What am I supposed to do?"

Her father stroked his chin, pondering the question in silence. Around them, the restaurant buzzed with the clinks of silverware and the animated chatter of patrons.

"If I told you to let the police do their job, would you stop?"

Claire shook her head. "Probably not."

"All I can say is whatever you choose, I'll be there if you need me." Her father shot her a sadness-filled gaze. Though her father's relentlessness with his work had cost him his marriage, he had never abandoned a case he started. A drive and a potential flaw Claire shared with him.

Frank was about to add something when the clank of broken dishes and shouts erupted from the kitchen. "I've got to run, Kiddo. I'll be right back."

Claire nodded as she watched her father run back inside the taco shop.

The sun was shining brightly overhead, casting umbrella-shaped shadows on the sand. Sunrays struggled to pass through the bar's straw roof, spotting

Claire's arms with warmth. She removed her shoes and walked barefoot to the shore. The happy screams of children mixed with the sounds of cutlery on plates sent her back to her childhood. She closed her eyes and smiled. Memories of her year-round days at the beach flashed in her mind. It had been such a paradisiac life until her sister Aurora disappeared. Claire had been twelve years old at the time, but the confusion and powerlessness she had felt was still sharp. Her attempt to comprehend what had happened to her sister haunted her still. And here she was, twenty-two years later, plagued by a feeling of déjà vu, taken aback by her friend's sudden and mysterious death.

She reopened her eyes and inhaled as if it were her last breath. "You're not a powerless teenager anymore," she told herself. "You're going to solve this one."

The phone vibrated in Claire's back pocket as if to agree with her. Claire reached for it and frowned. A text from an unknown number had brought the screen to life: *You were named the official executor of Vee Brooks' estate. Do you accept?*

Chapter Five

According to the Fashion Warriors Productions lawyer, Vee had named Claire her executor in the event of her death. Claire accepted the appointment without hesitation. It's not like she was busy with work anyway, and her late friend's trust needed to be honored. Such power would also allow Claire to dig deeper into Vee's life and help figure out the mystery behind her friend's untimely death.

Claire docu-signed the necessary documents via her smartphone and downloaded the letter of testamentary—the official proof of her executory power and legal authority to act on behalf of Vee's estate. She was glad to have opted for a device with a large memory when she had upgraded it months before. Her phone was already overflowing with recipes and the hundred pictures she had taken at the bottom of the cliff and the villa. Vee's liability waiver, video release, power of attorney, and executor agreement were added to it.

"I'll send you notarized copies of everything once I get your address. Feel free to use the digital copies in the meantime," the lawyer said. "You'll get paid a percentage of the estate when the matter is closed."

Claire glanced at her screen which displayed Vee's financial information and list of properties. "Are you really sure I am the executor? What does her husband think about this?" Claire asked the lawyer. She didn't know Vee's husband beyond what her friend had told her. It had been a sort of shotgun wedding that Claire had missed because of her post-bombing hospitalization.

"I couldn't tell you. All I know is that Vee and her husband wrote a prenup

29

and kept separate bank accounts. It's all in the documents I've sent you," he explained in a cold, even voice. "The only thing they ever had in common was their baby."

"Their baby…" she mumbled. Claire couldn't believe she had forgotten about Eva Claire, who was only three months old. Vee had sent her pictures of the adorable little girl, but Claire had been so preoccupied with her recovery and answering police questions about her law firm explosion that the baby's existence had evaded her. Claire dug her heels into the sand with frustration. Though her hospital stay and injuries explained her lack of attention to Vee's recent life, she felt like a rotten friend. "Do you have the husband's personal number?"

"I'll text it to you, but it might be of no use. He's gone AWOL."

"What do you mean he went AWOL?" Being missing was the worst possible situation to be in for someone whose spouse had just been killed under suspicious circumstances. Everybody knows that the significant other is always the first suspect.

"The police have been looking for him everywhere. He's neither at home nor at his company's HQ or on the political trail. If you find him, you should let the police know."

The conversation ended there, leaving Claire baffled. It was like the universe had destroyed her hope of setting crime-related matters aside. To be honest, she didn't mind it. She had always loved elucidating mysteries and solving puzzles. Criminal investigating was just a grown-up version of her childhood pastime. She only wished it had been under different circumstances and didn't involve the death of a friend.

"Everything alright?" Her father had rejoined her side and stared at the ocean with her. "Stress and jetlag aren't a good mix, you know. I'd advise a nap, but seeing your expression, I guess you're already working the case."

She turned to her father and smiled at his understanding. "How long does it take to obtain the results of a top-priority autopsy?"

"About three hours to get preliminary results, maybe. Full results may take up to twenty-four hours, as long as the coroner doesn't have a backlog."

"How full is their plate?" She was confident her father would know. Her father had once dated one of the forensic lab technicians, and Claire wasn't sure whether they were on amicable terms or not. The medical examiner's office was also adjacent to the police station, so the staff from both offices were chummy with each other. And since The Osprey was a cops' bar, every piece of office gossip and news would reach her father's ears in no time.

"There haven't been any deceased to examine recently, so not full at all."

Claire glanced at her watch. Four hours had gone by since Detective Torres had ordered the rush autopsy of Vee's body. If she left right away, she could get to the Coroner's office before it closed.

Well done, Vee, Claire thought, mentally congratulating her late friend for appointing her as her executor. The letter of testamentary would give her access to every document related to the investigation. She would be able to bring truth to the tragedy.

"Can I borrow your car?" Claire asked her father.

"You still know how to drive after years of using the subway?"

"Of course I do. What kind of question is that?" She laughed nervously and avoided her father's eyes. Even though she had taken the metro daily, she had driven through Washington D.C.'s rush hour traffic often enough to be trusted with a car. What she couldn't tell him was that she had let her driver's license expire.

Five minutes later, Claire was behind the wheel of the taco shop truck—a turquoise vehicle not unlike the Mystery Machine, the Scooby-Doo cargo van. Despite her desire to rush, she kept her speed reasonably low, which meant the twenty-five miles per hour speed limit enforced throughout Caper Cove. The fifteen-minute drive felt endless, and she had only five minutes to spare before the Medical Examiner's Office closed. She parked at the back of the building, in the empty employee-only parking lot, and rushed to the door.

She flew inside the greyish office, followed the Administration Office sign, and arrived at the Morgue/Autopsy desk.

"Hello, I would like to know if the autopsy results for Vee Brooks are ready to view. The corpse was brought in at around one thirty this afternoon, but it's a top-priority case," she blurted before catching her breath.

The clerk, a middle-aged woman with a wide face and droopy eyelids, glanced at the wall clock slowly, then at Claire, then back at the wall clock. "We're about to close. Can you come back tomorrow?" she asked languidly. Her tone was polite but carried a whisper of irritation.

"I'd rather not. It's really important."

The woman raised an eyebrow and shot Claire an annoyed sideways smile. "Your name?"

"Claire Fontaine. I'm the executor of Vee Brooks' estate."

"Claire? Is that really you?" a voice called out from the end of the corridor.

Claire pivoted toward the masculine voice. A young man in a lab coat over a green surgical scrub suit was staring at her, his eyes wide with pleased surprise.

She studied the man standing in front of her, struggling to place him. His tanned face, thick black hair and eyebrows, and brilliant black eyes were familiar, too stunning for Claire to have forgotten his name. "Yes, and you are?"

"It's me. Vikram Thomas. You were my summer babysitter. You taught me how to cook, and we made chorizo macarons together."

Claire jerked back in disbelief. The twenty-something, handsome man who stood in front of her couldn't be the shrimpy nerd she used to tutor and babysit on weekends.

"Little Vic?"

A radiant smile lit up Vikram's face. "In the flesh. No pun intended," he laughed. "Wow, you haven't changed. As beautiful as ever. Love the accent, by the way. Did you just return from a trip to France? It's charming."

Heat reached Claire's face. Though Vikram had to be twenty-eight years old now, being complimented so overtly by someone she could only picture as a little boy felt inappropriately strange.

"Thanks. It's a long story. I'd be happy to share it with you later. I've got an urgent matter to attend right now. I need to talk to a forensic pathologist."

"They're all gone for the day, but I may be able to help," he said, squaring off his shoulders. "I'm a forensic pathology fellow here at the medical examiner's office."

32

The desk clerk cleared her throat as if she were a thespian in a theatrical play calling everyone's attention.

"Oh yes. I'm handling this request, Debbie. Feel free to go home. You can lock the front door. I'll take Ms. Fontaine through the back exit when we're done."

The clerk compressed her lips in disapproval, grabbed her coat, and stomped out of the office, mumbling something about last-minute requests and special treatment.

"Let's go to the doctors' lounge and tell me what brings you here," Vikram said, leading the way.

Claire explained in detail, for the fourth time, her nightmarish discovery, her recent appointment as executor, and her suspicions of foul play. She also gave Vikram a very short synopsis of her life, her office bombing, and her foreign accent syndrome. About her need to lay low, and her new, stunted career as private chef.

"A lawyer turned sexy French chef. You could be the character of an action-packed romance novel." He threw her the same bright-eyed gaze he did as a ten-year-old infatuated with his seventeen-year-old babysitter. "Why don't you grab a seat while I check the recent autopsy files? Feel free to grab a drink or make yourself a coffee. I'll be right back."

The doctors' lounge was blinding white and smelled of antiseptic and stale coffee. Three blue tables and nine chairs and a large refrigerator took over the small space beside a Formica counter while a red rocker stood in a corner. Paintings depicting various organs and the human body hung on the wall, including a psychedelic view of a scrotum, reminding visitors they were at the Coroner's office.

Claire grabbed a water bottle from the snack counter and gulped down its contents. She had too enthusiastically binged on the dill pickled chips her father served at the bistro and hadn't realized how parched she was until now. Then, she settled in the red rocker and swayed gently back and forth, trying to fight jetlag. She was about to fall asleep when Vikram returned with a printout.

"Got it," he said, waving the pages above his head. He dragged a dining chair next to Claire and leafed through the paperwork. "Cause of death is cardiac arrest from respiratory failure. She died from asphyxiation." His breath smelled of fresh peppermint, as if he had just brushed his teeth or placed a mouthwash strip on his tongue.

"Asphyxiation? From what?" Claire asked, stretching her neck to better read the report. Respiratory failure could have many causes, from chronic bronchitis and pulmonary blood clots to trauma and drug overdose.

"It doesn't say. They're still running the tox screen. The pathologist in charge sent the samples to the hospital for further analysis. They just received a brand-new mass spectrometer, something we don't have here, so we use their lab."

"Any idea of what it could be?"

"It's likely a toxin. It could be from a medication overdose like sleeping pills or alcohol. Cocaine or amphetamines, maybe. Opiates and benzodiazepines can all cause respiratory failure. I can call right now to find out," he proposed with the same sweet voice and wide, smiling eyes he used when asking her to cook some new elaborate recipe as a child.

Claire smiled back. "That'd be great."

While Vikram called for the results, Claire leafed through the autopsy report. Time of death was estimated at around twelve noon, give or take thirty minutes. The corpse had exhibited no sign of rigor mortis when it had arrived at the morgue, and its temperature had still been within normal range. If a murderer was behind Vee's death, he couldn't have been very far from the villa when Claire discovered her friend at the bottom of the cliff.

The report also indicated hypodermic injection sites on the upper outer arms, abdomen, and upper outer thighs—traditional insulin injection sites. They were consistent with the finding of insulin pens and syringes found at the scene and the presence of the victim's name on the national diabetes registries.

"Got it!" Vikram cheered and hung up the phone's receiver to its base on the wall.

Claire craned her neck in his direction. "And?"

"Yes, what did you get?" Detective Torres tromped into the room. "Debbie,

34

your clerk, dropped by the station and told me you had an unauthorized foreign tourist in here asking questions. I usually ignore her since she's the meanest gossip in town, but she was right," he said to Vikram before glaring straight at Claire. "What don't you understand in *let the police do their job?*" he said, overenunciating. "Do you need me to translate that into French?"

"She isn't—" Vikram started to say before Claire stopped him with an arm squeeze.

"Again, I'm not a foreign tourist. I'm also the official executor of Vee Brooks' estate, and I have every right to be here." She scribbled the name and number of the lawyer who had informed her of the appointment and handed it to him. "You can call them to check. Also, in case you don't know, the California Public Records Act, government code sections 6250 to 6270, requires Caper Cove ME's office to make public records available for inspection by the public and to provide copies upon request."

Detective Torres' head jolted, and his back straightened in response. He grabbed the number, checked something on his phone in silence, and sighed.

"Fine," he said as if he had given Vikram and Claire the authorization to review the autopsy report together. "What did you find?"

"The victim died of tetrodotoxin poisoning."

Torres grimaced. "What's that?"

"It's a paralyzing neurotoxin that makes breathing impossible. It's found in puffer fish. One single fish can kill twenty to thirty people if its meat isn't properly prepared for consumption," Claire said in one breath. She had spotted a sushi plate on the picnic blanket next to the cliff from which Vee had fallen. Had Vee ordered fugu for lunch or had her dish been contaminated by improperly prepared fugu? If it was an accident, there might be other victims in town.

The detective eyed her with suspicion. "You sure know a lot about poison."

"Don't look at me like that. I know this because I represented a fugu enthusiast gourmet once."

"Fugu sushi?" Torres asked.

"Fugu is usually served as sashimi, fresh raw fish without the rice," she corrected, "but it could have been served alongside sushi, yes."

Torres grabbed his square chin between his thumb and his index finger. "So Ms. Brooks planned to jump off the cliff but died by fugu instead? Or she asked for bad fugu to make sure her jump would kill her."

Claire protested with a sigh. "I've already told you. She wasn't suicidal. That text wasn't hers."

Torres snorted. "Yeah? You got proof?"

"I do. First, Vee wore yellow, which means she was in the happiest of moods. Check her social media posts, and you'll see. She always wore yellow to celebrate. Second, Vee hated the word goodbye. She never used it. She always used *so long* instead. It's Forensic Writing 101. Maybe someone else used her phone and meant it as a joke. Or maybe it was meant for someone else and had a completely different significance; maybe it's being taken out of context."

Torres crossed his arms against his chest and regarded Claire. "I see, you're one of those true crime fans who thinks they can solve cases better than the police."

Claire raised her chin in defiance. "Maybe, because I don't speculate. I don't establish the cause of death without evidence."

"Huh!" The detective huffed. "So you think she died of food poisoning after eating bad fugu and what...fell?"

Vikram cleared his voice loudly, as if to diffuse the tension. "Tetrodotoxin can work very fast. People can lose muscle control and suffer convulsions within ten minutes following absorption. If she were near a cliff, she could have easily fallen down by accident."

"So she died of fugu poisoning and fell down the cliff because of a toxin-induced seizure," Torres hypothesized.

"Or she was poisoned first and pushed over the ledge by someone who wanted to make her death look like an accident," Claire said.

Torres snorted. "You watch too much TV."

"And you're a condescending egocentric who thinks he has all the answers."

"Okayyy." Vikram stepped between Torres and Claire, forming a physical buffer between them. "Either way, we now have the first piece of the puzzle. Vee Brooks was poisoned."

Chapter Six

U nlike Washington, D.C., where freezing temperatures reigned at that time of year, Caper Cove was a heaven of sixty-five-degree warmth. The sky was a canvas of red and orange and the setting sun had dyed the ocean amber—a wonderful setting which Claire enjoyed while dining with Suggie on the Osprey's outdoor patio. The evening had been perfect until Torres took a seat at the table across from them.

"I love this town and the small coastal community feel, but that Detective Torres really makes me miss the East Coast. In D.C., my speech disorder and my national origin have never been questioned. Accents are appreciated as essential elements of international cooperation, not reasons for suspicion or harassment." Claire scowled as she glared in the man's direction.

"Why don't you tell him about being a lawyer and your foreign accent syndrome? He would quickly leave you alone and may even invite you to join in the investigation," Suggie advised.

Claire frowned so hard it almost triggered a headache.

"There's no way I'm surrendering to this bully. First, I don't have to justify myself to him. My health history is private. Second, he should learn to respect everyone regardless of their national origins or qualifications. We're a nation of immigrants. Those who have the most to contribute to this country aren't always born within its borders. Take Tesla, Einstein, and Arnold Schwarzenegger; their strong accents didn't lessen their accomplishments. There wouldn't be Google without its Russian-born creator, and YouTube wouldn't exist without its Taiwan-born and German-born founders." Claire had thousands of similar examples. As a criminal defense lawyer, she had witnessed firsthand the prejudices some of her clients faced—be it based on national origin, culture, religion, or race. She refused to solve the issue with a simple *I'm a US-born American with a concussion-induced speech disorder.*

"Please, don't tell him the truth about me and my accent unless he asks, alright? And let's enjoy this beautiful evening." Claire lifted and repositioned her chair away from Torres so that her back was turned toward him and took another bite in her Philly cheese steak taco.

Suggie acquiesced with a nod and tittered. "Understood. But this tension between you and Torres and the way he looks at you... it seems a little... sexual."

Claire spit her mouth's contents and laughed. "Sexual? You surely don't know how to read a room. That guy has nothing but contempt for me."

"I think you may be wrong, kiddo." Her father stood beside her, a dessert bowl in each hand. "That guy's former military and a cop. He doesn't know the difference between approaching a suspect and assessing a potential date. For them, it's a target. They're like lions: assess their prey, throw them a few growls to see how they react, and when they think it's safe and worth the risk, they drop the aggression and make a move."

"Seriously? Maybe they should have an intensive course on twenty-first-century civility at the academy."

Her father chuckled and placed the glass bowls on the table. "Torres isn't bad. You might enjoy his company. Rumor is he's quite the catch, if you know what I mean."

"Eww. Really, Dad?" Claire shrugged, feeling nauseous, while Suggie giggled.

"I just thought a little fun would be nice," her father added. "Romance's good for the soul."

"Well, thank you for your input, but I don't need dating advice from anyone, especially not my dad." Though Torres was what she called a nice specimen, romance was the last thing on Claire's mind. Solving Vee's death, making sure Suggie's wedding took place, and finding a job were her top priorities right now.

"Whatever you say, kiddo. By the way, dinner's on me. If you both need anything, you know where to find me."

When her father disappeared back into the boisterous bar, Suggie was still laughing. "Your dad's the best," she said between sips of lemonade.

"Why, because he knows how to embarrass me?" Claire asked as she side-glanced at Torres' table. The detective was gone. Good, she thought as she suddenly retrieved her appetite.

"Because he remembered this." Suggie pushed one of the dessert cups Frank had brought to the table in front of Claire. It was filled with chocolate and coconut ice cream, topped with a preserved peach, and drizzled with raspberry sauce.

Claire gasped with joy. "Is that a C and S Peach Melba? I haven't eaten one of those since..."

"Since last time you were here, at home," Suggie said, finishing her sentence. Frank Fontaine had named the dessert after them after the then twelve-year-old girls had tried to create their own signature ice cream.

Claire scooped a huge spoonful of ice cream, shoved it in her mouth, and let it melt on her tongue. She closed her eyes and let the flavors transport her back to an easy childhood until a bolt of pain hit her forehead, forcing her to reopen her eyes.

Suggie was also grimacing, squeezing her temples in her palms. "Brain freeze," her friend groan-laughed.

Claire chuckled. "Same here. Some things never change."

"So, do you still miss D.C.?"

"I don't, and I won't, as long as I am with you and as far away from Detective Grumpy as possible."

* * *

How people handle jet lag tells a lot about their age, and Claire knew she wasn't fifteen anymore. After the brain freeze-induced giggle she shared with Suggie, Claire went straight to bed in her room above The Osprey. The bed was comfortable, and the sound of the waves lapping the shore was soothing. She was hoping to sleep nine hours straight to destress. However, despite her exhaustion from the long flight and emotionally taxing day, her brain refused to shut down. Her body's circadian cycle, a timer more reliable than any well-oiled clock, had decided against it.

So, here she was at 3 AM, wide awake. Had she been in Washington, D.C., it would have been 6 AM. She would have gotten up and run her three miles down the Mall; then she would have taken a shower, dressed, and gone to work. But she wasn't in D.C. anymore. She was in Caper Cove, California, without money or a job. Her heart skipped a beat at the thought, then raced.

"Omm," she chanted. She had learned this meditation technique at the hospital where she recovered from the explosion. The sound OM, when chanted, supposedly vibrated at 432 hertz, the same frequency as nature. The sound supposedly acknowledged her physical connection to nature and all other beings—except, of course, psychopaths, criminals, whoever was behind Vee's death, and Detective Torres.

She checked her smartwatch calendar and pushed on play. A robotic voice wished her good morning and proceeded to enumerate her to-do list of the day: "Find a job, solve Vee's death, concretize Suggie's wedding."

"A high order for today, don't you think?" she replied to the artificial voice. The modern timepiece had been a gift from Leti Bellini, one of her law firm partners. A woman who had mentored Claire since her law school days and who had perished in the criminal blast. A sort of guardian angel nurse, the fancy gadget was supposed to keep an eye on Claire's stress level and keep track of her legal workload.

"I notice your climbing heart rate but perceive no movement. Do you need suggestions to destress?" the watch asked in a monotone tone.

"Yes, please." Though she knew she was chatting with a bot, Claire enjoyed being monitored and asked about her emotional and physical health. Being a criminal defense attorney in a big law firm, her life often consisted of fourteen-hour work days. A taxing habit that only ended with a gruesome tragedy—a sort of bitter lemonade from lemons kind of story. Surviving the blast was a second chance at life, which wasn't lost on Claire. Though a daily struggle, she had promised herself to put her to-do list second to her health. It's not like she could investigate or search for a job at 3 AM anyway. "What do you suggest?"

"A warm bath would help promote relaxation," the watch said.

"That's actually a great idea." Claire slipped out of bed, grabbed a towel, and padded barefoot to the bathroom. The warm water would help soothe her tired muscles and calm her jetlagged, restless mind.

A soft light shined through the open bathroom door, which made her smile. Her father had mentioned installing nightlights throughout the apartment so Claire could easily find her way until she became familiar with the light switch locations.

She stepped on the tiled bathroom floor, which felt colder than the hallway parquet and reached for the bathtub faucet. She didn't notice the presence of a silhouette in the room until it cleared its throat.

Claire jumped backward from the sound, her hands balled in fists, ready to strike. "Who's there?"

"Your roommate, I guess? Why don't you turn on the light?" a voice said in the semi-darkness.

"Do not move." Claire groped for the light switch and turned on the ceiling lamp. The face in front of her was familiar. "Detective Torres?" She followed the head down to the floor and realized too late that the detective was standing in the bathtub, dripping with water, completely naked.

Claire let out a gasp of surprise. She immediately turned away and covered her eyes. "I'm sorry! I didn't realize you were in here," she stammered.

Torres chuckled, seemingly unfazed by the awkwardness of the situation. "It's all good," he said as he stepped out of the bathtub and wrapped a towel around his waist.

Claire tried to focus on the room's elegant porcelain tiles and the gleaming fixtures, but her gaze drifted to the man. She couldn't help but notice how toned and muscular the detective was, and she felt her face flush with embarrassment.

"I couldn't sleep and thought a bath might help," she explained, feeling foolish.

Torres nodded sympathetically. "I know how it is. Jetlag can be a real pain.

But next time, announce yourself."

"Excuse me? Announce myself? How about closing and locking the door when you're using the bathroom."

"I live here alone. I didn't know you'd be here."

"Didn't Frank tell you about a new roommate?"

"He vaguely mentioned something about having his daughter upstairs, but the bar music was too loud. I didn't catch everything. I didn't think it was today."

"Well, here I am."

"You think I'm stupid? No way you're Frank's daughter? You're French."

Chapter Seven

The Osprey was already serving customers when Claire left her apartment that morning. She had made a quick exit, hoping not to cross paths with Torres. Her cheeks were still flushed from their earlier bathroom encounter, which she tried to forget. The scent of crepes and waffles wafted in the salty air, along with the soft rhythm of morning conversations. Shirtless surfers lined up at the bar to pick up their coffee before heading to work, and tourists enjoyed a sunrise breakfast.

"Good morning, Dad. May I have your car keys?" she asked, poking her head through the kitchen side window.

"Sorry, kiddo. You can't," her father said, finishing crafting an intricate design out of steamed milk in a coffee mug. "Torres told me your license expired."

Claire sighed in frustration. Really? What a tattletale.

"Dad, please," she begged. "I really need to go to the police station. I need to give them my statement and find out the progress the police made on Vee's case."

Frank's mouth twisted. He wasn't a by-the-book cop, but she knew the police chief in him couldn't let her break the rule outside an emergency situation. "Sorry, no exceptions. I've an electric bike in the shed if you want to use it, or I can call one of the duty cops to pick you up," he proposed.

Claire paused and considered her options. She couldn't afford a taxi or a rideshare since she was broke. She could try to hitchhike to the station, but that would make her appear suspiciously desperate—something she couldn't afford if she wanted to find a job in town. Same with a police pick-up. If people saw her riding in a police car, they might assume her to be a criminal. And no one wants their meals cooked by a thug.

"I'll take the bike," she muttered, wondering how she would manage to ride in her clothes. She had chosen a grey, flared wool Chanel skirt, a pink silk blouse, and a fitted blazer in order to connect with the fashion design experts she was thinking of questioning later that day.

Though not born fashion-inclined, Claire had learned a lot about how to dress since becoming an associate at Beaumont, Farrell, and Volk—one of D.C.'s most prestigious firms. The first rules of clothing were: (1) dress for your clients according to your company culture and profession, and (2) dress to either blend or impress. Both of which meant to dress elegantly in designer clothes. Accordingly, Claire's firm had provided her with a monthly clothing allowance, which she was forced to spend at a professional stylist. Choosing the right outfit wasn't just about vanity or self-expression. It was a way to send a message: I am a top-tier lawyer, and I belong here, in this firm, and among its wealthy clients' social circles.

"You sure you want the bike?" her father asked.

"Yes, I'm sure. It'll definitely be faster than walking." She had a safety pin she could use to keep her skirt from flying in the wind and from exposing herself as she rode. She also wore thigh-slimming spandex shorts underneath in case the safety pin failed. She couldn't risk inadvertently flashing Caper Cove residents her thong-clad bouncing bottom.

She was trudging toward the side of the building when someone gently grabbed her by the arm. It was Vikram. Shirtless, tanned, muscular, seven-years her junior Vikram. His short black curls gleamed with wet morning sunshine.

"I'd be happy to give you a lift," he said with a grin. "Just give me two minutes to change." Like most surfers, Vikram showered and got dressed for work in the beach bathrooms.

"That would be wonderful. Take your time. I'm ordering you breakfast. My treat."

She ordered a crepe with chestnut purée and whipped cream (Vikram's favorite from her babysitting days) and two large cappuccinos to go. "Thanks,

Dad," she said as he handed her the order. "Please, put it on my tab."

* * *

Although the police station had undergone a remodel, Claire could still recognize the place. The once-grey walls were now periwinkle blue, and the plaster partitions were now glass panes, which gave the formerly stuffy office/local jail a bright and airy atmosphere. The oakwood desks and black filing cabinets had remained the same and, except for a few new faces, the officers focused on their daily tasks were just a decade older.

As Claire approached the front desk, the receptionist looked up and gave her a friendly smile. Claire returned the smile. "Good morning. My name is Claire Fontaine. I'm here to give a statement on the 179 Golden View incident."

"Do you remember the name of the officer in charge of the case?" the receptionist asked.

"Detective Torres. But I would prefer to talk to someone else," she whispered as she leaned slightly over the counter.

"The receptionist nodded and picked up the phone, dialed a number, and informed someone of her presence. A few moments later, a petite woman with fiery red hair and a thin nose as sharp as her gaze emerged from a nearby office, a look of recognition dawning on her face as she spotted Claire.

"Claire?" she said, her voice full of surprise, beaming.

Claire nodded, confused. The woman in a perfectly pressed suit reminded her of her sister's best friend. "Miranda Ernshaw?"

Both women rushed to each other's arms and hugged for a few effusive seconds.

"Mrs. Oh told me about the bombing. Hard to return to law after that. I'm glad you've decided to retreat back home to recover. Self-care's so important," Miranda said.

Mrs. Oh was Suggie's mother, the owner of the luxury resort spa, and the source of the town's most factual gossip. She was also a master at keeping track of her daughter's friends and their families. Which reminded Claire that a visit to Mrs. Oh might be necessary if she wanted to quickly find a job. Word of mouth in Caper Cove might be faster and more reliable than an ad in the newspaper.

"Thanks. What about you? What brought you back to Caper Cove? I thought you were pursuing your theater dream in New York." The summer before Aurora, Claire's sister, disappeared, all Aurora and Miranda talked about was moving to New York after graduation to be cast in a Broadway show.

"I did study acting for a while, but your sister's disappearance has always haunted me. After an Intro to Criminology class, I decided to major in criminal justice. After a few years as a cop and a detective, I requested my transfer here. I've been back eight years now, and I'm the station deputy chief. So, you're here to give your statement about yesterday's event?"

"Sort of. I've already given a statement and needed to make sure your officers got all the details down. I also wanted to know if you found the victim's cellphone. She was a friend of mine, and as the executor of her estate, I'm trying to gather her property and investigate a little."

Miranda's lips twisted in a corner smile. "You're the one Torres has been ranting about." She laughed and beckoned Claire to follow her. On the way to her office, the deputy chief grabbed a file off one of the clone desks. "What do you need?"

"Any update you may have," Claire said as she settled in the chair across from Miranda's large desk. Claire took a deep breath as nostalgia hit her. She couldn't count the many days she had spent in this very room when her father worked as a cop. Despite the new paint and flooring, the room still felt cozy and inviting.

"Let's see…" Miranda leafed through the dossier she had lifted from the main room. "This hasn't been classified as a homicide. At least not yet. The autopsy report lists tetrodotoxin poisoning possibly caused by fugu meat consumption. While we can't rule out murder, we're considering it an accident for now. We're looking for the provenance of the sushi meat that the officer collected from the scene."

"What about Vee's phone?"

The deputy chief looked back at the file. "We didn't find any. But we have footage from one of the neighbors' surveillance cameras." Miranda set the file aside, typed something on her computer keyboard. "Here it is." She swiveled the computer screen in Claire's direction and pressed play on the pop-up window. "The only persons appearing on it at the time of death are the production crew leaving the premises and, forty-three minutes later, you and Suggie."

The video showed Claire and her friend wandering the house through the windowed walls of the villa until they disappeared in the west wing. Under different circumstances, Claire would have considered the video an invasion of privacy—installing devices that record neighbors on their property constitutes an infringement of their privacy and data rights. Who installs a camera to point it straight at their neighbor's windows instead of the streets?

"We were calling Vee's phone but couldn't find her, so we decided to check outside," Claire explained, worried that Suggie and she might be considered suspects. Outside of people with obvious motives for murder, suspects always included individuals connected to the victim through personal or professional relationships, or persons who may have been present at the crime scene. Claire fitted these categories to a T.

Miranda nodded. "I know. A neighbor witnessed your arrival on the scene. He described you as "screaming and rushing like a maniac down the wooden stairs to the beach. Your 911 call came seconds later. You and Suggie are in the clear."

Claire exhaled in relief, happy to be off the suspect list, but she was disappointed the investigation hadn't progressed much.

"What about the villa's security camera? There was one mounted over the garage. There should be a few more peppered throughout the property, like is always the case in million-dollar mansions."

"The feed was off. The production crew's constant ins and outs had triggered the alarm so many times that they decided to unplug it until the filming was done."

That made sense. There were a few things more annoying than an alarm that kept going off like a weak, battery-powered smoke detector. Caper Cove was also known for being safe.

"Do you mind if I investigate on my side?" Though Claire didn't need the authorization to do so and was ready to go to any lengths to solve Vee's death as fast as possible, she wanted to be polite. Respect for one's territory and procedures often brought amicable relations and cooperation between police and private investigators.

"Officially, I'd rather you not. But as long as you don't impede the investigation and share with us what you find, I don't see why not." Miranda paused as if considering a new angle to Claire's question. "In fact, why don't you accompany Torres to his first round of interviews? The entire production crew is staying at the same hotel on the shore. Two of the show participants have records." She glanced back at the file on her desk. "Max 'Vinyl' Berkley for possession of Class A drug and Cordelia Jones for assault. Your sharp witness assessment and legal expertise might be useful to the case. The running governor will be grateful for your help."

"Thank you so much!"

Miranda shot her an amused glance. "Your dad's been following your career and makes every customer read any mention of you in the newspaper. But no articles showed how gorgeous you've become. You remind me so much of Aurora. God rest her soul."

Claire wanted to correct Miranda and tell her that no hard evidence confirmed her sister's death, even if her trail went cold years ago, that she had proof that Aurora was alive. When Claire was still in intensive care, fighting for her life at the hospital, an unnamed woman had left a "get-well box" for her. It included a book from *Lost in France*, Claire's favorite cozy mystery series, and a bag of strawberry Tagada—the candies she and her sister would buy at the gourmet store and binge on behind their parents' backs. Growing up with a physician mother, candies weren't allowed in the house. The nurses had described the woman as "a blond with a mole near the eye," which was how Claire used to describe her sister as a child. But it was the note that accompanied the gift that convinced Claire that Aurora was alive. It was written: IT'S NOT OVER UNTIL YOU DECIDE IT'S OVER. Her sister's motto.

But Claire remained silent. Though reopening her sister's cold case was partly the reason why Claire was back in Caper Cove, she kept that matter to herself. She was afraid both her father and her therapist would consider her delusional if they knew. Claire had a hard enough time dispelling the belief that she wasn't French; she didn't want to have to convince her loved ones that her mental health and clarity had withstood the explosion. It was surviving the blast that made Claire realize that she couldn't die without having solved the mystery of her sister's disappearance.

A few minutes later, Detective Torres knocked on the Deputy Chief's open door. He had traded his navy suit for a Californian cowboy look with Western jeans, brown leather sneakers, and a leather jacket to match. "You asked to see me, chief?"

"Torres, yes. Claire Fontaine here will shadow you through the investigation today."

The detective regarded Claire as if he had been asked to drive a putrid zombie in his car. "You must be joking."

Chief Ernshaw scolded him with her eyes. "Do I look like I'm joking?"

"No, ma'am. But she's a suspect. She was at the scene at the time of death."

"Correlation isn't causation. We've got a video that cleared that misunderstanding," the deputy chief explained. "Ms. Fontaine is a skilled investigative attorney who may prove useful and may teach you a few things. Take her with you on your morning interviews and let her ride shotgun. Backseats are for drunks and criminals, understood?"

Torres mumbled something unintelligible.

"I didn't get that Detective. Do you mind repeating?"

"Yes, ma'am."

Chapter Eight

The Fashion Warriors production staff, Claire and Torres were about to interview, stayed at the Agatha Hotel, a mere fifteen-minute drive which promised to be awkward if not silent. Most crew members had given their statements the day before and Torres was supposed to focus on the three main persons of interest: Karl Smith, the show's owner and investor; Cordelia Jones, one of the finalists; and Max "Vinyl" Berkley, the third finalist.

Torres was driving a police-issued Ford Mustang Mach-E, an electric car with a soft yet powerful hum and a bright blue body that reminded Claire of a blueberry. The detective veered left onto Ocean Drive, the scenic roadway that ran along the shore of the Pacific Coast. It was a main thoroughfare in the town, providing access to many of Caper Cove's key attractions and neighborhoods. The view of the ocean was stunning. Miles of blue water stretched out to the horizon, with sailboats and windsurfers dotting the surface with bright colors.

Claire was riding shotgun. The coastal air rushed through her opened window, leaving wet, salted kisses on her face.

"So you're an attorney. You passed the bar exam and all?" Torres said, breaking the pleasant silence.

"Yep." Claire could have added that she passed the California bar on her first try, when the passage rate was only forty-one percent, but she kept that achievement to herself. Bragging was a sign of insecurity, and she needed to keep a strong, confident front in Torres' presence.

"You didn't let your legal license expire like your driving license?"

"Nope." She still resented him for tattle-telling to her father about that. To be honest, if her law firm hadn't handled her law license renewal, she probably would have let it expire. She would probably let it lapse now that she decided not to practice law for the foreseeable future.

"And you know how to write?" Torres added.

Claire chewed on her bottom lip and inhaled deeply. It wasn't the first time her competency had been questioned due to her elocution. She wished Torres and everyone who had ever questioned her understood that the brain processes language via two different areas—Broca's area, which is responsible for speech production and the muscles associated with it, and Wernicke's area, which is involved in the comprehension and understanding of the spoken and written language; that one's ability to write had nothing to do with one's ability to speak and vice-versa.

She considered sending Torres the link to the National Institute of Health (NIH) study on the issue, but she refused to waste her energy and justify herself to him. He probably wouldn't read it anyway. If he refused to believe that she was the daughter of Frank Fontaine, the owner of the Osprey and his landlord, he was a lost cause.

"Uh-huh. That's what attorneys do. They write. Legal briefs, pleadings, and depositions, etcetera." She didn't tell him that she had won her law school Moot Court and Client Counseling Competitions, two competitions which required superior written and verbal skills, and that she had received the Washington D.C. Attorney Excellency Award for Exemplary Oration the year before. The loss of her eloquence was still a heavy cross for her to bear, which she was struggling to take in stride.

"In English?" he added.

"Really! That's all you can focus on? My accent and pronunciation?" she said louder than she intended, unable to hide the exasperated tone in her voice. "You're either a jerk or shamefully small-minded and ignorant."

Torres lifted his hands from the steering wheel and held both palms up in her direction, in a my-bad gesture. "You don't need to get angry. I was just asking."

Just asking? Didn't they teach de-escalating techniques at the academy?

"In that case, I have a question for you. Did you graduate middle school?" she asked.

"Ouch. I get your point."

The detective continued north, toward the outer limit of the town. The grassy open fields of Claire's childhood had morphed into a well-developed resort area. Four-story-hotels, and luxury villas dotted the hillside while brightly colored pedestrian trails meandered through the marram grass from the buildings to the beach.

"I remember when there was nothing here. We used to have school picnics right in the middle of the beach grass."

"The mayor's been smart. By keeping the building height under five stories and having the conference center built at the northern edge, she's allowed economic growth while preserving the quiet, laid-back lifestyle of the town." Torres slowed down and swerved right on Resort Way. "So, what's with the get up and the pretty makeup?" he asked, glancing at her clothes. "You're meeting your boyfriend later on?"

"I don't need a boyfriend to dress any specific way. My liking it is reason enough. I don't question your modern sexy cowboy look, do I?"

Torres raised an eyebrow and glanced at her, smirking. "You find me sexy?"

Heat reached Claire's face. "Not at all. I was talking about the clothes."

Thank goodness the car arrived in front of the hotel where a hotel valet stopped them and instructed them toward the guest parking.

* * *

Karl Smith was staying in a honeymoon suite, a space that included a living corner with a spectacular ocean view, a telescope to gaze at the passing boats, and a clothing rack as long as a food truck. Claire followed Torres into the room after the detective introduced her as his assistant. Smith barely acknowledged her presence with an approving head nod directed at her choice of clothes, which she didn't mind. Flies on the wall could observe and learn much more about suspects than any active participants.

She sat on the same couch as Torres, three feet apart, right across from Karl Smith, who had settled on a green loveseat. The man wore nothing under his gold silk robe, and Claire wished he would keep his legs crossed.

"I don't understand why we can't resume shooting," Smith said with a demanding voice. "Do you even know how much money I'm losing each day we postpone production?"

"That's why the faster you answer my questions, the faster we can solve the matter, and the faster you'll be able to resume your work," Torres replied in a calm, authoritative tone. "What can you tell us about Vee Brooks and the competition?"

Smith shifted on his seat and exhaled loudly. "Vee was the clear favorite. Her unique designs rode the line between ultramodern and elegant, and her stitching was flawless. If crowned the winner, she would have won a fashion line contract with Macy's or Neiman Marcus to carry her collection, and a full feature in Vogue.

"Any reason why you aren't staying at the private villa?"

"It was part of the contract. Vee was a recovering addict. She didn't want to share a house with people using drugs or alcohol, so she always made sure to stay in a different place. I guess the precautions didn't help, and she fell off the wagon."

Claire's jaw tightened in frustration. Vee didn't fall off the wagon, she scream-thought. She wanted to correct the producer's statement, but she had promised Torres not to intervene in the suspect's interrogation.

"Did she stay at the villa alone?" Torres asked.

"Yes, the rest of us checked in at the hotel."

"Why not have her stay at the hotel instead? Would have been cheaper for the budget."

"Not really. Vee footed half the bill for the place. Her staying at the villa made it easier to avoid distractions like drugs or alcohol on the set. Once the crew left the set and was done with work, they could do whatever they wished." Smith picked up a porcelain cup from the marble coffee table that separated them and took a sip. "Vee saved me a lot of money. Her hermit-like attitude kept her confined to the villa, so I didn't need to hire security to

53

keep an eye on the equipment."

Torres jotted a few notes in his police-issued notepad. "Do you know if Ms. Brooks had enemies?"

Smith snorted. "Which of today's celebrities don't? Vee had a lot of enemies: other artists, rivalries…the list is long."

"What about the show finalists, her competitors? Cordelia Jones and Vinyl," Claire said.

"I wouldn't worry about Vinyl. He's high most of the time. I can't imagine him killing anyone. But if I were you, I would definitely check Cordelia. She and Vee were long-time rivals and fought a lot. They didn't even care if the cameras were rolling. They went at each other's throats like hyenas, claiming cheating."

"I'll need those videos and the list of potential enemies," Torres pulled a business card from his jacket pocket and handed it to Smith.

Smith scooted to the edge of the couch to grab the piece of paper, his robe rising on his hairy thighs and stopping thankfully short of his crotch. "Sure thing. My assistant will forward them to you."

Torres suppressed a laugh at the rising fabric and scribbled something in his notebook. "Do you know where we can find them, Vinyl and Cordelia?"

"Vinyl's room is right next to mine, but he's been gone since yesterday. Last I heard, he went on a day trip to Mexico. Cordelia is in 303, but you won't find her there. She's probably lounging by the pool getting oiled up by the local gigolos." He scoffed and shook his head. "At her age, no woman should sport a two-piece swimsuit."

Claire mentally gasped but kept a poker face like she had been trained to do with a hostile witness. Her age? Cordelia Jones was only forty-something. How could a bikini on a forty-year-old be a crime but skinny rhinestone jeans and a tight mesh shirt on a sixty-year-old man with a bulging belly be okay, she wondered, as she recalled the outfit the producer wore during the finale of last season of Fashion Warriors.

"You mind elaborating?" Torres asked.

The producer lifted his chin and nodded. "You see, in fashion, like in the entertainment industry, rules for men and women are different. To calculate a woman's real age, you need to multiply it by two. Forty for men is really eighty for women."

Claire exploded in laughs. "Really?"

Torres threw her a quick glare for speaking but didn't say a word.

Smith nodded solemnly, frowning. Next to his exposed thighs, the cover of ElitEgo magazine showed a suit-wearing elderly man surrounded by lingerie-clad teenaged girls. "Exactly."

Torres shook his head. "This is the stupidest thing I've ever heard."

Smith's face went from professorial seriousness to surprise and to embarrassment. "I didn't make the rules.," he said, violently setting his cup back on the table.

"Of course not." Torres stopped laughing and stared straight at the producer. "To return to the case, the sushi plate Ms. Brooks was eating when she died. Do you know where it came from? There was no identifying brand on the plate or on the take-out box."

"My assistant ordered it for Vee. I'll ask her to send you the information."

"Where was your production crew between 12:00 noon and 1:00 PM," Torres continued asking.

"We were all out for lunch. I always treat my staff to a nice fancy meal to celebrate the first day of shooting. We were supposed to shoot the first scene last night, in the backyard, with the setting sun in the background."

"Anyone missing?"

"Only Vinyl. He's a Minnesota kid in Cali who wanted to enjoy the beach and probably the legal weed. A skinny nothing with a soft personality. He doesn't have an aggressive bone in his body if that's what you're wondering."

"Okay." Torres closed his notebook and was about to stand up when Claire stopped him with a hand touch.

"One last thing," she said. "Any suspects you think of that the police might not consider or know about?"

Torres cleared his throat and threw Claire an angry look, but again, didn't stop her.

"Besides Cordelia?" Smith pressed his lips together and tilted his head sideways as if to dislodge some lost information stuck in his head. "The private chef Vee hired for the show. He never showed up and can't be reached. His phone's been disconnected. Maybe he came, killed her, and left."

Torres gave Claire a side glance before refocusing on Smith. "You've got his number?"

Chapter Nine

C laire and Torres left Karl Smith's room and took the elevator down to the hotel lobby. A breathtaking mural inspired by Hokusai's "The Great Wave" had been painted on the walls. Towering blue waves and frothy white foam created a sense of movement in the confined place, reminding the hotel guests of the power and beauty of the nearby ocean.

"What a pompous asshole," Torres said over the ambient music, a blend of cascading notes that evoked the sound of the wave slapping the shore.

"You took the words out of my mouth," she said with a nod.

"Don't you find it strange that he didn't know who you were?"

"Not really. I signed all the work-related email correspondence between me, Vee, and the production assistant with C.C.F, my initials."

"CCF?"

"Claire Clementine Fontaine. Vee had insisted I only use my initials. After meeting Karl Smith, I now understand why she wanted the hiring contract to be gender-neutral. That guy's a misogynistic jerk."

"Yeah, who would want to hire a seventy-year-old chef, right?" Torres mocked.

Claire joined him in laughter. She had heard many shocking statements in her law practice, but never something as ridiculous as the "twice-faster aging woman rule" Karl Smith had mentioned.

The lobby button brightened, and the elevator pinged as they reached the first floor.

"Why do you think he lied about not being able to reach you? His assistant must have had your number, didn't she?" Torres asked as he stepped out of the elevator.

Claire nodded. "Yes, that puzzled me too."

She fished her phone out of her crossbody purse and woke up the screen with a touch, revealing dozens of unopened messages. They were mostly texts of sympathy from acquaintances back east, customer discounts from her favorite D.C. stores asking her to visit, and her insurance's notifications that they were still investigating the explosion and couldn't release any funds and were sorry that Claire was completely broke. Nothing that needed to be handled right away. Except for one message from her phone carrier: *Your service has been stopped.*

"Smith may not be lying." She swiped through her email notifications and sighed. "You mind calling my number?"

Torres pulled his phone from his front pocket and handed it to her. Claire dialed her number and waited for her device to ring or to hear her voice asking the caller to leave a message. Instead, an automated voice told her "The number you are trying to call has been disconnected."

Claire facepalmed her forehead. As an attorney always on the phone with clients, her phone bill used to be considered a work expense, which her law firm paid every month. Until the law firm's expense accounts closed along with its destruction. Claire had received an "intent to stop service for non-payment notice" from her phone carrier over a month ago when she had just resurfaced from her coma. At the time, she had paid no heed to the notification, more focused on her physical recovery than her invoice.

"I forgot to update my method of payment," she said, grinning with embarrassment. She had never flaked on a bill before and couldn't correct the problem right away. She was broke. She needed a paying job stat!

Chapter Ten

There was nothing wrong or shameful about Cordelia Jones in a two-piece suit. The forty-ish woman was the textbook picture of the Hollywood trophy wife: Botoxed and Barbie-dolled up from head to toe with arms dotted with tattoos. A plastic kind of beauty who probably never enjoyed a fudgy cupcake or a chocolate croissant.

Claire tiptoed carefully behind Torres, feeling overdressed and off balance. The ground tiles of the heated pool were slippery with steam and the fogged-up bay window was clearing up as the morning sun tried to pour through.

Torres approached the woman sporting the baby-size swimsuit. "Cordelia Jones?"

"In the flesh," Cordelia sat upright on her chaise lounge and rearranged her breasts, pulling them upward behind the tiny triangles of fabric that covered her nipples. "Who's asking?"

Torres flashed his badge. "Caper Cove Police. I'm Detective Torres, and this is my assistant."

Cordelia flashed a seductive smile. "Oooh, I love men in uniform. What can I do for you, detective?"

"I have a few questions to ask you about Fashion Warriors and Vee Brooks. Do you mind sitting at a table?"

"Sure." She grabbed a bright red sarong from her seat, wrapped it around her bust like a dress, and settled at a nearby table. The large rectangular fabric had a poppy and splatter pattern, which Claire recognized from her "Red Death" collection that won her first place in an earlier season of the show.

Torres didn't mince his words and went straight at Cordelia's metaphorical throat, which didn't faze the woman at all. It was as if she was used to aggression and how to fend it off. Her prior assault conviction made sense. That woman was tough, Claire thought as she listened and observed attentively the woman's words and expressions.

"Did you want Vee dead?" the detective asked. Cordelia had been convicted of aggravated assault for breaking the nose of the woman who had stolen her hair appointment. It wasn't difficult to imagine her pushing Vee down the cliff for a one-million-dollar prize and a feature in a world-famous fashion magazine, but Claire needed to be sure. Presuming Cordelia's guilt of Vee's death simply based on her prior record was wrong, especially since Cordelia had already paid her debt to society by completing a prison sentence.

"Vee was a pain in the butt. Of course, I wished her dead. And yes, I punched her. But I didn't kill her, if that's what you mean. I was with the crew, enjoying lunch when it happened. I've got like thirteen alibis."

"What were your fights about?" Torres asked.

"Vee was trying to ruin my brand. She was spreading lies about me, accusing me of stealing designs. This top for example," she said, inflating her chest to better show off her teensy swimsuit top. "This is all me. My designs, my colors, and my prints. All handmade except for the fabric." The fabric, white or patterned, was provided by Karl Smith, who was also a fabric manufacturer and the show's fabric supplier.

"Are your designs original?" Claire asked, recalling an early phone conversation she had with Vee. Her late friend had inquired about intellectual property (IP) and design protection for independent artists whose designs were stolen by famous artists and big corporations.

"You bet they are. As original and genuine as me and as French as you are!" she replied to Claire with a sideways smile. As Cordelia fluffed her hair, a heady scent of sweet rose infused the air.

Torres nodded, seemingly unconvinced. A claim of genuineness by someone who had dental veneers, colored contacts, hair extensions, and implants wasn't very compelling.

"The real thief was Vee. Did you know she stole her husband? Clay

Poderas was engaged to Tara Betrossen when Vee met him. Clay broke off his engagement to Tara and eloped to Vegas with Vee a few weeks later. A shotgun wedding, most likely, except that rumors say that he isn't even the baby's father."

Claire tensed up. She didn't like hearing disparaging statements about her late friend, especially when Vee wasn't around to defend herself. She knew Vee's marriage had been a spur-of-the-moment event, but it had also been an act of love, not desperation. Vee had been strong enough, financially and emotionally, to raise a child alone. It wasn't her style to ambush a man with a lie.

Having heard enough, Claire left the table and returned to the lobby. So much had happened in Vee's life since Claire survived her firm's explosion. Her short coma and weeks of physical therapy had prevented her from being socially active, and Claire felt like a stranger in her late friend's life.

After serving herself a complimentary cucumber water from the lobby's refreshment counter, Claire settled in the sunbathed corner of the bay window. She closed her eyes to relax and recenter herself as the sun warmed her face. She needed to cast her emotions aside if she wanted to remain objective in her investigation. She needed to only focus on the evidence at hand. She took a long, deep breath and listened to her surroundings. The hums of tourists' conversations competed with the sound of flip-flops on the tiled floor—the soft rhythm of the tourist season.

Be patient and precise, she told herself as she mentally reviewed the facts of the case.

Vee couldn't have been the victim of suicide. Claire was sure of it. Her friend had fought too hard through life and risen too high to destroy everything on a whim. Especially with a new baby in her life. A review of Vee's medical record should confirm whether or not her friend was suffering from post-partum depression.

If suicide was ruled out, the list of suspects included: (1) Cordelia Jones, the rival who wanted to get rid of the competition; (2) Tara Betrossen, Vee's husband's ex-fiancée who might have wanted to take revenge on Vee for stealing her fiancé; (3) and Clay Poderas, Vee's husband and gubernatorial candidate, who could have killed his wife for revenge for not being his baby's biological father and/or save his campaign with empathy votes.

A classic masculine fragrance and the sudden lack of sun brought Claire out of her rumination. Before reopening her eyes, she knew Torres was standing in front of her. She recognized his Calvin Klein cologne from the car ride, and only someone with a distorted sense of self-importance would block her sun like that.

"I guess you want to accompany me to San Diego to interview Clay Poderas?" he asked. The shadow of his tall stature and wide shoulders enveloped her entire body.

Claire stood up, walked into the sunlight, and checked her calendar on her watch.

"Thanks for asking, but I'll pass." She had a virtual meeting with her speech therapist she couldn't miss. Today, she was supposed to work on her D and T sounds.

"Some urgent matter to attend?"

"You can say that." She could postpone her meeting if an emergency presented itself, but a round trip to San Diego would eat the rest of her day and she wasn't looking forward to being stuck in a traffic jam with Torres. She would rather spend that time looking for a paying job and another place to live or recheck the crime scene and search for clues. She would read about Torres' findings in the police report.

Torres narrowed his eyes. "Why is that? You've already talked to him or know him personally?"

"I've never met him." Vee had talked to Claire about Clay Poderas after meeting him for the first time. Her late friend had told her that he was "the one" and called him her soul mate, a term Claire never understood. Her firm's bombing happened shortly after that. Claire had been in the coma and intense physical therapy at the time of the wedding and the birth. She had missed Vee's most important life events. Being her private chef was going to be an opportunity for them to catch up.

"How close of a friend were you if you don't know her husband?" Torres asked, scratching his head.

"It's a long story."

Torres must have read the sadness in Claire's eyes because he didn't press her for an answer. "Do you need a ride back to the station?"

"No, thanks. I'll walk." She didn't need his pity or his help. Besides, Vee's private villa was only a thirty-minute walk away. She pulled her phone from her purse and texted Suggie to meet her there, deeply grateful for the hotel's free Wi-Fi and her ability to text using her email address.

"Don't forget to send me your number whenever you get it back," Torres said with a patronizing smile.

Claire force-grinned and dialed the detective's number on her video call app.

Torres picked up his phone. "Detective Torres listening."

"Since you obviously don't know how someone can place calls without a phone number, here's my direct line. Don't hesitate to call me here if you need help with legal or technological aspects of the case." She waved at him as she left the lobby, amused.

Claire quickly hung up afraid the lack of free Wi-Fi network would drop her call as soon as she exited the building. Outdoor places were literally dead zones that would cut her off from the internet world and digital communications.

She followed the pedestrian path to the cliffs, cogitating on how to get her cellphone number and data plan back. Had she been a teenager, she would have called on her father's grace for an extra allowance or a friendly loan from her best friend. Now, at thirty-five, she had too much pride to resolve to mendicity. She needed to get a job fast.

Chapter Eleven

The tide had receded enough to give Claire and Suggie a clear path to the bottom of the cliff. No yellow police tape had been draped around the wooden stairs leading to Vee's private villa. It was as if the police had forgotten about it, maybe due to the incoming tide, or they had judged it unnecessary. No matter the reason, this procedural misstep amounted to negligence. The killer—Claire was sure there was one—could have easily returned to the premises to erase the traces of their presence.

"The police must think it's a simple accident," Suggie said as she fought against the strong wind to keep her silky black hair out of her face.

Though Claire doubted the police took the matter seriously, she applauded their decision to station a guard at the villa's official entrance. The uniformed policeman had parked his car right across the entry gate to block access to anyone—a smart precaution that wouldn't stop her from checking the crime scene one more time. If the police didn't take the matter seriously, she needed to investigate on her own. Her job, reputation as a private chef, and Suggie's wedding were at stake.

"Either way, they probably assumed no one would willingly climb hundreds of these steps," she said.

Bent in half, Suggie held the wooden handrail with both hands. "You can say that again. Only crazy people would agree to climb this wobbly staircase."

"Not crazy. Spirited," Claire corrected as she took a pause mid-way to catch her breath. It wasn't the first time Suggie was following Claire on one of her dangerous explorations. Her best friend had been doing so since they were kids—from the cliff jumping dare when they were nine years old to the "kiss a complete stranger" challenge when they were twenty-one. They had just taken a ten-year break.

"Thank you for agreeing to accompany me," Claire added. "I was afraid you wouldn't get my text."

"Honestly, it was kind of weird to receive a text from a stranger claiming to be you and asking me to meet you at the beach. I wouldn't have come here if you hadn't used our old safe word. I can't believe we still remember it." It was a word their families had created when they were twelve years old, right after Claire's sister disappeared. A word they had to use in every communication relating to a change of schedule, tardiness, or impromptu hangout with friends. A word that conjured up a broken childhood and prompted Claire's parents' divorce and her move to the East Coast with her mom.

Claire laughed, pushing her dark past away. "Yes, pineapple's not the easiest word to drop in every conversation."

"So, who was that guy?"

"The guy who lent me his phone? His name's Dylan. He's a drone enthusiast I met near the resort. When I realized he was flying his craft over the hills, I asked him to take a look. That's when I spotted the police car. And that's why I asked you to meet me at the beach." If the police caught them nosing around the villa, Claire could still claim that she didn't know the residence was off access, that the absence of yellow tape indicated that she had the right to go.

Even though Claire had always been a rule follower, law practice had taught her that walking the legal line could be useful and necessary when the greater good was at stake. Finding Vee's killer and making sure Suggie's wedding took place qualified as such.

"Trust me," she added. "It's easier to ask for forgiveness than it is to get permission."

Suggie raised an eyebrow and gave Claire a quizzical look. "If you say so. But if we get caught, you'll have to return to law and be my legal defense. Unlike you, I don't personally know the chief of police, and I'm not the executor of Vee's estate. I've no reason to be here."

"Deal, but it won't come to that. Plus, you're going to get great material for your newsletter *and* well-defined glutes," Claire pointed out, laughing. With the steepness and length of the staircase, there would be no need for a Pilates class to tighten their derrières.

* * *

"Revisiting a crime scene is an important step in any investigation. It allows the observer to rediscover the place with new eyes, uncolored by the novelty or emotions," Claire explained as she captured every inch of the backyard with her cellphone camera.

To her dismay, the once pristine lawn was now a green canvas of flattened grass and scattered footprints. The potential culprit's imprints were impossible to isolate or distinguish from the tracks left by the TV crew returning from lunch, the police officers, and the neighbors. Though unpreserved by yellow tape, the dirt patch edging the cliff, the point from which Vee had fallen, had been left undisturbed. The plate of sushi and picnic blanket were gone, hopefully, taken to a lab for analysis, and the soil around it presented only two sets of footprints. By the depth and narrowness of the impressions, the shoes had formed in the dirt, one of them had to be high heels. Probably the one Vee wore when she died.

"You don't think the police collected all the evidence?" Suggie asked from the safety of the tiled patio.

"I'm not sure, but processing a crime scene properly takes knowledge and experience, which I doubt the town police have enough. Unlike big metropolitan areas, Caper Cove is far from being murder central."

"Which is why it's paradise. A safe haven from the chaotic world," Suggie sing-songed.

"Which is also the reason why a lack of criminal expertise might let Vee's killer go free." Claire squatted on the brink of the cliff and squinted at small depressions in the soil. They were tiny and repetitive but didn't appear to come from an animal. She zoomed in on the small prints, snapped a few pictures, and airdropped them to Suggie. "There's something odd about this second set of footprints. It's way too close to the edge, and it has a half-moon dent in it."

"What do you think it is?" Suggie asked as she checked the images on her phone.

"I'm not sure. Maybe a pebble caught in the sole, or a flaw in the killer's shoes proving Vee wasn't alone on the cliff." Claire took a few more pictures from various angles, for good measure, added a few thoughts in her phone's notes, and stood up. "Let's go inside."

Suggie's eyes widened. "Are you sure?"

"I don't see any yellow tape, do you?" If the police were negligent, might as well use it to their benefit. Also, since the house was supposed to be Claire's legal residence for the next two weeks, it wasn't technically trespassing.

Suggie shook her head and followed hesitantly.

As soon as Claire pressed the digits Vee had given her into the keypad, the kitchen's French door clicked open. These newly automated houses, which required no physical key, were easier to access than traditional homes. As long as one remembered the keycode, one could enter through any door.

Bright columns of sunlight brightened the room. The red kettle was still on the stove and the three mugs and Linzer cookies had remained untouched on the counter.

"It doesn't feel right being here," Suggie moaned, trailing behind.

"I know, but we don't have a choice. Being here without Vee may feel wrong, but it's the only way to find out what happened to her." It was also nice to give their ears a break from the violent wind outside. A low-pitched rumble accompanied the forceful and persistent gusts, resonating through the house like a screaming ghost. If ghosts existed.

Claire led the way down the corridor to the master bedroom and pushed open the yellow door of Vee's suite. "Don't worry, we won't stay long. I've a speech therapy appointment I can't miss."

The room was soft yellow, from the plush carpet and the sheer curtains to the silk bedcover. Vee's favorite color. Beyond the bright sunny theme, the room was in shambles. The nightstand and dresser were overturned with drawers pulled out, their contents scattered on the floor.

"Wow. It's chaos in here. Are artists always this messy?" Suggie asked.

"Not Vee. She was organized to a fault." It was a personality trait she shared with Claire—a need for control in our turbulent world, which bordered on OCD. Besides, the destructive sense of the place felt like a violation. Someone had forcibly entered the room and carried out an extensive search. "This isn't her clutter. The police must have searched the place."

Claire sniffed the air. Chanel No. 5, the perfume Vee used to wear still lingered in the air. There was also a flowery scent with a hint of sweet rose.

"What are we looking for?" Suggie asked.

"A receipt or bag from the sushi delivery or anything that could alter perception like drugs or alcohol. Any written content, like a diary or a tablet, that could tell us about her state of mind or display her emails. Could be anything. Something that seems missing or out of place, like stained clothing," Claire explained, heading straight for the bathroom. Killers often washed their hands after a crime, leaving precious DNA behind.

Suggie gasped and rushed to a far section of the room where bright tailored outfits hung from a rolling clothing rack that had been miraculously left untouched by the intrusive search. "Is that her new collection?"

"Yes, but let's focus on finding clues, alright?" Claire directed gently. She retrieved discarded insulin pens from the waste basket and a bottle of ibuprofen from the medicine cabinet. It was strange the police hadn't bagged them. In a suspicious death, any medication found on the premises should be preserved, tagged, and entered into evidence. She bagged both in a Ziploc, just in case, and placed them in her purse. She would ask Vikram to analyze them. If the police refused to do their due diligence, she would do it for them.

"Anything?" Claire inquired as dread filled her. Maybe the police hadn't inspected the place thoroughly enough. Maybe the mess was the result of someone else's search. Someone who had taken Vee's electronics, including her iPad Pro on which she had designed her latest collection. But who? And what was Vee hiding that would cause someone to ravage the place?

"Nothing in the closet, but the wedding dress is missing from the new collection," Suggie crinkled her nose. "You think someone stole it?"

"I don't think so. The designs had been submitted three months in advance. No one could steal a design at the last minute and claim it to be theirs. The dress must be in the blue room," Claire said as she rushed out of the master bedroom.

Suggie trotted after Claire. Their hasty footsteps were muffled by the wind's howl and the creaking of doors. "The blue room? Why?"

"It was supposed to be my room. Vee made the dress to your dimensions. You were supposed to try it yesterday, upon our arrival. It was supposed to be a surprise," Claire explained as she headed down the marble hallway. "As your maid of honor and the close friend of a fashion designer, I couldn't let you get married in a work suit." She stopped in front of the blue door on which a page had been taped. The large print letters read *Claire's room*.

"You mean I'm getting married in a Vee Brooks original?"

Claire opened the door and nodded. "Vee refused to design wedding dresses unless made for real brides. Your wedding was supposed to showcase her first and only one."

"OMG, Claire, you're the best!" Suggie hugged Claire from behind, so excitedly that they both tumbled inside the room.

The space was true to its name. Blue lace curtains framed the windowed view of a private garden, and a quilted bedspread of azurean shades dressed the bed. Even the white wall betrayed a bluish shine.

After finding her bearings, Suggie rushed to the bed where a bridal gown had been laid. "Is this it? It's gor-ge-ous!" She grabbed the dress, walked to the wall mirror, and looked at herself with the dress in front of her.

Claire observed Suggie and sad-smiled. Vee's designs made people so happy as if magic had been weaved into the fabric. Her death was a terrible loss not only to her friends and family, but to the world as well. Claire was about to help Suggie adjust the veil on her head when the corner of the bedspread caught her attention. This type of luxury villa rental always included top-notch housekeeping services—professionals who would never leave a bed imperfectly prepared. Which meant someone had disturbed the bedding and tried to tuck the sheet back but had done it poorly.

Claire kneeled in front of the bed and slid her hands beneath the mattress. She ran them along the box-spring, her elbows disappearing under the fabric, until her fingers came in contact with paper. Claire retrieved the object and placed it on the cover. It was a folder filled with handwritten pages, newspaper clippings, and computer printouts.

Suggie glanced away from her reflection. "What is it?"

"Looks like a case file, evidence Vee had collected on someone." Claire quickly leafed through the paperwork and fabric samples.

"Evidence against who?"

"Cordelia Jones. It appears that Cordelia didn't create her designs but stole them from high school students." Fabric samples from Cordelia's collection were stapled to small-town newspapers' articles praising the creativity of their students. Pictures showed designs Cordelia called her own months before the woman supposedly created them. "Cordelia Jones's a fraud and a thief, and Vee was about to expose her. That's a motive to kill."

A triple buzz of the doorbell called Claire's attention. The third chime was followed by two rapid buzzes and another three additional rapid buzzes. It wasn't an ordinary way for people to ring a doorbell. It was more like a code. Then, the sound of high heels hitting the floor echoed above the wind.

Suggie was about to say something when Claire jumped forward and muted her with one hand. "Someone's in the house," Claire whispered.

Chapter Twelve

With her phone in camera mode, Claire followed the sound of the clicking heels to the entrance door, which slammed shut. She placed her phone against the vestibule window, trying to capture a clear view of Cordelia leaving the house and kissing the police officer on duty. She zoomed in on the man's face and uniform to get his badge number and on Cordelia's face. The evidence of Cordelia's trespass and police corruption would be undeniable in court, if needed.

She held her breath, making sure the video captured the words exchanged between the woman and the guard outside and not her own ragged breathing. She hadn't sprinted like this since the explosion and really needed to get back into shape.

"You've got to go *now*," the man said. "My replacement's on his way. He's a nosy one who's going to tour the property."

"Thanks, Tom. See you tonight." Cordelia threw him a coy smile and scampered out of view.

Claire ended the video on these words and rushed back to the blue room, where Suggie quietly waited as Claire had asked her to do.

"We need to leave *stat!*" Claire grabbed the folder. It probably was what Cordelia had been searching for—damaging evidence Vee had collected against her competitor and the perfect motive to kill Vee. That's why Vee had hidden it under Claire's bed. That had to be the legal matter Vee had wanted to talk to her about.

Claire lifted her dress and tucked the file in her shapewear, grateful for its high-waisted elastic band. "Ready?"

Suggie shook her head nervously, pouting. "What about the wedding dress? We can't leave it here. What if thieves take it or the police stain it during their search?"

Fashion felt frivolous at this very moment, and rushing down the wobbly, wooden stairs to the beach with a fancy gown in tow seemed hazardous, but Suggie had a point. With the house's lax security, anyone could take the garment. If not burglars, she could easily see untrained police officers touching the fabric with dirty fingers and leaving greasy, unremovable stains on the delicate, shiny silk. Vee would have hated that. Claire's inner fashionista understood that. With her fiancé's last-minute deployment and her lack of wedding reception, Suggie needed something positive to look forward to. The wedding gown was it.

"Let's roll it like a towel inside the veil and wrap it around your waist under your blouse. We'll get the dry cleaner to get rid of the creases."

A minute later, Claire and Suggie barreled out of the kitchen door and down the beach staircase with altered gaits, like two clowns escaping the circus. Claire ran straighter than usual, almost backward, with the folder pushing against her bra, while Suggie followed her arms wide open by her side as if she were wearing a pool ring underneath her blouse.

* * *

Claire rubbed her jaws in her hands. Her mouth and tongue were sore from too many speaking exercises and her brain was exhausted by too much focus on how to pronounce even the most familiar words. She hated the discomfort, feeling of shame, and lack of control she experienced after intensive sessions like this one. The grief for the loss of her once-celebrated eloquence felt sharper than usual. After her rushed trip up and down the hundreds of wooden steps, speech therapy was akin to a coup de grace. Luckily, her father didn't need her to talk to understand her need for comfort food. As soon as he spotted her dragging her feet to one of the customer tables, he brought her childhood favorite: a glass of lavender lemonade and easy-to-chew lobster tacos.

The cool, sugary drink and the sweet crustacean dish soothed Claire's jaw and tongue, the way ice cream heals a child's booboo. Something her physical therapist called "a serotonin and dopamine miracle"—two neurotransmitters that decrease the stress hormone cortisol and make people feel calmer and less tense.

The sound of the ocean was soothing. The tide was ebbing, widening the beach as its water slowly receded, unveiling miles of shell-covered shoreline—a tourist and shell-collector paradise. The salty sea breeze and the sun had also joined in Claire's recovery until a shadow blocked the sunshine's curative warmth.

"Do you mind if I sit down?" the shadow asked.

Claire straightened on her chair and looked up at the middle-aged woman standing in front of her. Deep grooves lined her face, which could either be from years of unprotected sunbathing, tough living conditions, or addiction. By the dark circles under the woman's eyes and the plain, old-fashioned clothes, Claire guessed it had to be one of the latter. Some of the destitute clients she had defended pro bono had the same weary eyes and second-hand clothes.

"Suggie Oh told me I could find you here. Vee was my friend," the woman explained.

"Of course." Her tailbone and thighs were still sore from her morning escapade, but Claire managed a smile. "Please, take a seat."

"Thanks. My name's Nina Rock. I'm a social worker with San Diego Blooms, an organization that provides services for at-risk youth. Vee was one of our sponsors." The woman settled in the chair closest to Claire as if they were about to discuss matters of national security, pulled a photograph from her purse, and set it on the table. The picture depicted a brightly smiling Vee surrounded by teenagers. They were standing on a podium behind which a banner read *Caper Cove Fashion Week*.

"This was taken last year. Vee'd been volunteering with at-risk youth for over a year. Every week, she would teach kids about fashion, how to make outfits from scraps, how to design and sew. She even bought twenty sewing machines for the club," the woman said in one breath. "And she wasn't just generous with her time and money. She was an inspiration, a model for the de-motivated, down-on-their-luck kids. Especially juvies."

Claire nodded. She knew that about Vee. Claire was the one who had recommended volunteer work as a way to keep her friend grounded, and Vee had embraced the idea of paying forward and making a change in the world. Vee went as far as renting a large beachfront property in Caper Cove every December, so the kids without family could enjoy Christmas outside of the city. "Yes, Vee had a huge heart. She was proud of these kids. Did you come here to tell me all this?"

"No, I came because Vee told me that you were the first person to ever believe in her. I just wanted you to know that she wasn't an addict and that her death wasn't a suicide." The woman paused and blinked hard as if trying to stop tears. She fiddled with her bracelet, a sobriety coin encased into braided leather. "Vee was supposed to help out next week, and she never missed a single appointment with the kids. Something's not right. Her death can't be a suicide or an accident, either. There's no way she walked close enough to the edge for the ground to give in. She always stayed clear of heights and balconies." She took a deep breath and sighed. "Vee told me you were a great lawyer-investigator. Please find who did this."

The woman pulled a wad of cash from her purse and presented it to Claire. "It's not much, but I can pay you. People at the center all pitched in, but it's all we can give you right now."

Claire's throat tightened. The offer was nice, especially since Claire was completely broke and needed the money, but she couldn't charge someone a fee for something she was already doing for free. Someone who probably needed it more than she did. Besides, the FBI and her therapist had been categorical: she was to stay away from the practice of law, which meant not taking on any clients. Paying or not.

"I'm sorry, but I can't accept your offer. I'm not practicing law anymore and the search for truth and justice should be free." It was also nice to have someone who personally knew Vee and believed her death wasn't an accident or suicide.

"Does that mean you're taking the case?"

"I can't accept money, but I'm investigating her death on the down-low, yes. But this must stay between us." The police rarely appreciated parallel investigations by PIs and lawyers. Like in most professions, while most police work was reliable, there were enough bad apples or overworked employees to warrant a separate investigation.

The woman jolted on her seat, tears running down her face. "Thank you so much. You can't imagine what that means to the kids and me."

Claire bit her lips as she nodded. She knew exactly how it felt. When Aurora disappeared twenty years ago, she would have donated everything she had, including her organs, to find out what had happened to her sister. She still wondered about it and was hoping to dig into her sister's cold case right after she solved Vee's murder. No matter how much time passed, there were questions that never got answered and wounds that never healed.

"You're welcome. But I need to ask you a few questions. Do you have time?"

"Yes, I took the afternoon off, and there won't be a train back to San Diego before three-thirty."

Claire checked her watch. She had two hours to learn as much as possible about Vee's recent state of mind and circumstances. "Great. Please, make yourself comfortable,"

She ordered a pitcher of lemonade, an extra plate and set of silverware, and a large sampler of tacos. Finding new sources to interview and potential leads always opened Claire's appetite, and sharing food built trust between people.

"What can you tell me about Vee's recent mood? Any specific stresses in her life besides the fashion competition?" Claire asked, feeling guilty, as she pulled her phone to take notes. Vee's mental health was something she should have known. Her busy schedule of physical recovery after the explosion had left her out of Vee's loop.

"For starters, her husband's political campaign was a huge cause of stress. Vee was afraid journalists would find out about her troubled past and ruin her husband's chances at the governorship."

Journalists could be relentless, indeed. Claire discovered that early on in her legal career when she had to fight the misinformation the press had disseminated about her clients. Since Vee was only sixteen at the time of her criminal trial, her records had been sealed and considered no longer existing for most purposes. In fact, if interviewed, Vee could have legally and truthfully denied having a criminal history if someone had questioned her about it. But the stress of campaigning could be brutal and send anyone over the edge, a fact the police would probably use to declare her death a suicide.

"You said *for starters*. Is there more?" Claire asked, refilling the woman's glass with lemonade.

"Yes, but you didn't hear it from me." She looked over her shoulders and scooted her chair closer to Claire's. "Vee was being harassed by someone named Jason."

Claire entered the information on the digital notepad of her phone. "Did she share that with you?"

"No, but I heard her fighting with him several times over the phone. The guy was angry and so loud it was like he was on speaker. Whenever the phone rang and his name flashed on the screen, Vee would ignore it or run to the bathroom to take the call. He even called the annex once and asked me to give Vee a message."

Vee had dated a Jason a year or so ago, before her lightning-fast wedding to Clay Poderas, her present husband. A Jason McCarthy, if Claire remembered well, a trust fund playboy with whom Vee had a tumultuous relationship. A jerk who had insisted Vee get an abortion. Could it be the same one?

"Do you know his last name?" Claire asked.

"I'm sorry, I don't. Vee was very private about it. Secretive even."

Claire glanced at the vastness of the ocean and its retracting tide, as if nature was holding back something from her. Through her practice of law, Claire had discovered that secrets were invisible threads in most people's lives, strangers and loved ones alike. She often wondered how many secrets her sister or parents kept that they never shared with her.

"Any details you may remember from her phone conversations?"

"Before Vee blocked the number for good, I overheard the word *child custody* and something about him wanting to be on the child's birth certificate. It sort of surprised me, because, besides her baby with Clay Poderas, I didn't know Vee had any other children."

Claire nodded, typing down the information on her phone's tiny keyboard as fast as she could. "Anything else?"

"She also told him to leave her alone and to focus on his *fuku restaurant*," the woman said, making air quotes with her fingers. The kids were all laughing hard when they heard her say *fuku*, because Vee never swore."

"Did she say *fuku* or *fugu*?"

"Why, is there a difference?"

"Possibly." Fuku could mean many things, including "clothes" or "to blow" in Japanese, while fugu could mean blowfish and be a direct link to Vee's cause of death. The Jason McCarthy Vee used to date was a sushi aficionado who had invested in a chain of luxury Sushi restaurants. The Jason who had harassed and fought with Vee over the phone might be the source of the tetrodotoxin that killed her.

* * *

When her interlocutor left two hours later, the tide was low. Sandpipers waded in the water, foraging for small mollusks and crustaceans. The birds moved quickly along the exposed shoreline, running after their prey and probing the sand with their bills to snatch them up.

Claire didn't feel that different from them as she was poking around for clues that could help her solve her friend's murder. Her two-hour conversation had been like a receding tide that had revealed the uneven, rocky shoreline of Vee's life.

"You look tired and tense. Everything all right?" The warm, comforting voice of her father asked. He placed a fragrant mug of chamomile-blueberry tea in front of her, the same way he did when she was studying for exams as a child.

"I'm fine, Dad. I'm just enjoying the sights," she said in the direction of the flock of sandpipers running after the waves. There were dozens of them now, bobbing their heads up and down to keep focus on their food and keep their balance on the uneven shoreline. "Do you know anything about the owner of a fugu restaurant named Jason?"

"I do, both as a former cop and as a restaurant owner." Her father settled in the chair beside her. Most patrons were gone, leaving behind two busboys who were actively cleaning the tables. It was her father's time to take a break as The Osprey would only reopen at sunset, when it turned into a cops' bar. "What do you need to know?"

"Anything you have, starting with his full name."

"Jason McCarthy is a local restaurateur who owns the exclusive HaruNam-iCali in the resort district. He serves the best sushi and most expensive fusion dishes on the coast but underpays and mistreats his staff. He's the stereotypical self-entitled rich boy who's never worked a day in his life and thinks the rules don't apply to him. His juvie file is sealed but his adult criminal record is pretty thick. Mainly DUI and speeding tickets he got out of and assault charges that were dropped. Money, I tell you."

"What do you mean? The charges weren't pleaded or officially dismissed?"

"Nah, the charges were dropped like a lava-hot potato. A hefty bank account's more appealing to most victims than public justice in court."

"Do you remember what the cases were about?"

"Something about forcing his girlfriends into getting abortions. The usual trifecta: coercive control, intimidation, and assault. Why? Does that have something to do with your friend's death?"

"Maybe." But if Jason hated the idea of paternal responsibility, why would he fight with Vee about child custody? Did Vee have his baby? And if so, why would Jason want to be officially recognized as the father? More importantly, did Vee's husband know?

Claire squeezed her head in her hands. There were too many motives and too many theories to consider to keep it all in her mind. "Do you have a chalk or dry-erase board I can use?

Her dad shot her a concerned look. "Yes, in the old office, in the basement. Why?"

"I just need to jot a few things down," she said as she sprang out of her chair and dashed toward the building.

Chapter Thirteen

The Osprey back office was the only room Frank Fontaine hadn't remodeled since he had purchased the building from its former owner. It was a cool windowless room that served as a recyclable storage area. A weak light illuminated the space. The small desk and chair that once occupied the right corner were now gone, replaced by cases of bottles and kegs. The old, magnetized whiteboard was still present. It hid under layers of yellowed newspaper clippings, expired coupons, and flyers—vestiges of a pre-digital accounting and communication era. Once Claire plucked at the magnets holding everything in place, the papers all fell to the floor like dead autumn leaves.

"Someone ought to clean this place," she mumbled to herself, coughing against the dust.

She tried to pull the board off the wall but failed. So she uncapped one of the dry-erase markers and started to jot down everything that occupied her mind—the list of possible suspects, their motives, and opportunities.

Jason McCarthy (V's ex): threat of paternity suit, fight for baby custody?

Clay Poderas (V's husband): revenge, pride?

Tara Betrossen (V's husband's ex-fiancé): revenge?

Cordelia Jones (competitor/rival): keep Vee from exposing her/eliminate the competition?

"What are you doing here?" Detective Torres' warm, authoritative voice bounced off the walls, startling Claire.

"I could ask you the same thing," she said as she watched him carry four cases of empty beer bottles and deposit them in the corner of the room.

"I'm helping Frank, earning my keep," he said in a snarky tone, as if implying she didn't earn hers. "I don't know how much rent Frank charges you, but with his soft spot, I'm sure it's way below average. You should consider pitching in around the bar."

Claire raised an annoyed eyebrow but inwardly smiled. Torres hadn't yet realized she was Frank's daughter. Even after she told him. Talk about being a detective! Yes, cops were suspicious by nature and didn't rely on simple statements without solid corroboration of the truth, but was her accent that awful that he couldn't conceive her connection to her dad? They had the same last name.

"You must be kidding me! Is that a murder board?" Torres said as he stared at the board.

Claire turned her back to him and continued adding to her writing. "What if it is?"

"So that's what you've been doing. You've been investigating on your own instead of accompanying me to the Poderas residence!" There was a hint of hurt in his voice as if he had taken personally her refusal to accompany him that morning. "You knew Vee's husband was AWOL, didn't you?"

Claire gasped, offended by the accusation. "I had no idea he was missing. I don't have inside information or a crystal ball." Though the Fashion Warriors lawyer had mentioned Clay Poderas was nowhere to be found the day before, she had wrongly assumed he would have returned home by now. "Of course, I'm going to investigate. I'm the executor of Vee's estate and must provide due diligence. Especially when the detective in charge doesn't know what he's doing."

"What did you say?" Torres squinched his face up at her. "You think I can't follow a lead?"

"What do you think?" She said, solidifying her stance, her arms crossed over her chest.

A deep, hearty laugh boomed through the basement, cutting the tension in half. "I see you've met my daughter," Frank chuckled as he patted Torres' shoulder and guided him out of the room.

Torres shook his head as if trying to rearrange his thoughts. His gaze darted between Frank and Claire. "Your daughter? But she looks nothing like you."

Claire followed and stepped onto the sunlit patio. "Dad's hairier."

"She's really your daughter?" Torres grimaced as he had just learned pigs could actually fly. "But she has an accent."

Claire rolled her eyes. "Jeez, what's your obsession with people's elocution?"

"I personally love that accent, and that French bob with bangs is so becoming." Roxy Putnam, Claire's former French teacher and her father's best friend, threw her arms around her into a welcome-back hug. Roxy still wore a bright red ponytail, untouched by gray, tight Navy capri pants showing off her curves, and a striped long-sleeved shirt. Laugh lines etched the woman's face from the corners of her mouth to her eyes—two crescents that surfers called summer moons.

Claire loved Roxy like a favorite aunt, and she always wondered if there once was, or if there ever would be, something between her dad and Roxy.

"I'm so happy you're back on your feet and in California after the tragedy. Your dad told me you were home, but I hadn't had a chance to say hi. Let me look at you."

By the time Roxy had finished examining Claire from every angle, Frank was back with the whiteboard. "If you're going to draw a murder board, it's better to do it in your room. You don't want to scare the tourists by rushing in and out of that basement like a crazed sleuth."

"I can take it upstairs," Torres volunteered as he took the board from Frank's hands. "For the record, I never said I didn't like her accent." He was on his way to the private stairs when he turned toward Claire and paused. "Wait. Who's Jason McCarthy, and why is his name on the board?"

"It's Vee's ex-boyfriend. He was harassing Vee and had access to tetrodotoxin, the poison that killed her."

Frank laughed. "Looks like Claire's got a leg up on you, Ben."

Torres' jaws tightened. "Not for long, because I'm on my way to interrogate him."

"You may want to slow down your horse, son. If he sees you coming, he's going to shut down like a clam. The best way to approach this guy is to engage him in a casual conversation. Make a reservation for dinner and have Claire lead. He's always around at night to mingle with his rich clientele, and he has a penchant for French women."

Claire rolled her eyes. She wanted to scream that she wasn't French, but she understood the assignment. At least her French accent would serve her for once. She looked up the stairs at Torres with a forced half-smile. "I'm up for it if you are."

"Are you sure, sweetie?" Roxy asked. "You've just arrived to rest, and you're already playing spy."

"Thanks for your concern, Roxy, but it's the only way I can find out what happened to my friend. Only then will I be able to truly rest."

Torres wasted no time and was already dialing on his phone to make a reservation. "They don't have any openings this month."

"They're usually booked two months out," Roxy explained. "I can call and pull some strings to get you a reservation if you want. My niece works there."

"That would be perfect, Roxy. Merci."

Chapter Fourteen

Getting ready for a date that wasn't a real date, with someone who rubbed her the wrong way, was by far one of the most uncomfortable situations Claire had ever experienced, which included interrogating felons within the tight confines of a high-security prison. On the positive side, Torres was agreeable to the eyes and non-threatening, and the restaurant would certainly smell better than the rancid sweat and bleached concrete of a jail cell.

Maybe Suggie was right, Claire thought. If flirting or the possibility of romance were more frightening to Claire than being caged with a convict, there was something seriously wrong with her. Her past ten years of legal work, striving to reach her law firm's top rank, had left her single. But for one office romance that didn't end well and short-lived relationships, Claire was the poster child of the workaholic woman: overworked, overstressed, and under-loved. Let's hope this new life as a private chef will be more rewarding than the last, she wished.

"Knock knock." Torres poked his head through Claire's ajar bedroom door. "Ready to go?"

"I am." Claire stood up from her desk chair and slicked down her black silk gown with her hands. She might have been slightly overdressed for the evening and the fabric might have been a little too tight, but it was the only fancy dress that fitted her. Her physical and emotional post-explosion recovery had involved a lot of chocolate-binging, making her un-squeezable in any other dresses she owned.

"You look... really nice," Torres stuttered before glancing at his watch.

"You're the first of my dates to ever be on time."

"Thank you. You don't look bad yourself," she said, not unpleased by his appearance. His tight-fitting blue suit outlined his muscular frame nicely. He was by far cuter than any orange prison jumpsuit she had counseled. Fake-dating was better than jail-visiting, she decided. "Also, this is not a date, and you're five minutes late."

"Late?" He peered at the tripod that stood by her window. The dry-erase board of earlier wasn't only displaying the names and motives of three suspects. It now held their pictures, a detailed list of questions to be answered, and the clues Claire had obtained against them—pieces of fabric and newspaper clippings. "Don't tell me you were working on your murder board while waiting for me."

"Why, you've never been around people determined to find the truth or catch a murderer?" She stepped out of her room with her high heels in hand and slipped them on as they reached the apartment door.

Torres frowned. "Not before a date. Puts you in a gloomy state of mind before having a good time." He grabbed his black wing-tip shoes from the entrance cubby and put them on. Claire appreciated that Torres left his footwear in the vestibule and walked shoeless through the apartment, the way her mother had taught her—after a hard-working day, always leave your problems and the street germs at the door.

"Again, this is not a date. It's an undercover investigation," she repeated, secretly smiling. "Our conversation should only relate to the case."

"The case?" he asked with a hazy gaze as he straightened up, his eyes gliding from her toes and her thighs to her chest.

"Yes, *the case*. Vee's death. How Jason McCarthy had both the motive to kill Vee and the poison to do it. Isn't it what this evening is about?"

"Oh yes. TTX… tetrodotoxin, of course." He pulled on his shirt collar with his index finger as if he didn't have any room to breathe and chuckled. "Did you know his restaurant isn't licensed to serve pufferfish, and there's no fugu-certified chef on his payroll? Fugu isn't even on the menu."

Claire kept a poker face, but giggled inwardly as she stepped outside. She appreciated his sharing of information but guessed the gesture was more a distraction from his wandering eyes than a true intent at collaboration.

"The fact that fugu isn't on the menu doesn't mean anything," Claire said, heading down the stairs. "They may have a secret menu."

"A secret menu?" he asked, locking the apartment door behind them.

"Yes. Very exclusive restaurants have off-the-menu dishes diners can discreetly request. Sometimes they offer dishes whose consumption is illegal in the US. Like meats from endangered species, shark fins, Ortolan bird, Redfish, or White Beluga caviar."

"You've been to a lot of these restaurants before?" Torres asked, following her down the stairs.

"A few, when I was consulting with clients, but no one ordered anything illegal, at least not in my presence." As a criminal attorney, she had one rule: to only represent law-abiding defendants, which was the reason why most of her cases involved judicial errors, framed victims, and pro bono work with the Innocence Project. If her dinner date had ordered one of these dishes, her legal representation or romantic rendezvous would have ended on the spot.

"I never understood the appeal of showing off one's power and influence by eating protected animals. It's cruel at best."

"I guess, with a cop salary, I won't encounter many secret menus in my life."

Me neither, she thought as she reached the landing. As an unemployed private chef with an empty bank account, the only food she could afford was mooched dishes from her father's place.

The evening sky was what Vee called mandarin-cyan, a dark blue expanse streaked by orange filaments. The pattern was similar to the first scarf Vee ever sewed and which Claire had purchased to encourage her friend's fashion design ambitions. Claire hadn't paid much for it since she was student broke. Vee used to joke that the price she charged would allow her to live a month on 99-cent burgers and ramen noodles.

"Actually, many fast foods have them," Claire said, recalling her college days. "Wendy's has the Barnyard, which consists of bacon, beef, spicy chicken filet, and ham, all with cheese between each layer in one single bun. And McDonald has the McCrepe, which is a yogurt parfait inside a folded hotcake."

Torres slapped his chest with his open palm as if she had revealed a higher truth. "You're joking. How didn't I know this?"

"Maybe it's a good thing. No one truly wants that much cholesterol per bite."

"I guess you're right." He laughed, checked his beeping phone, and waved at a black Mercedes driving by. "Our ride's here."

"You're not driving?" Claire asked, wondering why on Earth Torres had ordered a chauffeured car.

"Nah. The police car would look too conspicuous, and I hope to enjoy a little wine." He held the car door open, waited for her to take a seat, and trotted to the other side to jump in.

"This is *not* a real date, you know that, right? We'll be there to investigate, not enjoy the evening together."

"I know, but there's nothing wrong with mixing work and pleasure once in a while." He shot her a mischievous smile. "Plus, you can catch me up on Jason's relationship with Vee in the car without stealing my attention from the road."

* * *

According to its website, HaruNamiCali was a Japanese-Californian fusion restaurant. Their menu was an ode to the region's natural bounty, with a focus on locally harvested products. The seafood, fish, and produce were sourced from nearby wild fisheries and farms, ensuring the freshest and most vibrant ingredients found their way onto dinner plates. If they did serve fugu, Claire doubted it was from California. While the fishes they offered were wild caught by Caper Cove fishermen, catching pufferfish was as hazardous as rare. The Pacific Ocean was too cold for the fish to survive outside of the El Niño years when the waters were unusually warm.

"Welcome to HaruNamiCali." A blond woman in a pink kimono greeted Claire and Torres with a bow and led them to their table.

The restaurant had no walls, its windows stretching out towards the vast expanse of the ocean as if the place was just an extension of the beach. The décor was simple yet elegant. Driftwood tables and earthy fabrics spoke of the sands and the rocks that lay just beyond the windows. The amplified sound of the crashing waves blended with the gentle clinking of dishes and soft conversations.

"Welcome to our romance-for-two evening. We ask that you silence your phones and directly message me through this link if you have any questions or requests. Thank you," the hostess presented them with the menu and a QR code. "Since the tasting menu is pre-set and fixed, the dishes will come as they are ready. May this evening surprise your palate and intensify your love."

"Oh no, we aren't together," Claire blurted.

The woman lowered her eyes. "I'm sorry, I assumed."

"It's completely understandable, considering tonight's theme. It's just that my father made the reservation without realizing my friend and I weren't together," Claire explained, chuckling nervously, wondering why she needed to justify her lack of relationship to a perfect stranger. "I've been dying to sample your dishes, and I heard you serve fugu sometimes?"

The woman didn't respond but simply said, "I'll let the chef know of your interest." Then she quickly left, disappearing in the dim restaurant lighting.

Claire shifted on her seat. She usually preferred her restaurants bright where she could see every detail of her plate and her surroundings, people's faces and well-marked exits—something any high-profile defense attorney needed to excel and survive. But here, in Caper Cove, she welcomed the lack of overhead lamps. The muted light allowed the sunset to cast its warm, orange glow throughout the restaurant, a priceless and gorgeous mood setting that only the California coast could provide.

Torres glanced at the thin paper screens that separated each table, providing semi-privacy and creating an intimate dining experience.

"Did you know about the Romance-for-two theme of the night?" he asked, looking as uncomfortable as Claire felt.

"No, but Roxy must have known. She's been trying to pair me with a local man since I turned eighteen, hoping I'd never leave, to keep me close to my dad. It's like they can't understand that my work's in DC... *was* in DC." Her voice trailed as she genuinely wondered what life had in store for her. If she couldn't find a private chef position fast, she would need to return to D.C. as a lawyer to earn a living or open her own practice in town.

Claire grabbed a menu and started to read through the dish descriptions, hoping the evening would go by quickly.

"Frank's surely happy you're back. The guys at the station noticed a spring in his walk since your return." Torres swallowed hard and threw her a quick, sheepish glance. "By the way, I'm sorry about before. I didn't realize you were a serious attorney, with your accent and all. I hope we can start fresh."

"Of course," she said, raising her eyes from the menu to look at him, but keeping the page in front of her. "Does that mean I'm part of the investigating team?"

"Well, civilians aren't supposed to investigate murders on their own. We could say you're my C.I."

"Your confidential informant?" Claire laughed. "We're not dealing with drug trafficking, white-collar crimes, or gangs. We're talking about Caper Cove, a quaint and quiet resort town, not Washington D.C. or New York. If I'm going to help you, I want it to be a two-way street. A true quid pro quo."

A silence settled between them as a hostess deposited a small bamboo tray with moist towelettes on the table between them.

"What if I pay you?" he asked.

If it hadn't been about finding her friend's killer, Claire would have jumped on the opportunity to make some money. Her bank account was drier than Death Valley, and living rent-free at her dad's started to erode her self-esteem. But she knew that her criminal defense experience made her a better investigator than homicide novice Torres. Teaming up with him would slow her down when she needed the case to be solved quickly—in time for Suggie to have her dream wedding and for Claire to cater a memorable feast that would catch the attention of potential clients. Claire's livelihood depended on it.

Claire shook her head. "I can be your consultant, but the exchange of information must be mutual," she said as she unrolled her towelette and wiped her hands.

Torres imitated her and jerked back in shock. "Ahhhh." He puffed, passing his towelette from one hand to the other, like a child playing a solo game of hot potato. "It's burning hot. How can you be holding it in your hands?"

"Force of cooking habit, I guess." The explosion had also decreased sensitivity in her left fingers. "Just give it a few minutes to cool down."

Torres dropped the towelette on the table and extended his right hand over the table. "I accept your terms, but you must keep me informed as soon as you find out new information."

"Deal!" Claire put down the menu and shook his hand. "So, what have you learned about Clay Poderas? You mentioned you couldn't find him."

A smile crossed Torres' face. "Wow. You don't waste any time."

"We're here for work, aren't we?"

"We are." He paused, allowing the waitress to settle two plates in front of them.

"Your first course, yellowtail sashimi with avocado and jalapeno, drizzled with a citrusy yuzu," the woman said before quickly disappearing. The bite-sized raw fish had been sliced into thin, delicate pieces arranged on each plate in the shape of a flower.

Claire grabbed her steel chopsticks and picked up a sliver of fish and deposited it delicately on her tongue. She half-closed her eyes and let the creamy avocado and spicy jalapeno peppers permeate her tongue. Food always transported her to different worlds and for a second, she imagined herself alone, wading in the warm summer waves of the Pacific Ocean surrounded by the hills of citrus trees that border the town.

After a short battle with his chopsticks, Torres resolved to use his fork. He picked up the pieces of fish two by two and swallowed after just one chew.

"According to his campaign manager, Poderas is attending a fundraising retreat with powerful tech moguls. The ones who like to go off-the-grid for a few days, to commune with nature," he said. "There's no way to reach him. He should be back tomorrow."

"I see." Complete isolation retreats were usually a code for rehab. Vee's husband was an addict trying to get clean, a situation which begets new theories regarding Vee's death. Maybe Poderas was involved in a drug ring, and Vee was a casualty of his addiction, or maybe Vee's death was a warning, an under-the-belt strategic hit from a political opponent. "Do you think you can get a list of the retreat attendees?"

"Not without a warrant. At this time, we don't have enough probable cause to get one."

The second and third courses quickly followed, leaving Claire no time to talk. Sushi rolls and miso-marinated black cod with soba noodles, with an accompaniment of wines, which Claire forewent. She never found much pleasure in drinking and preferred to eat her calories, unlike Torres who was thrilled to take the sample portion off her hands and mouth.

The sushi was a creative spin on the classic California roll and included sweet chunks of mango and juicy crab meat, wrapped in seaweed. But it was the generous portion of flaky cod marinated in a sweet and savory miso glaze that drew a gourmet grin on Torres' face.

"Wow, I never thought I'd say this, but this is truly magical," he said, his mouth full. "If Jason McCarthy killed Vee, one must wonder: how can a man smart enough to provide a foodie experience like this be a killer?"

"Alas, psychopaths and sociopaths aren't allergic to haute cuisine." Claire sighed. In her experience, it was often the extravagant eaters who were the greediest and the most dangerous kind of people. They weren't nibblers and considerate of their place in the world. When they desired something or wanted to take someone down, they swallowed them whole.

"On the plus side, culinary preferences can give us clues into someone's insights," Claire added. "An Austrian study of Americans' taste preferences, performed by the University of Innsbruck, found that people who like bitter foods and drinks are more likely to exhibit psychotic, antisocial, and sadistic personality traits."

"Talking of suspects. Look who's at my ten o'clock," Torres said between sips of wine.

His ten o'clock being her four o'clock, Claire swiveled on her chair and discreetly peeked over her right shoulder, past the paper partition.

Tara Betrossen, Poderas' ex-fiancée and the woman from whom Vee had supposedly stolen her husband, was here. She was standing in the entrance in a nude, clingy dress that made her appear naked.

"Good eye," Claire noted as she wondered whether it was the woman's face or physique that had first attracted Torres' attention. "The man who's kissing her goodnight is Jason McCarthy, Vee's harasser and the owner of the restaurant."

Claire recognized him from the pictures an enamored Vee had texted her before her friend's passionate romance with Jason had turned to ashes, like most explosive affairs did. The man had the look of a model: six feet tall, wide shoulders, slim waist, strong jaw, and blinding white teeth. He wore an expensive summer wool suit—probably Gucci, she guessed—and a bleached blond pompadour.

"So Jason McCarthy and Tara Betrossen are a couple," Torres whispered. A power couple with strong motives to kill Vee.

"Here's the fourth and fifth courses." The waitress deposited four plates in front of them. "Wagyu beef tataki with truffle ponzu and Uni pasta with caviar and truffles."

"Your service is lightning fast," Claire said, surprised by the two courses being served at once—an unusual occurrence for an upscale restaurant. It was as if someone was trying to get rid of them. Her mention of fugu might have struck a chord somewhere in the kitchen.

"No complaints here." Torres arched over the dishes to inhale their aroma. Like most men, he couldn't resist the thinly sliced seared Wagyu beef, drizzled with a fragrant truffle ponzu sauce and topped with fresh herbs and crispy garlic.

"Thank you." Claire spoke in an exaggerated French accent, loud enough to attract Jason McCarthy's attention. "So far, the food has been spectacular."

Her father had been right. The French rhythm brought the restaurant owner to a pause and redirected his steps toward Claire's table. McCarthy introduced himself and asked Claire if the meal was to her liking, to which she replied *beaucoup*, which meant very much in French. His undeniable charm made Claire cringe. Criminals with the most charisma were the worst.

Claire presented herself as a private chef in need of a good wine supplier for her affluent clientele. A lie by omission since her only client who fitted that description was now dead, probably at Jason McCarthy's hands. "I've read that you have an extensive wine and liquor collection."

"We do and it seems like your companion's been enjoying both of your shares." He chin-pointed at Torres. The eight glasses of wine and liquor they had been served were empty next to Torres' plate, confirming that the detective had drunk them all on his own. "The plum wine is especially potent. I hope you were able to savor it as well. If not, may I interest you in a tour of our cellar?" He extended a hand to Claire, inviting her to follow him, completely disregarding Torres' presence.

Claire hesitated. It wouldn't be the first time she found herself alone with a killer, but she was no longer a lawyer, and there were no wardens around. Was Torres too inebriated to accompany her or was he pretending to be drunk so McCarthy would lower his guard and be unsuspicious about Claire's questions?

Chapter Fifteen

T hough she could have run a fifty-meter sprint in high heels, Claire adopted a snail-like pace as she walked. The more time she spent with Jason McCarthy, the more questions she could ask, but she needed the lubricant of small talk before assaulting him with harder questions. The playboy strutted by her side, leading the way to the cellar, seeming not to mind. He answered her every question about the artists behind the paintings that hung on the walls, the origin of the wines, and the seed from which the restaurant was born.

"Do I know any of your clients?" he asked as he pushed open the cellar's door.

"Maybe. I think you knew Vee Brooks." Claire paused to read his face as she answered. "She recently passed."

The man didn't blink or recoil. "I've heard. She was such a vivacious woman. It's a terrible loss."

"Were you on good terms with her?"

"Actually, yes, Vee got all her sushi from us." He crossed the cellar threshold, beckoning her to follow, but Claire stayed put. The musty scent of damp stone walls reached her nostrils, sending shivers down her spine.

"Did she ever have fugu?" Claire stared straight at the man as she spoke.

McCarthy's Adam's apple bobbed up and down as he swallowed hard like someone with something to hide. "Sometimes, why?"

"They found tetrodotoxin in her system. Do you know where it came from?"

Jason flinched back, like a spring that was suddenly released after being pulled too hard, his spine straightening. He pivoted to face her. "Are you kidding me? Am I a suspect?"

Claire took a step back. "I don't know. Did you have any reason to kill Vee?"

"No way. We've got a child together. I wanted my name on its birth certificate. We were working on a shared custody agreement."

Claire knew this to be a lie. According to Nina Rock, the youth group advocate with whom Vee worked, Vee had blocked Jason's number after only a few calls. They couldn't have been talking about anything if he couldn't reach her. Furthermore, how caring could a father be if he referred to his child as *it*?

"You should check her husband. Isn't it always the spouse, anyway? He's the one with a motive. Vee had a druggie-juvie past that was sure to tarnish his campaign. She hadn't told him that the child wasn't his but mine."

It always amazed Claire how quickly malefactors could throw others under the bus as a way to divert people's attention away from them. Oddly enough, McCarthy's words sounded truthful, but she wasn't willing to be conned by a professional liar. "Why the sudden interest in the child?"

"Vee had confessed to me that her husband wasn't the fatherly type, so I agreed to step in. I was so happy to be a dad."

Claire held back a frustrated laugh. How could people manufacture the most extravagant of lies and think they could get away with it?

"Happy to be a dad? That's why you sent her a check to get an abortion last year?" Claire asked. She still had Vee's text and the screenshot of the infamous message on her phone.

Jason stiffened. Though he remained calm, he couldn't hide the mix of surprise and panic in his eyes. "People change," he said in a gravelly voice.

From what Claire had witnessed in her years of legal work surrounded by criminals, truly bad people never changed. They simply adjusted to shifting circumstances. What Jason's circumstances were, Claire needed to find out.

"Where were you yesterday morning between nine and twelve ?"

"I'm not answering any more questions without my attorney present. Get out of my restaurant now!" He waved at the uniformed sommelier who was leaving the cellar. "Call security."

"What about my meal?"

"Consider both your reservation and your bill canceled. Just leave with your poorly dressed schmuck," he said, dragging Claire by the wrist.

Claire freed herself from his stronghold, thanks to the weekly Krav Maga class she used to take every Friday evening after work. "Do not touch me."

"Yes, let the lady go, or I'm arresting you for assault," Torres warned in a menacing voice. The detective was standing by her side with one hand on his holster while holding a large paper bag in the other. "For your information, this suit cost me five hundred dollars."

"It's a very nice suit," Claire agreed, stepping in Torres' direction.

McCarthy grimaced as if he had stomped on a venomous jellyfish. "What the hell! What's the police doing here? Am I under arrest?"

"Not yet," Torres said before leading Claire out.

They speed-walked away from the restaurant, all the way to the parking lot without a word, trying to put the most space between them and McCarthy. They both knew that de-escalation was the best way to approach an angry suspect but were also aware of the exception—the reactive thug who couldn't seem to cool down and had family money to bail him out.

"What the hell, Claire? You were supposed to seduce him and gently get information out of him, not grill him! You aren't the police. You've got no right to interrogate civilians." Torres was walking backward, his eyes darting between Claire and the restaurant, as if to make sure she was safe, and no angry goon would run after them with a gun.

"You're not my boss. I don't need your authorization to question whoever I want. If it weren't for me, Jason McCarthy wouldn't even be on your radar. Assuming you have one, and you're really investigating Vee's death."

"Of course, we're really investigating. She's a politician's wife."

"So, that's it? The only reason you investigate, quite slowly, may I add, is that she was married to Clay Poderas? Otherwise, you would close the case as an accidental fugu poisoning, right? Being a woman, a regular human being without generational wealth, isn't worth your efforts?"

Torres paused at the beach entrance under a lamppost's soft light and looked Claire in the eyes. "We have no proof of foul play or that someone had motive to harm her."

"Yes, we do."

"Oh yeah? So why don't you tell me instead of keeping everything between yourself and your murder board? You really think Jason McCarthy's got something to do with Vee Brooks' death?"

"I don't know." Her inner truth compass, on which she had relied for so long, was of no help. Her shoulders low, she removed her shoes and entered the beach in silence. The contact of her bare soles against the cool sand took away her stress. Besides her sister's disappearance, none of her cases had been personal ones, until now, and staying objective and unbiased was her biggest struggle. Could Vee's death have been a suicide or an accident that Claire couldn't accept and turned into a fictitious murder?

"All I know is that McCarthy lied when he said Vee and he were working on a custody agreement. Why would he want custody of a child he didn't want in the first place?"

"Maybe his biological clock's ticking. Women don't have the monopoly on that." Torres followed her through the soft sand, his shoes still on, the large paper bag still in his hands.

The beach was empty. Stars started to appear one by one, dotting the sky like tiny white splashes of paint on a purple-blue canvas.

"I get that, but why Vee? It's not like he's lacking candidates to carry his child." In an interview in The Financial News, Jason McCarthy had corroborated the tabloids' statistics on his dating life—the fact that he averaged 47 different girlfriends a year.

"I wish I could say he truly loved your friend, but the guy doesn't seem the emotional type."

"I agree. Wealthy men like him develop an ugly sense of self-entitlement and impermeability to all laws. What affects them is usually related to money or pride." The type of men who had a PR rep and a lawyer on speed dial to handle their messes and always found a scapegoat to take the blame for their wrongdoings.

"Maybe he became infertile, and Vee's child is his only chance at having a legacy," Torres suggested.

"It's possible. STDs can cause infertility, and, with his lifestyle, McCarthy is prone to them. But if he really cared about his progeny, wouldn't he try to find out about his child considering her mother's death?"

Claire sat on the sand, a few feet away from the waves' reach. Straight ahead, the horizon was a darkening line. "Could he be having money problems? Fortune isn't an endless well from which he could mindlessly draw funds." Losing everything from one day to the next wasn't improbable. If it happened to Claire, a frugal lawyer who saved all her earnings, it could certainly happen to a spendthrift like McCarthy. "Maybe killing Vee was financially beneficial to him somehow."

"I'll check. Though I'm not sure how killing Vee could benefit his bank account." Torres settled right next to her, grazing her skin. She could feel his warmth radiating against her bare arms and legs. "What's your take on Tara Betrossen?" he asked.

"The husband's ex-fiancée?" Claire paused, wondering why every murder/suicide story had a disgruntled ex-girlfriend. Women should hold each other's hands like sisters and shun the men who had hurt them instead of turning against each other. "Tara has a strong motive for wanting Vee dead. Blaming Vee instead of Poderas for their breakup is textbook motive for revenge. Plus, her dating Jason looks suspicious, without mentioning gross." As if trading sexual partners made people even. "Being cozy with a fugu restaurant owner gave her the tool for murder. Not sure how fugu's stored, but she could have easily added some to Vee's sushi plate. What preoccupies me more, though, is Clay Poderas. His absence is highly suspicious."

"Yep. I was thinking the same." Torres scooted closer to her, his legs fully touching hers. She wouldn't admit it, but it was a nice contrast to the cooling evening air. "Hey, what about we stop talking about death for now?"

"I think it's a great idea." Claire buried her toes in the sand, thinking of her mother's wisdom on the importance of balancing rest and work. No one could go on climbing without taking a breath every now and then, or without a colleague or a rope to hold them back when they fell. Rest was as important as support.

Claire let the silence settle between them and watched the moon's reflection ripple on the ocean until Torres brought the large paper bag in front of them.

"What's in the bag?" she asked.

"Beautifully boxed courses four, five, and six with their accompanying wines *and* environment-friendly bamboo forks."

"What? How?"

"I knew McCarthy would kick us out. No matter how charming your accent is, there's a limit to the number of intrusive and accusatory questions a guy can take without feeling personally attacked. I asked for the rest of the meals to go as soon as you left the table. The staff's really efficient. They handed me the bag right before McCarthy raised his voice. Not sure about the check, though."

"Don't worry about that. He told me to forget about the bill and that he never wanted to see my face in his restaurant ever again."

Torres wiped his forehead with the back of his hand, and his shoulders dropped with relief. "Good, because I didn't have the funds to cover that meal."

Claire glanced at the bill that had been stapled to the bag. It amounted to almost a thousand dollars. "Me neither."

Claire and Torres exchanged a half-guilty, half-relieved gaze and burst into laughs.

"You hungry?" he asked.

"Starving." Confrontation with unsavory characters tended to whet her appetite. "You think they may have poisoned the food?"

Torres grabbed a bamboo fork, shoved a huge scoop of noodles in his mouth, and smiled. "Let's hope not."

Chapter Sixteen

I t was past 9 PM when Claire and Torres left the beach aboard their black, chauffeured Mercedes. The ride wasn't an extravagant expense as Claire had originally thought, but an off-duty cop working a second job who was doing Torres a favor.

"Straight back to the Osprey then?" the chauffeur asked.

"Yes, back home."

"Homebase," Claire corrected. The word *home* by itself was a little too weird of a term for her at the moment. No one calls their temporary lodging *home*, unless they expect to live there for at least a month, which was way longer than Claire anticipated to stay at her father's place. *Homebase,* on the other hand, was a solid professional designation, which reminded Claire of her mission: to quickly find a job and her own independent housing. Homebase also alluded to a place of work, which dispelled the idea that Torres and she were living together.

"How was the meal?" the chauffeur asked. "Worth the wait?"

"Skip the place. It's ridiculously expensive, and the owner's a criminal," Torres said before sprawling out on the backseat next to her. He had removed his jacket and unbuttoned the collar of his shirt, revealing a sexy tuft of chest hair.

"You don't know that yet." Claire hated to take McCarthy's defense, but no matter how much she disliked him, she couldn't allow hearsay or incomplete information to accuse a man without supportive evidence. She had represented too many innocents who had been framed or sentenced based on misinformation to allow Torres to do that. "McCarthy's definitely an immoral jerk, but we don't know with certainty if he has broken any law."

"I take it you liked the food?" Torres gazed at her with a flushed face and glazed eyes—the results of the generous portions of wine samplers the waitress had packed in the to-go bag. He was kinder and softer than he usually was, which bothered Claire. She hated that inebriation was sometimes the only way for people to reveal their true selves. Why did people have to hide who they were, especially when they had a tender, gentler side?

"Yes. The food was phenomenal." She had enjoyed all the courses, and her beach picnic with Torres had been such a delight that she was considering leaving a four-star review on the restaurant's website. Something indicative of her experience: "divine food, unsatisfactory service by grumpy owner." She exchanged a knowing smile with Torres, still bewildered by their sheer luck of not having to foot the steep restaurant bill. "But, as Ben said, the prices are exorbitant."

The car took the long way back along the shore road. Claire opened the window and watched the moon cast silver lines onto the lapping waves. The world was so beautifully quiet. The cool salty air slithered into the car with a whistle, leaving a trail of goosebumps on Claire's arms.

"You're cold?" Torres wrapped his strong arms around her shoulders, enveloping her in his jacket.

Claire didn't fight it and let him pull her against him. He would fail to remember this moment of temporary intimacy once he sobered up. Her head cradled against his chest, she could hear Torres' heartbeat and felt oddly at peace. She stayed in that position until the car veered a sharp right, indicating their near arrival at The Osprey.

"Do you mind dropping me off here, at the curb?" she asked the driver, leaving the warm comfort of Torres' hold. "Right next to the hedge of roses, please." The natural green fence of pink flowers marked the limit of Claire's old neighborhood. Where she used to live with her parents and sister, eons ago.

"Sure." The driver brought the car to a stop next to one of the old-fashioned streetlamps that peppered the street. "Right here, okay?"

"That's perfect. Thanks."

"Hey, where're you going?" Torres mumbled. "Don't you want to go back home with me?"

"Homebase," she corrected. "And no, I can't. I have an errand to run before I call it a night." She knew she needed to cut her evening with Torres short. She didn't trust herself to be in the presence of a slightly inebriated, good-looking, protective man at the moment. Her financial insolvency and the grief over losing her friend had left her feeling powerless and vulnerable—a dangerous combination when paired with the romantic atmosphere of the seaside moonlight. She wasn't ready for romance and even less for a one-night stand with her roommate.

She grabbed her high heels in one hand and stepped out of the car. She needed to talk to Suggie to keep her head straight and her best friend's house was close. As children, both girls used to run to each other's houses and to the beach barefoot. Their childhood homes were only two blocks from the ocean and four blocks from The Osprey where they waitressed as teenagers.

Claire pulled her phone from her crossbody purse, connected to the recreation center's public WiFi, and texted Suggie.

CLAIRE: <Free to chat?>

Her screen lit with an immediate response.

SUGGIE: <Free to chat or meet>

CLAIRE: < When/where?>

SUGGIE: <The skyhouse in 5?>

CLAIRE: <The skyhouse? It's still standing?>

SUGGIE: <Still standing and improved>

CLAIRE: <See you in 10>

* * *

Even after a ten-year absence, finding her way back to her best friend's house had been easy. Claire did it with her eyes closed, following her feet down the paved road and up the pebbled side street to Suggie's backyard. The Coast Live Oak tree that stood tall in the middle of the lawn was as huge as she remembered it, and the skyhouse—the treehouse hidden in the middle of its foliage—had been improved, indeed. The little trapdoor that they could close to keep out any unwanted visitors was still there, but real glass windows filled the openings in the wall, and a solid, retractable stairs replaced the old rope ladder. Yet, Claire experienced the same excitement as she felt as a child, as she climbed up the tree and stepped into her childhood sanctuary.

"You don't joke with your remodeling. This treehouse could have its own vacation rental listing," Claire said, gasping at the modern luxury feel of the room. "Is this a replica of our college dorm?"

The shelter looked like the room they shared as NYU students. A soft plush carpet and a small table/desk separated the twin beds, and fifteen-year-old posters lined the wall. It was like traveling back in time to the years Suggie called the *magic era*—when their heads were full of dreams, and everything was possible.

"Yes, please, settle down. This is your home as much as mine," Suggie said as she poured a thermos of hot chocolate into two mugs. "Daniel has a carpentry background. He wanted to make sure the skyhouse was ready before he deployed, so we can video-chat privately when he's gone, since you know...Umma."

Claire laughed. Suggie's mother was as lovable as she was nosy. No conversation in her house could remain private, which was a challenge if Suggie and her fiancé got into sexy FaceTime or intimate phone conversations. Marines' sensual language was beyond Mrs. Oh's purview or comprehension. Moving back with her mother had been a strategic move for the soon-to-be-married couple: Suggie would be living with her mother while Daniel was deployed. On his return, their combined savings would go toward the down payment on a house.

"Since you lost your childhood bedroom when your parents divorced, I wanted to give you a place that'll always be there," Suggie added as she handed her the sweet-smelling drink.

As children, Claire and Suggie had spent countless hours up there, playing games, telling stories, or just enjoying the view of the town from up high.

Spending whole afternoons lost in their own perfect little world. The world was simpler then, their problems small and insignificant compared to the vast expanse of the tree canopy above them.

"It's so thoughtful. Thank you." Claire grabbed the drink and hugged her friend. "And kudos to Daniel. I admire a man who completes his work way before his self-imposed deadlines! It's beautiful. I could live here."

"You're welcome to spend the night whenever you need it. The lock code is October 21, you know, to never forget." It was the date Aurora disappeared. "So what's the urgency?"

The women sat on the faux-fur carpet, their backs against one bed, and Claire shared her concerns. The fact the police didn't take the investigation seriously and how Torres was getting on her nerves and in her dreams.

"Love isn't a bad thing, you know. When you're attracted to someone, your brain releases dopamine, your serotonin levels increase, and oxytocin is produced. This happy hormone surge is great for healing." Suggie dropped a few mini marshmallows in her cup. "About that, how are you doing?"

"There may be a crush and a little lust, but it's definitely not love. And I'm doing fine," Claire said, withholding the fact that, for the first time since the explosion, her tailbone and hips hadn't bothered her. "We've got a serious list of suspects, including Tara Betrossen."

"Betrossen as in Clay Poderas' former fiancée?"

"Yes. You know her?"

"Not well, but I can tell you that she couldn't have done it. She was at the spa all day when Vee died. She had her hair straightened, which took about four hours, and she got into a fight with Mrs. Stevenson, the co-chair of Caper Cove Arts Foundation. Which, of course, doesn't mean she isn't involved in Vee's murder. I can totally see her hiring someone to do it."

Claire brought the hot drink to her nostrils. She could smell the rich, nutty flavor of the oat milk Suggie used instead of regular milk. "What makes you say that?"

"Tara never tips, even on thousands of dollars worth of services. Umma doesn't say anything and says having Tara as a client is great publicity, but I disagree. That woman has bad karma." Suggie grimaced. "I saw her kick a dog once. The poor thing was just waiting for its owner outside of Café Louis when Tara walked up to it and booted it. I didn't say anything because Tara threatened to ruin the reputation of the spa if I opened my mouth."

"That's horrible. She could be suspended or even disbarred for that. Blackmail's a crime."

"That's not the only thing. According to Julie, her hairdresser, Tara, still had the hots for Poderas and hated Vee. She got Vee disinvited from the Caper Cover Arts Foundation annual gala, where one of Vee's couture gowns was to be sold at auction. Mrs. Stevenson told me that Tara threatened to withdraw her family's support if Vee was invited. Vee was gracious enough to still donate the gown without making an appearance."

Claire added a handful of marshmallows to her cup and watched them bob up and down. "Vee was classy that way. Do you have anything on her husband?"

Suggie shook her head. "Not really. Why, you have a theory?"

"Yes, but you can't write about it. You can't print anything I'm telling you here tonight, alright?"

"Everything's off the record, I promise."

"Secrets from Vee's past could have jeopardized his career."

"Well, that problem seems fixed. Since his wife died, he's been gathering a lot of sympathy and support. The spa's staff and clients are talking about pity-voting for him since he's a good-looking widower with a new baby and all that."

"That's interesting. I can see how his PR team could reframe the narrative to his advantage," Claire said before taking a sip of her drink. Politicians were skilled in turning terrible events into public relations gold. "I need to go to San Diego tomorrow to interview him. You mind giving me a ride?"

"Not at all. I've a few errands to run that way, but only after ten. Tell me something, though: why would Vee rent a private villa twenty miles from her residence?"

"She needed to be alone to create. With a baby at home, renting a place must have been the best way to be away while staying close." Claire got up to stretch her legs and stared out the window, a feeling of longing weighing in her chest.

On the other side of the fence stood her childhood home with its grey shingles and red brick walls. The backyard needed mowing, but nothing had really changed. On the second floor, straight across from the skyhouse, Claire's old bedroom was illuminated.

"How are the neighbors?" she asked.

Suggie giggled. "Neighbor. Singular."

"One single person bought that four-bedroom house to live on their own?"

"Yes, but it's not anyone. The new owner's Vic Thomas."

"The little Vic I used to babysit?" The shrimpy boy who had turned into a good-looking forensic pathologist?

"The one and only. He bought the house when your father put it up for sale, five or six years ago."

"Six." It was right after her mother passed. It was like her father had suddenly realized that his dream of seeing his family reunited under the same roof could no longer be. "What did he buy it with? Bar Mitzvah money? After medical school, he must be drowning in student loans."

"Apparently not. You want to know the creepy part?" Suggie giggled some more and joined Claire by the window. "He asked if he could keep the furniture."

"So? Buying an already furnished home makes sense." The apartment in which Claire lived in D.C. had been a corporate, furnished rental. "It's practical and saves time and money since you already know the furniture fits the place. And it makes the house move-in ready.

"It's not that." Suggie chuckled.

"What is it?"

"He's been renovating the entire house with the exception of your bedroom. He likes to watch TV in your old bed. He's probably there, right now, watching Bones re-runs. Take a look." Suggie handed her a pair of binoculars.

"Really, Su? Since when are you spying on people?" Claire placed the pair of lenses in front of her eyes and stared straight out of the window. Her old bedroom hadn't changed, from the striped wallpaper and the mirrored vanity to her twin bed and her pink-hearts comforter. The only difference was the big screen TV adorning the wall in front of the bed from which Vikram was watching.

"Look at the frame on the nightstand," Suggie said with amusement in her voice.

Claire moved to the right and located the picture. "What in the world? Where did he get that image?"

"He must have downloaded it from your firm's website. I'm still debating whether it's sweet or creepy, but I lean toward sweet. You never forget your first love..."

Chapter Seventeen

Though Claire fell asleep with a pang of nostalgia for her carefree days of childhood, she woke up with the drive and tenacity of a teenager. Waking up in the skyhouse's replica of her college dorm reminded her that life was not a predestined path. It was what you made of it. Be the heroine of it, not its victim or passive observer.

She grabbed her shoes and ran the four blocks to her apartment, thinking treehouses were great except for the lack of plumbing. She kept her head low, hoping no one would be out that early in the day and see her. Though a popular tourist resort, Caper Cove remained a small town with rampant gossip. If anyone spotted her in her evening gown and assumed her morning jog to be a run of shame, finding a job as a reputable private chef would be a challenge. As if sharing an apartment with a good-looking, single cop wasn't enough to feed the rumor mill, she didn't need people to speculate about her libido, or lack thereof.

It was past 6 AM when she crossed the threshold of her apartment and found Torres half-asleep, making coffee in the kitchen.

"Where were you? I was worried about you," he said in mid-yawn from behind the counter. He was standing shirtless as if showing off his chiseled chest, making Claire wonder if he had any underwear on. Not that she wanted to find out.

"Good morning to you, too." She turned her gaze away and rushed to the bathroom, mentally scoffing. Living in the same apartment made them roommates, not husband and wife.

* * *

Claire reached the law office of Betrossen, Betrossen, & Betrossen, a stutter of a name, as soon as they opened.

"You want to see Tara Betrossen but you don't have an appointment, is that right?" the secretary shouted in an exaggeratedly slow and loud voice as if she was addressing a hard of hearing client.

Claire winced at the auditory assault and force-smiled, assuming the woman was simply born with a bigger larynx and vocal cords, or maybe larger lungs, than the average person. All of which produced a louder-than-average voice. "Yes, that's what I just said. I would like to see Tara Betrossen, but I do not have an appointment."

"What is your name, and why are you here," the woman asked in the same raucous and oddly patronizing tone.

Claire took a few steps back to protect her hearing. She was about to answer the question when a man in a suit appeared next to the front desk.

"What's the matter, Marjory? Why are you shouting? I thought someone was dying."

"Oh no, Mr. Betrossen, sir, everything's fine," she said in a soft, high-pitched voice. "I was just trying to help this woman." She pointed at Claire with a grin. "She doesn't speak English. I wanted to make sure she understood me."

"My English's fine," Claire said. "I'm here to see Tara Betrossen. My name is Claire Fontaine. I'm the executor of Vee Brooks' estate." She handed the man one of her old business cards that read "Claire Fontaine, Attorney at Law." She always kept a few on hand to avoid a repeat of the airport incident. The piece of paper and the blue, professional pantsuit she had chosen to wear that day were supposed to help people take her seriously.

The man's eyes darted between Claire and her card. "I'm really sorry about this. We don't get many foreign lawyers here. Please take a seat. I'll see if Tara can see you," he told Claire before pivoting back to his secretary. "Keep your voice down and bring me the Karl Smith file right after this."

The secretary watched Betrossen Jr. disappear down the hallway while

Claire tried to figure out whether the Karl Smith the man mentioned was the same Karl Smith from the Fashion Warriors TV show. In the absence of leads on Vee's death, any connection between people could be a serious clue.

The woman rose from her seat, opened a drawer from the wall of file cabinets behind her, and pulled a thick folder from it. She dropped the dossier on her desk long enough for Claire to read a few of the tags—*fabric manufacturing trademark and patent protection, Fashion Warriors*—and glared at Claire.

"I didn't know you knew English. You've got an accent," she said in a voice that bordered on a whisper.

"No worry. I understand." Claire forced herself to say, making her miss her former, pre-explosion, pre-accent life when she took her perfect elocution and oratory skills for granted.

While in D.C., it never occurred to her to question people's intellect or competency based on their elocution, being accented by foreign languages, regional inflection, or affected by speech impediments. Since the U.S. had literally been built by immigrants, weren't accents the norm?

* * *

Five minutes later, Claire was seated in a white office filled with gold furniture and colorful paintings. A basket of pink hyacinths stood on a coffee table, imbuing the room with a sweet fragrance of spring. Dozens of diplomas, equestrian awards and trophies decorated the back wall. An impressive display that could easily intimidate any client.

Tara Betrossen was seated at a marble desk right across from Claire. She had traded her nude skin dress for a bright pink blazer and skirt that reminded Claire of Elle Woods from Legally Blonde, a look she personally loved.

"If I understand, you're not here for legal advice but to ask me questions about Clay and his late wife. Is that right?"

"That's right. I'm the executor of Vee Brooks' estate. Since her marriage to Clay Poderas and the comingling of their properties, I thought you might help me unfasten a few knots or tie potential loose ends. I understand that your firm handles the Poderas-Brooks family trust. Is there anything I should be aware of?"

The woman twirled her soft brown curls between her fingers as she assessed Claire with her gaze. "You're well informed, and I'm going to answer all your questions, but what I'd like to know first is why Vee chose a foreign attorney to represent her?"

"I'm not a foreign attorney. I am an American and California licensed attorney just like you are." She didn't feel like explaining the origin of her accent to yet another person. "Vee Brooks chose me for my unbiased stance and my lack of personal connection to her world, I suppose." It was obvious that Vee couldn't have trusted her husband's hate-filled ex-fiancée to handle her affairs.

"Really? That's interesting." She shot Claire the same skeptical glance the airport CBP agent had given her—people who can't fathom someone with an accent could achieve as high or higher than they did. "Are you thinking of settling here in Caper Cove?"

"No, I'm just passing through. To return to the reason for my presence, you may know that Mr. Poderas is missing, which doesn't look good for him."

"And how much are you being compensated for your executor's duties? Five, ten percent of Vee's estate?"

The question shocked Claire. The idea of being remunerated for fulfilling her friend's wish hadn't crossed her mind. "I think you didn't hear me well. I was asking if you knew Mr. Poderas has gone missing."

"Clay has nothing to do with Vee's death if that's what you're implying. He knew of Vee's troubled past and that the baby wasn't his. That's why it really hurt when he dumped me. Who could have conceived that he would choose a pregnant drug addict over me?"

Claire used every scrap of patient willpower left in her body to remain unreactive to the verbal jab the woman was throwing at her late friend.

"When was the last time you saw Mr. Poderas?"

"Two months ago, a month after the baby's birth. He asked me to financially support his election campaign and made me promise not to drag Vee through the dirt if I ever felt an ounce of love for him." She dabbed the corner of her eyes with the tip of her fingers and sighed. "So, of course, I did. It's not like I can stop loving him just like that, with a snap of my fingers."

"So you're trying to forget him by dating Jason McCarthy?"

Tara Betrossen blinked. "How is that any of your business?"

"Did you know Jason McCarthy was Vee's ex?"

Tara grimaced, a frown of confusion carving her brow. "I think this meeting's over. If you have more questions, you can email them to me. I'll reply at my earliest convenience."

* * *

San Diego was only a thirty-minute ride away, short enough for the box of fresh madeleines resting on Claire's lap to saturate the air of Suggie's Prius with a sweet citrus scent. Claire had barely had the time to craft them with ingredients from her father's commercial kitchen. She was hoping the small lemony treats would comfort Mrs. Poderas (Vee's mother-in-law) and make her more receptive to Claire's questioning. Maybe the little cakes would even sway her into letting them snoop around the house for possible clues.

"The smell's making me hungry. Is it too late to ask for one?" Suggie asked hesitantly, her lips twisting in regret for refusing Claire's earlier offer.

Claire laughed as she pulled a small bag from under her coat. "Of course, you can have one. Even three. I knew you would want some, so I brought extra for the ride."

She handed her friend a small yellow cake and looked at the passing landscape.

The palm tree-lined road and miles of sandy beach were in such a sharp contrast with Washington, D.C.'s urban landscape, yet she loved them both. There were no centuries-old stone buildings or cherry trees here, but there was an undeniable warmth to Southern California—a loving atmosphere brought by the year-round sunshine and happy childhood memories that Washington D.C. couldn't beat.

"You okay? You're really quiet." Suggie veered left onto the High Occupancy Vehicle Lane, reserved exclusively for vehicles with two or more occupants.

"I'm enjoying the beauty of the day. I had forgotten how warm and welcoming San Diego County felt after so many years away."

"Thinking about settling back home for good?"

When Tara Betrossen had asked her that question, Claire had replied she was just passing through, but she wasn't so sure anymore. Caper Cove was the only place she could call home.

"I genuinely don't know. The only thing I'm sure of is that I'll have to renew my driver's license."

"It's definitely a must-do, especially if you have to drive your catering around," Suggie said as she reached for another madeleine.

"Well, I'm not sure I'll be catering anything soon. My professional prospects look pretty bleak so far. But at least one of us is succeeding. Congrats on your blog post!" Suggie's article on Vee's death had gone viral and brought hundreds of new subscribers to The Caper Cove Whisper. "Your dream of becoming a nationally recognized journalist is coming true."

"I guess… I wish one of my readers had seen something and could help with the investigation." Suggie accelerated, keeping up with her higher speed lane, bypassing the heavy traffic going south. "It's also sort of tragic that celebrities' deaths fascinate the public. Of course, they're like us but with idyllic lives."

"*Seemingly* idyllic lives," Claire corrected. "Beneath the perceived glamour, there's a lot of work and stress. It's hard to keep your life private when you're famous. Did you know that many celebrities hire doppelgängers to play their part at events so they can breathe a little, away from the crowd, or be safe? Once your face is recognizable…goodbye, private life." Some of Claire's defendants had become so notorious because of their high-visibility trials, they had to wear wigs or fake mustaches just to make it to court alive.

Even when broke, Claire recognized that being rich didn't mean a problem-free life. She bit heartily into a madeleine and let its sweet tanginess soothe her. Food was the only true panacea in life.

"Funny you're mentioning doppelgangers. Did you know Karl Smith, the Fashion Warriors producer, had one? Mrs. Schumann, one of our seasonal guests from New York, couldn't stop talking about how she recognized him and how he refused to accept being whoever she thought he was."

Claire straightened in her seat. "Who did she think he was?"

"Someone called Gerhard Dexter. Mrs. Schuman said the man was infamous in the pharmaceutical community."

"Gerhard Dexter? That name sounds familiar." Using Suggie's phone as a hotspot, Claire typed the name in her phone, but the search yielded no result. She logged in LexisNexis, the legal database she used as a lawyer, happy to see that her annual subscription was still active. Since notoriety in the pharmaceutical industry came hand in hand with lawsuits, the name should be easily flagged. Claire entered the name and waited a few seconds for the search engine to come up with information. A list of registered complaints and criminal and civil lawsuits flooded her screen. Bingo!

"I found a Gerhard Dexter, chemist and owner of a pharmaceutical lab involved in a wrongful death lawsuit. His company was cited for violation of clinical trial protocols and for inadequately informing patients about the risks related to his drugs and the resulting life-threatening complications," she read out loud. "The case was settled out of court."

"Does that Gerhard look like Karl Smith?"

"Let me check." Claire clicked on *images,* and the spitting image of a bald Karl Smith popped up on the screen. "It's weird. That Gerhard Dexter has the same exact mole on his left ear as Karl Smith does. They might be the same person."

Suggie glanced sideways at Claire. "With a past like his, no wonder he changed his name. You think he's guilty?"

"I don't know. He had no obvious reason to kill Vee. In fact, he's the one who gave her a start in the fashion industry. But he should have told the police that his name was an alias.

Chapter Eighteen

The Poderas' mansion was as impressive as the Caper Cove Golden View villa. Nestled at the end of a dead-end street, the Spanish revival mansion featured a richly ornamented façade, stately columns, and intricate tilework. It was a true masterpiece of architectural craftsmanship similar to the Embassy Row houses in Washington, D.C.

"Good morning, my name is Claire Fontaine. We talked yesterday on the phone, and you told me I could visit today. I'm the executor of Vee Brooks' estate," Claire said as a middle-aged woman with ribbon-braided hair opened the door.

"You're the woman who saved Vee's life, the one she named her baby after," the woman exclaimed. Her smile was broad and warm, similar to the expression of the baby she was holding in her arms. "I recognize you from the picture, but I didn't know you were French."

"The picture?" Claire asked. She didn't remember any pictures of herself with Vee. They had stayed in contact throughout the years but hadn't had time to meet in real life in ages.

"The one of you and Vee at the courthouse when she was declared not guilty."

"Oh, that picture." It had been taken right after the judge declared Vee free to go, over ten years ago. Claire had gained a few pounds since then, but her French bob hairstyle and conservative suit had remained the same. "And this is my friend Suggie."

"Enchantée. I'm Lynn Poderas, Vee's mother-in-law and the proud grandmother of this bundle of joy," she said, kissing the baby on the head.

"Eva Claire."

Her throat tight with emotion, Claire waved at the baby. She had been touched that Vee named her daughter after her, but she had failed to appreciate the honor of the gesture until this very moment. "Hi, Eva Claire. I'm Claire, and this is Suggie."

The baby cooed and gurgled back as if in reply. She was wearing the red polka-dot dress Claire had sent Vee. The garment was GOTS-certified, which meant it met stringent criteria Vee valued the most from a clothing company—the sourcing of organic materials, environmentally friendly practices, the prohibition of hazardous chemicals, and minimum social and labor standards.

"She likes you already. She must sense that you're here to help. Come on in," Lynn Poderas said, ushering them inside.

Claire and Suggie followed the grandmother and the babbling baby inside. The interior boasted soaring ceilings, glittering chandeliers, and an abundance of art pieces. From the formal living room with its hand-carved fireplace and colorful furnishings to the outdoor terrace, everything was designed to evoke a sense of awe. The perfect place for a politician to woo wealthy campaign contributors.

"This is Maria, the nanny," the grandmother said as she handed the baby to a woman in a white uniform. "Let's settle at the table. Carmen will bring us some horchata and tea. These madeleines smell divine. Did you make them yourself?"

Claire settled on a rattan chair next to Suggie and across from the grandmother. "I did. Vee told me they were your favorite."

"What a sweet child Vee was. What a tragedy for everyone, especially Eva Claire. How unfair to grow up without a mother." The woman retrieved a cloth handkerchief from her right sleeve and dabbed her eyes with it. "Vee was such a great mom, always making sure to call and sing to the baby every night when she was away. She promised Eva Claire that it was their last time apart, that she needed to participate in this last competition to become a household name. After that, she promised Clay and Eva Claire that she'd work from home."

Claire nodded, smiling sadly as she listened. Vee had finally found and created her dream family until tragedy struck. It was so unfair.

"Vee was indeed a gifted designer and devoted friend. Were you and Vee close?" she asked.

The grandmother's hands slowly clasped together, fingers intertwining, grip tightening, as if seeking a sense of comfort. "As much as daughter-in-law and mother could be."

"What about Clay and Vee? Any tension between them?"

"Not more than any regular couples, you know. They both worked too much on top of the campaign."

"Did Clay know about Vee's past?" Claire focused on the woman's face as she posed the question, waiting for micro-expressions—subtle revelations of the speaker's emotional state, which are impossible to fake or suppress. Clues that would tell Claire whether Lynn Poderas was genuine in her answers or whether she was hiding something from the police.

"You mean the drug past?" Mrs. Poderas failed to display signs of surprise, anger, or contempt, but she looked over her shoulders as if to make sure her staff wasn't near. "Of course, he knew. He had run a background check on Vee before proposing. Her flaws were what attracted him to her. He's always had a savior complex."

Claire was about to ask whether the woman knew that Eva Claire wasn't her son's biological daughter, but Suggie's warning kick stopped her. Too much bad news at once could break someone's heart.

"Do you know where your son is?" she asked instead.

"No, which troubles me. The last time I saw him was seven days ago when he left for a fundraising retreat for his election. He should have been back by now. Clay promised Vee to attend the fashion competition's first day of shooting."

Though Mrs. Poderas' concern for her son's whereabouts sounded sincere, Claire wondered whether the woman believed Clay Poderas attended a real *fundraising retreat,* or whether she knew it was politicians' codeword for *rehab.*

"Did you report him missing?"

"Not officially. I was afraid the news would leak to the press and affect his campaign. But I told the police about it when they asked me about Vee. Clay's assistant told me he left the retreat two days ago in the evening."

A day after Vee's death.

"You mind if we check his office?"

"If that can help you find him, please do. I can't reach him. I'm starting to really worry."

Ten minutes later, Claire and Suggie had combed through Clayton Poderas' office. They rifled through antique books and scoured through files— accounting spreadsheets, legislative proposals, and Verdant Green golf resort pamphlets that proved that rehab facilities could look like vacation resorts. They inspected everything from his bookshelves and desk drawers to his computer. New parents' passwords were always easy to figure out. It was always the birthdate or name of their child. And years of legal practice had endowed Claire with incredible speed at reading and appraising the value of information found.

So far they had discovered two clues of potential importance: a private eye's business card and an email informing Poderas of Jason McCarthy's paternity and custody claims over Eva Claire.

"So Poderas knew about McCarthy for sure and that the baby might not be his," Suggie whispered. "He must have hired a PI to find out more."

"Maybe. Unless he wanted to dig into something completely different." Claire pocketed the card and the email printout. Politicians usually have more than two skeletons in their closets.

"Hem-hem." The sound of someone clearing their throat startled them. A young woman in a black dress with a white Peter Pan collar and white apron stood under the doorframe. "Mrs. Poderas wants to know if you're done. A light lunch has been served on the beach patio, and she's waiting for you to start."

"We'll be right there. Do you mind telling me where the washroom is?"

"There's one at the end of the hall, but you can use Mr. Poderas' lavatory if you wish." The maid stepped into the room, walked past them, and pushed on the chair rail to the left of the bookcase. The crown molding receded into the wall, and a door swiveled open where a seemingly uninterrupted wall surface previously was. "You didn't hear it from me, but Mr. Poderas was sterile. He knew that Eva Claire wasn't his," the maid said before leaving the room. "I'll tell Mrs. Poderas you're on your way."

Claire inspected the medicine cabinet while Suggie washed her hands. She found a tiny bag of white powder and blue pills behind bottles of ibuprofen, aspirin, and acetaminophen.

"Is that baking powder and Viagra," Suggie asked. "The older ladies at the spa always joke about getting their husbands a dose of blue pills on their anniversaries."

Claire smiled. It was refreshing to see that not everyone was familiar with illegal drugs. "The white bag is probably heroin or cocaine. That's called a baggie, a small single-use bag. The blue pills with the Superman symbol stamped on them are ecstasy," Claire explained matter-of-factly. It was a well-known fact that drug use wasn't rare among politicians. Many of them turned to cocaine to cope with stress and anxiety as well as to boost their energy, confidence, and focus when appearing in public debates. But it always came at a deadly price.

"I can't confirm it yet, but it certainly looks like Poderas didn't fall for Vee because of a savior complex," Claire continued. "He married someone who had been there before. Someone who would understand his disease without judging him."

* * *

"Did we have to leave so soon? I was dying to try the ceviche." Suggie whined as she exited Highway 5 toward Caper Cove. "Did you see how cute the prosciutto tea sandwiches were?"

The food display Mrs. Poderas had arranged for them had been luxurious, which was exactly the reason why Claire and Suggie couldn't stay.

"Believe me, I wish we could have sampled all the food and held that precious baby in our arms. But we can't accept anything that could be construed as a bribe. The caviar on blinis and petit-fours weren't what I would call a *light meal*. It definitely felt like a bribe." As any self-respecting attorney, Claire knew that fact-gathering needed to remain as unbiased as possible. Any gift could not only affect the way evidence was collected or appraised but could also taint their legitimacy and worth at trial.

Her eyes on the road, Suggie took a sip from the horchata Mrs. Poderas' maid had poured into a to-go cup for her. "What about that drink?"

"I personally wouldn't have accepted it either, but since it's just a one-time thing that can't be valued over five dollars, I guess it's okay. But as a journalist, you should think twice about accepting gifts. It could affect your credibility." Horchata wasn't a simple watery drink like tea and coffee, or fruit punch pouches Suggie always carried in her trunk. It was a complex, sweet drink made with rice, almond, and lime that took time to prepare.

Suggie choked on her straw and quickly dropped her drink back into the car cup holder. "You think she has something to hide? She was so nice and welcoming."

"See what you just did? You cleared her from suspicion simply because she offered you food!"

"Wait... you think she's a suspect? What reasons would she have to kill Vee?"

"I don't know, but she could be an accessory after the fact and cover for her coincidentally missing son." Even the nicest people would go to great lengths, sometimes becoming criminals themselves, to protect their children.

"Where to now?" Suggie asked as they arrived at Caper Cove's first intersection. Right to the hills or left to the shores or downtown.

"To the Irish Oyster downtown. The P.I. card we found in Poderas' office lists their agency above the pub. I can get you a side of French fries there if you're that hungry."

"Okey dokey," Suggie turned left and followed the coastal road that bordered the ocean. The sun was high and bright, and many tourists had flocked to the beach to enjoy this summer-in-April day. "No need to bribe me with fries. All the info I've gotten so far is all the gold I need for my next article."

"I'm sorry, Suggie, but you can't write about the evidence we found today."

Suggie slammed on the brakes, jolting Claire forward. "Why not?"

Claire glanced through the car's rear windshield, grateful there hadn't been anyone behind rear-ending them. The great thing about Caper Cove is that, as a small resort town, most of the traffic along that road was pedestrian.

"Oops, sorry." Suggie resumed the drive slowly. "Why can't I write about today's discoveries?"

"Because the killer's still at large and may try to silence us if they find out we're closing in on them. I also don't want Torres to give me an earful on how civilians shouldn't investigate on their own."

"But it's my biggest story." Suggie glanced sideways at Claire, pouting. "I can't write about it *at all*?"

"You can talk about it, but you can't mention any new evidence we found, like the P.I. business card or the cocaine in Poderas' office. Or the folder proving Cordelia's plagiarism, which, by the way, I've double-checked. Vee was right. Cordelia's a plagiarist and a thief."

Suggie's hands tightened on the steering wheel. "What if I slip?"

"If you slip, we could both go to jail for removing the folder and your wedding dress from a guarded house. It's *breaking and entering* and *tampering with evidence*."

"But we saved the evidence. Cordelia would have stolen the folder if she hadn't been stopped by the cop's warning. And the folder was in an envelope addressed to you."

"It doesn't really matter. Even if what we did was understandable, it's also actionable. They'll take your wedding dress into evidence and keep it there until the case is closed. They can also charge us with obstruction of justice."

Suggie conceded with a sigh. "Well, I don't want to go to jail or ruin my mother's spa reputation by association."

Claire took a deep breath of relief. "And I can't afford to be disbarred. Seeing how my life as a private chef is going, I may need to return to law."

Suggie looked at Claire with worried eyes. "You don't think Detective Torres would come after us if he finds out, do you?"

"I hope not. But if not him, the killer probably will."

Chapter Nineteen

According to a small plaque on Morgan Fisk P.I.'s office door, the private detective could be found "lunching every day at the outdoor patio of the Irish Oyster," the pub occupying the building's first floor. Located on a steep hill, the Irish bistro offered a breathtaking view of the harbor and roads below. The perfect place to observe tourists or to spy on local folks. A quick inquiry at the establishment's front desk directed Claire to the corner table at the end of the deck. A corpulent man in his sixties wearing thick eyebrows and a straw fedora was seated alone at a rustic wooden table, watching people in the street below with a notepad in hand.

"Excuse me, Mr. Fisk?" Claire asked.

The man turned around, tucked his notepad and pen in his jacket's inside pocket, and gave a once-over to both Suggie and Claire. He raised his bottom from his chair and his hat from his head, in a quick reverence, and smiled. "Bonjour."

"Yes, hello," Claire greeted back. "Do you have a minute to talk?"

"I've the whole day for beautiful French ladies. Please, join me," he said in a deep-resonant voice as he gestured to the two empty chairs at his table. "Would you like some chips? My treat."

Claire stared at him without answering, stunned by a strong but eerie sense of familiarity. She couldn't pinpoint exactly what it was about the man that generated that feeling—maybe his Santa Claus-like physique—so she contented to smile.

Suggie took a seat next to Claire, across from the P.I. "We're not French.

122

And yes, please, for the chips."

Claire checked her wallet, wondering if she had enough change to cover Suggie's slider. The rampant hospitality of Caper Cove residents was destabilizing, to say the least. In Washington, D.C., every lunch or coffee was often offered with ulterior motives—something she had been trained to decline or to be prepared to return in one form or another.

"Wherever you're from, how can I help you?" he asked as a cool, salty sea breeze rushed through.

"My name's Claire Fontaine. I'm the executor of Vee Brooks' estate. I'm here to ask you a few questions about her and her husband, Clay Poderas."

"Claire Fontaine, as in Camille's kid?"

The question startled Claire. No one had mentioned her mother's name since she passed six years ago. "Yes, why?"

The man removed his hat and patted his bald head with his hand. "Don't you recognize your uncle?"

Uncle? Claire tried to process the man's words with what she knew about her parents. Her dad and mom only had sisters unless…a flashback hit her. A bald man with a thick, black goatee, laughing with her mom. His bass-baritone voice. His tanned, shiny skull and bushy eyelashes and eyebrows. The three of them binge-watching Harry Potter movies past her bedtime.

Claire squinted at the man, who was at least fifty pounds heavier than she recalled. He wasn't a blood uncle. He was one of her mother's closest friends until they moved. He was a friend who always dropped by with movies and ice cream when her dad was working the graveyard shift. After her sister's disappearance, her mom had been so afraid to spend the night without a man in the house.

"Uncle Mo?"

"You betcha!" Morgan Fisk grabbed Claire by the shoulders from over the table, lifting her slightly from her seat, and gave her a huge kiss on the cheek. Just like he did when she was seven years old. "Your dad told me you were back in town, but I didn't expect to see you all grown up like this and certainly not speaking French."

Claire froze on her chair. She couldn't remember the last time someone had greeted her with such forceful enthusiasm. This type of embrace didn't exist among her Washington legal circle, where the closest you could get to touching someone was a firm handshake—unless you were dating them or wanted to be sued for sexual harassment. She laughed at the contrast, recalling her late mother's bear hugs and kisses.

Next to her, Suggie stifled a giggle.

"Well, I'm thirty-five now, and I don't speak French," she said, flattening her blazer and skirt as she shifted on her chair.

Uncle Mo grinned awkwardly and scratched the back of his head with both hands. "I'm sorry. I got so excited I forgot about physical boundaries. I should have asked before picking you up like that."

"Here's your chips." A waitress in a green dress deposited a basket of French fries in the middle of the table, cutting through the weird atmosphere.

"I understand the enthusiasm." Claire nodded, grabbed a few fries, and raised them at face level. "Cheers to being reunited!"

Uncle Mo's shoulders loosened as he retrieved his smile. Then Suggie and Uncle Mo imitated Claire. They seized a few fries with their fingers and bumped them together in the air as if crossing swords. "Cheers."

"I'm so happy to see you back, Claire. I assume this must be Suggie Oh, your childhood best friend and an affiliate of Oh LaLa, the town's best upscale spa?"

"Yes, I am. Your detective skills are sharp," Suggie said, her mouth full of fries.

"Seeing how hungry you are, let's get you a drink and whatever dish you want. They have a great choice of seafood soup or lamb stew. My treat. I insist."

Suggie glanced at Claire, waiting to hear if anything more than a single basket of fries could be called a bribe.

"It's fine," Claire whispered.

After ordering their dishes and squeezing the last ten years in a few sentences, Claire turned serious. "I'm here because I need to ask you about Vee Brooks and Clay Poderas, her husband. Did you know he was missing?"

"Yep. Heard it through the grapevine, yes. Why? You think he's dead?"

"I've no idea. We found your card in his personal papers, among *other things*," Claire explained, alluding to the cocaine in the medicine cabinet. "We thought you could help."

"What d'you need to know?"

"The reason why Poderas hired you."

"He wanted me to find his wife's birth mother. Said she was only fifteen when she had Vee and was forced to give up her daughter by her parents. T'was supposed to be a gift for their one-year anniversary."

Claire looked straight at the P.I. "Anything relating to Jason McCarthy?"

Mo straightened on his chair, jolting the table with his ample belly. "How do you know about that?"

"Vee was my friend. McCarthy was harassing her. He wanted custody of her child."

"I didn't know anybody knew about that. Poderas asked me to keep it on the down-low."

"What exactly did Poderas ask? I was Vee's attorney and her close friend, and now her husband's missing. Anything could help. Everything will stay between us, I promise."

Mo Fisk's eyes darted between Claire and Suggie; his lips sealed into a taut line as if he debated whether or not to talk. "He asked me to dig up whatever I could on McCarthy. His encounters with the law, DUIs, complaints, settlements, etc.… He also wanted to know why the guy, who's the opposite of dad material, wanted his paternity recognized. He was preparing to fight back in court to keep the baby under his name. Which didn't make much sense to me, especially if he couldn't prove his paternity."

"That's because a child born from a married woman is legally assumed to be the husband's child. The married couple are automatically recognized as the child's natural parents unless contradicted on the birth certificate," Claire explained. "For unmarried parents, the parentage of their children needs to be legally established by signing a declaration of parentage or obtaining a court order."

"So the only way McCarthy could be recognized as the father is by getting a court order?" Suggie asked between mouthfuls.

"Exactly."

Mo's eyes widened as he leaned back on his chair, pensive. "That's why Poderas wanted proof of McCarthy's motivation to fight him in court. It all makes sense now."

Claire leaned forward on the table. "Did you find anything helpful?"

"Yeah. One of McCarthy's relatives recently died with a clause in his trust concerning a conditional inheritance. The will stipulated that McCarthy could only inherit if he had fathered a child at the time of the deceased's death."

Claire gripped the armrests of her chair. "This is huge. There's nothing worse to a family court judge than a deadbeat dad who feigns interest in a child's welfare because of greed."

"Yeah, but all I got was hearsay. Nothing concrete that could stand up in court. The testament is part of a trust. Because it won't go through probate and become public record, I had no way of getting a copy of it. The lawyers denied my request."

"Who's the lawyer? I could talk to them."

"You can try, but they are a nasty bunch. It's the triple Betrossen." Mo dunked his fries deep into the cup of mayonnaise before placing them on his tongue.

Suggie shivered loudly. "The more I hear about that Tara Betrossen, the eviler she sounds. How much do you bet she's helping McCarthy with his paternity claim? She probably thought that the news of McCarthy's paternity would prompt Poderas to leave Vee."

Mo hummed in approval. "Jilted, narcissistic lovers are dangerous, irrational creatures. They're also some of my best clients."

Claire agreed with a nod. Angry, neglected lovers often ended up in criminal court, which made both Poderas and Tara Betrossen prime suspects. "Unless Tara was helping Poderas to find dirt on McCarthy. She was the one who emailed the paternity and custody claims to Poderas in the first place. Helping him keep his child would have earned her a lot of gratitude from Poderas. Maybe she was hoping to seduce him with her assistance and support and get him back."

Suggie grabbed her head in her hands. "It's getting way too complicated for me to follow. What would that change?"

"If Poderas could prove to the court that McCarthy's interest in the child was based purely on greed and that McCarthy initially paid for Vee to get an abortion, the judge would reject McCarthy's paternity claim straight away," Claire explained. "The court would consider the payment for an abortion similar to giving up his parental rights or abandoning a child. The only option for McCarthy to get his paternity established after that would be to kill Vee. When a mother dies, custody of newborns and young babies is given to the biological father."

"So McCarthy is suspect number one?" Suggie concluded.

"Who's suspect number one?" Torres' resonant voice boomed across the patio.

Chapter Twenty

The instant Torres had joined them, Suggie left the table, professing to be late for work. Though initially inclined to piggyback on her friend's excuse, Claire decided to stay. She didn't want to be rude to Mo and was curious to learn why Torres looked unusually jovial. Morgan Fisk seemed to be well acquainted with the detective, which was to be expected. In a small town like Caper Cove, police and PIs regularly worked on the same cases, often in a collaborative manner. But even when their perspectives and goals diverged, police and private investigators usually kept their relations professional and interactions courteous.

"You two know each other?" Mo asked as soon as Torres took over Suggie's chair.

Claire nodded. "We're investigating Vee Brooks' murder together."

"*I* am investigating Vee Brooks' death. Claire's a sort of consultant because of her connection to the case," Torres corrected.

"That's right. I'm the executor of Vee Brooks' estate and an experienced criminal attorney with insight into murder investigations."

"That and whatever past connection you have with Deputy Chief Ernshaw." Torres' condescending tone surprised Claire. He had been so polite and courtly the night before. Why the sudden change?

Claire wanted to remind him that she was the one who told him about Jason McCarthy's connection to Vee. She could point out the botched search of the private villa during which his team failed to find the folder under the guest bedroom mattress *and* brag that she had discovered that Clay Poderas had hired Mo Fisk *and* that Poderas was a cocaine enthusiast. She could

128

also tell him that Poderas' unreachability was probably due to his stay at one of the secret complete-shut-off-from-the-world detox programs that politicians and celebrities frequent. But she thought it wiser to keep quiet and listen. Torres' coming to her table meant he had new information to share. And new information meant new clues and being closer to bringing Vee's killer to justice, catering Suggie's wedding, and hopefully finding a job soon.

"Chief Ernshaw's very smart. Claire's a brilliant investigator. Always has been. Remember your first case?" the P.I. asked as he winked at her.

Claire threw Mo a thank-you smile for not revealing to Torres the tragic common past she shared with Miranda Ernshaw. "Of course. No one forgets the day they learned the truth about Santa Claus."

Annoyed by her sister's snarky smile whenever her parents talked about Santa, nine-year-old Claire had decided to treat the area around the Christmas tree like a crime scene. She had watched a lot of crime TV series with her father, whenever her mother was on night duty at the hospital, and she knew everything about collecting evidence, including fingerprints. Her search for truth was stronger than her fear of being hurt, a drive that only intensified as she grew.

"What did she do? Wash down instant coffee with Coke to stay up and catch Santa?" Torres asked.

Claire chuckled. Almost. She did overconsume caffeine while studying for the bar exam, a tactic she wouldn't recommend to anyone. Sleep deprivation and stomach cramps were memories she preferred to forget.

"She processed the wrapping paper of her Christmas gifts for prints. Then she compared them to her parents' fingerprints with the microscope she had received that very Christmas." Mo laughed. "She knew everything about prints. The arch, the loop, and the whorl, and how to lift them off surfaces. After that day, everyone thought she would follow in her father's footsteps into law enforcement.

Torres' eyebrows rose. "That's impressive, indeed."

Mo patted Claire's shoulder. "That investigative mind of hers and dedication to the truth are precious assets. She's a skilled ally to have."

"Thank you. It's nice of you to say so, Uncle Mo." Claire wasn't sure whether her investigative drive had always been a good thing. When her sister disappeared, Claire spent every minute of her days looking for clues, neglecting school and losing sleep, scrolling the internet chats about missing children, and conversing with random strangers online. Her inquisitive mind had marked the end of Claire's perfect childhood, and it was the reason she only saw her dad in the summers. Her mother couldn't watch her youngest daughter's health deteriorate any further and moved to New York, where Claire couldn't search for physical clues.

"I don't mean to be rude, but I need to ask. Why are you here? Did you have something to tell Mo or me about?" Claire asked.

"Actually, yes. I'd just ordered my sandwich when I spotted you on the patio. I thought you might like to know that Vee Brooks' death has been upgraded to homicide. The level of tetrodotoxin in her body was too high to come from a single serving of fugu. We've also arrested Jason McCarthy and charged him with murder.

"How?" Though Claire was ecstatic about the news, something felt off.

"We subpoenaed Brooks' phone records and found out McCarthy was harassing and extorting her over his alleged paternity of her child. With Brooks' death and Poderas' sudden absence, we were able to convince a judge to issue a search warrant for McCarthy's house and restaurant. We found correspondence between a Trust & Estate lawyer and McCarthy. McCarthy was due to inherit millions, but only after proving having conceived a living child and actually raising said child. We also found McCarthy's detailed, handwritten plan to get rid of Brooks if his custody and paternity claims were denied by the court."

"A handwritten note?"

"Yep, like a to-do list. Look at this." Torres placed his phone on the table for Claire to view. The screen showed the picture of a loose sheet of paper which read:

amicable request to recognize paternity

second judicial request

exert pressure on political campaign

get rid of Vee.

* * *

Mo hummed as he glanced at the screen. "It's as good as a confession."

Claire paused, pondering. *"Get rid of Vee* could mean anything. It's too vague to amount to an intent to commit murder."

"Which side are you on?" Torres groaned.

"I'm just stating, legally, that fourth point isn't enough to convict. Plus, don't you find it strange that McCarthy didn't wait for the court to deny his petition before killing Vee?"

"No. He probably knew his petition would fail if his abortion payment was entered into evidence. By killing Vee now, he made sure the evidence would never be presented to the court. No judge in their right mind would grant custody to someone who did everything imaginable to prevent their child from existing in the first place."

"Here's your order," a waitress handed Torres a brown paper bag.

"Thank you." Torres grabbed his lunch and rose from his chair as if about to leave. "It was nice chatting."

"Wait. What about tetrodotoxin?" Claire asked.

Torres paused and grinned, seemingly delighted by the fact Claire needed something from him. "That's the funny part. McCarthy claims he never had any. Said the fugu dish on his secret menu is just a scam."

"You believe him?" she asked.

"Don't know. Granted, the guy's a scammer. But he could have gotten fugu and thrown the evidence out. And for guys like him, money's everything. It's an instinctual motive for murder."

* * *

Claire watched Torres return to his blue police car, conflicted about her feelings. The reclassification of Vee's death as a homicide and the arrest of a suspect should have pleased her. The yellow tape would soon be removed from the Golden View villa. Suggie would get her dream wedding, and Claire would be able to display her culinary skills to many potential clients as she catered the event. Yet something felt amiss.

She hadn't seen a crime solved so fast before. Not that she complained. McCarthy's arrest felt somehow expedient. The other suspects, including Cordelia, Vinyl, and Clay Poderas, hadn't been thoroughly investigated enough for the D.A. to reasonably charge McCarthy.

"Something's wrong?" Mo asked.

"I don't know. Justice isn't usually that fast and easy."

"If you're sad the case is closed, I've got a job for you if you're interested and willing. It pays ten times the DMV's driver's license fee and only requires three hours of your time."

Mo had obviously talked to her dad, or the gossip about her return home (and her lack of a driver's license) had made a lightning-fast circuit of Caper Cove. Appealing to someone's desperation—her lack of transportation and source of income—wasn't really nice but was understandable. Claire did need a job. Badly. She quickly ran the numbers in her head. $500 for three hours was extremely tempting, but there had to be a catch. She could see it in the glint of Mo's eyes and his corner smile.

"I'm listening."

* * *

It was 7:00 PM when Claire returned to The Osprey. She was exhausted; her back ached a little, but she was happy. Her wallet was no longer empty. She had her first private chef gig teaching how to make French macarons at a local hotel, substituting for an absent pastry chef.

Suggie waited for her on the beach, by the warmth of a firepit, with dinner: Mrs. Oh's homemade bibimbap's mouthwatering smell threw her back to their childhood sleepovers. The overcast evening had melded the sky and the ocean into a velvety grey.

"How was it?" Suggie asked as she handed her a steaming bowl of rice and vegetables.

Claire grabbed the dish, placed her face over it, and let the spicy gochujang sauce tickle her nostrils. "Like pleading in court but with utensils in hand."

"How did you get a paid position so fast?"

"Mo Fisk had registered to the event to spy on one of the attendees. When he learned the chef was ill, and the workshop would be canceled, he convinced the organizer to hire me instead. He told them I had been Vee Brooks' personal chef and that I was French-trained," she said, rolling her eyes.

"So? That's the truth. You studied cooking for two whole months at the Cordon Bleu Institute in France before starting college. That makes you French-trained. If Julia Child called herself a French chef, you certainly can. Your last name alone proves your French heritage."

Claire gave a thoughtful sigh. "What about people believing I'm French because I was too tired to explain that my accent wasn't native? I feel like a fraud. Some of them were even trying to converse with me in French, and all I could do was smile and nod." She finished mixing the bibimbap ingredients with her chopsticks and put a pinch of food in her mouth, focusing on the dish's flavors. The spinach and mushrooms, seasoned with soy sauce, garlic, and sesame oil, and the marinated chicken pulled her mouth into a smile.

"That's on them. People's obsession with accents is ridiculous. Even if you had told them, I bet the majority wouldn't have believed you anyway," Suggie commented. "Remember the agent at the airport?"

Claire didn't need to be reminded. "On the good side, a few participants asked me when my next class would be, so I may be called next time they need a substitute, and I've got enough money to reactivate my phone with enough data for one month," she cheered. "What about you?"

"Cordelia Jones came to the spa today. She required laughing gas before her Botox injections because she supposedly passes out at the sight of medical needles. We had to ask for Doctor Opilka, the next door dentist to help out since we don't carry nitrous oxide. And now Umma wants to expand our services beyond our organic, all-natural treatments," Suggie said. "Other than that, same as usual. People would say it's boring, but I enjoy the predictability of my job. Numbers don't lie, and certainly don't try to kill you." Suggie laughed. "It's crazy Jason McCarthy's out, right?"

"What? How?" The murder charge should have kept him in police custody overnight, until his arraignment.

"He had a solid alibi. He was getting his monthly grooming regimen at the spa when Vee's sushi platter was prepared and delivered. He couldn't have poisoned her dish."

"Are you sure?" McCarthy could have easily paid someone to lie about it, Claire thought.

"One hundred percent. Georgia, our top esthetician, took care of him. She's the only one who can stand him. She told me he first got his eyebrows, chest, and pubic hair waxed and went for a sixty-minute massage afterward. No wonder the guy looks so good and relaxed after that. He held a press conference on the steps of the police station when he was released two hours ago. He claimed Torres had been harassing him. He even mentioned your visit to his restaurant and called you a French spy."

"Torres must be furious."

"That's a light way to put it. That detective's intense, like he has something to prove," Suggie said as she zipped open an insulated bag filled with hotteoks, releasing the sweet cinnamon fragrance of the Korean pancakes.

Claire could imagine Torres' bruised pride for failing to catch Vee's killer despite his confidence and his bitterness about having to restart the case from scratch. However, she decided to pay no heed to her roommate's possible mood. She bit into one of the warm pancakes, let the mixture of brown sugar and nuts fill her mouth, and refocused on her friend and the investigation.

"What about the fugu? Didn't they find any?" Claire asked.

"No, not a trace. I was going to ask you about that. Can't they punish McCarthy for lying about serving fugu?"

"They could charge him with false and deceptive advertising since he lied about the nature of the product. Did he say what it was he served instead?"

Suggie pulled her notebook from her bag and scrolled through her notes. "Whitefish with Szechuan pepper sauce."

"Smart. That sauce is sure to tingle or numb the tongue." Though Jason

McCarthy might have been a liar and a bully, Claire recognized the man's business acumen: his fake fugu provided the excitement and thrill of fugu eating without the liability or risk of killing someone. An over-priced experience, but a lifesaving one. "Any other earth-shattering news I need to know?"

"No. Clay Poderas is still missing and impossible to locate, but there are rumors about Fashion Warriors resuming filming soon. And yes… your father added a new item to the menu. It's called *a claire*."

Chapter Twenty-One

Suggie had been right. Saying that Torres was furious was an understatement. The detective was so mad at McCarthy's release that he brought the case file back to his apartment to study the evidence well into the night. He was still shirtless and combing through Vee Brooks' phone records when Claire joined him in the kitchen. The marble counter had disappeared under witness statements, computer printouts, and photographs.

"Do you need any help?" she asked, rubbing her awakening eyes. The sun hadn't risen yet, and the scent of extra-strong coffee saturated the air.

As Torres lifted his head from his homework, his neck muscles strained, tensing along with his sculpted chest. "Don't you want to go back to bed and be fresh for your driving knowledge test in the morning? Drowsy test taking is like drowsy driving, you know. Never leads to great results."

Had Claire lived in another town, Torres' knowledge of her 10 AM DMV appointment would have felt stalkerish. But here in Caper Cove, the whereabouts of the newcomers, or the freshly returned, seemed to spread faster than the speed of light.

"My brain's still on East Coast time. California three AM used to be the start of my workday in Washington D.C. Vee was also my friend. I'd do anything to find her killer." She reached for the copy of Vee's phone records. "Do you mind?"

"Be my guest. Chief Ernshaw suggested I seek your help and maybe deputize you since I'm a *homicide virgin,*" he groaned, making air quotes with his hands. There was a bit of whine in his tone, which Claire decided to ignore. From her personal experience, men always struggled to admit needing help from a woman.

"There's no shame in that. Every cop, lawyer, or medical examiner was once in your situation. Plus, two heads have always been better than one."

Claire speed-read through the pages of texts. Her phone number and text exchange were present on the list as Vee and Claire had communicated heavily prior to her arrival in Caper Cove. The printout also showed the black and white, pixelated pictures Vee had sent to Claire of her baby as well as her studio in the private villa.

"What suspects do you have so far?" she asked.

"You tell me. You're the criminal expert with the murder board in her bedroom." Torres inflated his chest as he pointed his chin in the direction of her door.

"Hold on." She trotted to her room, wondering if the heart shape of Torres' chest hair was natural or the product of a manscaping session at the spa. She didn't remember any of her D.C. colleagues being hairy. Though a few must have been, none of them had chest curls poking through the openings of their shirts. Chest hair on a man felt daring and exciting and sexy, in a Wolverine-Hugh Jackman kind of way. Something she had never thought about before.

She cast her rumination aside and returned to the kitchen with her board and its tripod stand, which she set up in front of the counter next to the refrigerator.

"Why do you have Karl Smith on it?" Torres asked as he approached the display. "Wait. He changed his name? Why didn't you tell me?"

Torres threw her an angry glare before returning his gaze to the hub of information Claire had collected.

"I was going to. I found out yesterday and didn't see you until now."

"And you've got proof Cordelia Jones is a thief?!"

"Yes, I ran an online search on her designs. Most, if not all, of her *supposedly* original patterns were stolen from younger artists' works. Her winning fabrics are the products of small-town creative high schoolers who are too young or too poor to be taken seriously or be heard."

"You think Cordelia Jones killed Vee to keep her thieving quiet?"

"It's a theory." Claire grabbed the coffeemaker carafe and rinsed it before brewing a new pot.

"Wait." Torres raised an eyebrow. "Did you hire Mo Fisk to dig into all this?"

Claire almost dropped the glass container. "What kind of question is that? I didn't hire anyone. I did the work myself! Why is that so difficult for you to believe that I could have better investigative skills than you do?"

"I'm not used to it." He puffed out his chest and stretched his muscular arms as if to make up in height and width what he lacked in professional expertise and confidence.

She set the coffee jug aside and went for the box of chamomile-lavender tea she had just bought instead. A calming herbal infusion felt like the smartest choice while dealing with Torres.

"In case you didn't know, women have been proven to have superior problem-solving skills than men," she said. "Maybe it's time for you to accept that. Unless you prefer to learn how I solve the case all by myself in the newspaper."

Torres' chest deflated. "I don't want that."

"Great. So we agree on something. Let's review our potential suspects, their motive, and opportunity." Seven portraits had been pinned to the board, Vee Brooks as the victim and one of each of the six suspects: Jason McCarthy, Clay Poderas, Tara Betrossen, Cordelia Jones, Vinyl, and Karl Smith. Under each picture, each suspect's profile, alibis, motives, and connections to the victim were written in black.

"Tea?" She proposed as she poured boiling water in a yellow mug.

"No thanks." Torres grabbed a red dry-erase marker and crossed out Jason McCarthy's name. "They couldn't find a single trace of tetrodotoxin in his kitchen or the hiring of fugu chefs. McCarthy was getting his bikini wax at the time the victim's sushi plate was ordered, prepared, and delivered. The guy was running a fugu scam but isn't the killer."

Which didn't mean he didn't hire someone to poison Vee.

"What about Clay Poderas? Did you find anything on him?" Claire asked.

"He's our main suspect, but he's still MIA. It fits the bill if you ask me. Prideful husband who felt betrayed by his wife's illegitimate child and wanted revenge."

"Actually, he knew the child wasn't his. Clay Poderas is sterile. I can't tell you the name of my source, but his medical record should confirm his condition."

Torres' eyes grew wide, and his lips disappeared into a line. "Okayyy," he sighed.

"Also, Poderas might be a drug addict."

Torres leaned forward, his shoulder muscles tightening. He was getting so close to Claire that she noticed the light musk of his skin beneath the scent of soap. "What proof do you have that suggests that?" he asked.

"I saw a white powder baggie and some Blue Superman pills in the medicine cabinet of his home office. I'm not sure how wealthy he was or how much he consumed, but if he owed his drug dealer money, Vee's death could have been a warning of what could happen to him if he didn't pay up." Claire spoke fast, focused on lifting the teabag up and down in the hot water in repetitive movements, making sure it would properly steep.

"You went to Poderas' house to investigate without telling me?"

"No, I went to my late friend's house to pay my respects and meet my namesake. Vee named her baby after me, and I had to meet her. Mrs. Poderas, Vee's mother-in-law, invited me and gave me permission to check her son's office. She's very worried about her son's disappearance."

Torres took a deep breath, inflating his chest like a rooster, and drew a rectangle on the "suspect line" of the white board. Under it he wrote *drug dealer* with a question mark.

"What about the third contestant? Did you find anything?" she asked.

"Vinyl?" Torres snorted and crossed the name off the board. "The Mexican border police spotted him in a local dive where he got into a bar fight the day of Brooks' murder. According to his phone's ping, he's still in Tijuana. Probably getting high as a kite."

They discussed each suspect one by one until Tara Betrossen was the only name left on the board. Torres and Claire had nothing new to add about her.

She had an alibi like all the others.

Torres leaned back in his chair and yawned. "The autopsy report revealed traces of tetrodotoxin in Brooks' system *beyond* what would be found in a fugu dish. Now, that's not something you can just get your hands on. It's not like buying rat poison at the hardware store."

"Actually, it might be." Claire finished typing on her computer and grimaced. "Local pet stores sell pufferfish, and there are plenty of websites that explain how to extract the toxin from them."

"Damn the internet!" Torres yawned once more and scribbled *check pet stores* in his police-issued notebook.

Claire took a sip of her warm, comforting drink, feeling the soothing power of lavender fill her. "What now?"

"What about this?" Torres pushed a series of letters and numbers in front of Claire. "Vee Brooks sent herself this text. I can't figure out what it means. Want to give a try decoding it?"

"Why not?" The combination looked familiar. It reminded Claire of the reference code of a drug test. Vee had undergone dozens of them when Claire had defended her in juvenile court.

"If you crack it, I owe you one."

"Does that include driving me to the DMV in six hours?" she asked, glancing at her watch. She had the incredible luck to get a next-day appointment due to a fortunate last-minute cancellation and couldn't miss it. Having to rely on other people's goodwill or the use of a bike for transportation made Claire feel like a pre-teen needing to be driven around by her parents. On top of living and eating at her father's for free, dependency wasn't something she was comfortable accepting.

"Sure. Why not?" Torres stretched his arms high above his head, exposing a small tattoo on the inside of his left biceps. It was something in Elvish writing, probably from Tolkien's literary work, *Lord of the Rings*. He stood up languishingly and shuffled his feet all the way to his bedroom. "Right now, I'm going to try to get some shuteye before sunrise."

"Goodnight."

Curiosity kept Claire awake. She could still catch up on sleep later since she didn't have a job. Torres had given up figuring out what the series of letters and numbers meant, but Claire thought she could decipher the code.

"If it's an order for a lab, Vee must have sent a specimen," Claire whispered to herself as she entered the code into her phone. What could that specimen be? A sample of her husband's urine for drug testing or maybe saliva or a hair sample to confirm the identity of her baby's father. Or something so secret that Vee sent herself a reminder without caption. Something that could solve Vee's murder once and for all.

Chapter Twenty-Two

The DMV office opened at 8 AM sharp. Torres had insisted Claire check in as soon as they opened because her 10 AM appointment was too inconvenient for him. He had flashed his badge at the entrance to get first in line, pulling an embarrassed Claire along with him.

The employee, a thirty-something curvy, 1950s pin-up lookalike in a red polka dot dress, beamed at him. "Good morning, Ben. What brings you here?"

"Hey, Robbie. I need help. Claire, here, has an appointment to take her knowledge test at ten, but I need her at that time. Police business. It would be great if you could squeeze her in first."

The woman flipped her electric blue hair with one hand, exposing her dangling cherry earrings. She flashed a PR smile at Claire. "Sure. Do you have a piece of identification?"

Claire handed the DMV worker her expired New York driver's license and her passport.

"Claire Fontaine," the woman read out loud as she scrutinized the identity card. "I knew a girl with the same name. She left town after her sister ran away."

"She didn't run away. She disappeared," Claire corrected her.

"How do you know..." The woman scrutinized her. "OMG, Claire? It's you, isn't it? You traded your long hair for a sharp city haircut and got an accent. I didn't know you moved to France."

Claire squinted, trying to place the woman.

"It's me. Robbie. Skelly Robbie. Doesn't ring any bell?"

Claire vaguely remembered the skeleton-related moniker. Eighth graders had given every entering sixth grader one. Claire had been nicknamed Harriet the Spy because she enjoyed spying on others and recorded her observations in a notebook she always carried around.

"Robbie Mayers?" Claire asked, dubious. The lanky and scrawny girl she knew from middle school had certainly bloomed.

The DMV employee's eyes brightened along with her smile. "Yes. How have you been? It's been ages."

"Sorry, but we are kind of in a hurry," Torres admonished with a stare.

"Oh, yes. This way, please."

* * *

Fifteen minutes later, Claire was riding shotgun aboard Torres' police car on their way to the resort to re-interrogate the Fashion Warriors crew. The detective was particularly interested in questioning Karl Smith and Cordelia Jones again and felt the need to have a female escort tagging along. Someone to shield him from Ms. Jones' aggressive flirting.

"I've never met someone who scored one hundred percent before. Out-of-staters make at least one mistake on the California DMV written test."

"Well, I'm not an out-of-stater. I actually learned to drive here, in Caper Cove and on Highway 5. Once you learned to drive north to L.A. or south to Mexico on a Friday night, you can drive anywhere," she said, referring to the notorious southern Californian traffic.

"You've got that right!" Torres laughed before quickly turning serious. "By the way, I'm sorry about your sister. I didn't know."

Claire shook her head in appreciation and looked at the window. "It was a long time ago."

The sun was rising lazily on Caper Cove. The marine layer lingered, hovering over the ocean and the centennial lighthouse, giving the coastal landscape a mystical ambiance.

"So that's how you knew Chief Ernshaw? Rumor around the station is that she was a theater major before becoming a cop. I can't imagine her singing and dancing. All I've seen her do is shout orders and beat everyone at the gun range with her sharpshooting skills."

Claire laughed. Discovering that her sister's old girlfriend was the police chief had been a surprise but not a shock. Most people had broader potential and talents than the boxes we put them in.

"Miranda Ernshaw has always been a multitalented woman. That's maybe why she was a great actress. Acting, singing, and dancing are about understanding emotions, openness, and adaptability, which most leaders hone." She glanced at Torres as she spoke, wondering what kind of skills the detective hid beyond his military training. Given his physique, he could easily be a Mixed Martial Arts Fighter. Or a stripper, Suggie would guess. Or maybe he collected old vinyl records and was an avid bird watcher. "Don't you have any secret talents or hobbies of your own?"

"Not really."

"Not even reading?" she asked, remembering the tattoo she had spotted under Torres' arm the night before. She hadn't told him that she had recognized the word *courage* and decided not to push him. "Everybody engages in pleasurable activities on their days off, be it cooking, watching crime documentaries, or hiking.

"Here we are," Torres said as he parked the car.

Claire didn't insist on an answer and smiled. Avoiding the question meant he was either boring or had something to hide.

Chapter Twenty-Three

Karl Smith's refusal to meet him in the lobby of the Agatha, the luxurious hotel where the Fashion Warriors crew was staying, made Torres angry. Ghosting the police to enjoy a fancy breakfast instead of helping them solve a murder was definitely a faux pas in Torres' etiquette book. To make sure Smith became aware of his error in judgment, the detective stomped into the hotel dining room. His feet pounded the white tiled floor, swerving through polished maple wood tables and brocade upholstered chairs.

"Can you tell us why you never mentioned your name change?" Torres asked without greeting as soon as he reached the table where the show owner was seated with his assistant.

Smith stopped mid-bite, his eggs Benedict dripping from his fork onto the plate below. "I don't see how this is relevant."

Torres frowned. "You don't get to decide what's relevant or not. When the police ask for your name and alias, you give them all your names. Not just the one you want."

"Well, I prefer my past buried and forgotten. I am a new man now," Karl Smith said before refocusing on his plate and placing the poached egg in his mouth, ignoring Torres as if the detective was some annoying fly to be shooed away with a handwave. He hadn't even noticed Claire, who observed the conversation a few steps behind.

"The only man I see here is the one who changed his name so we wouldn't find out about his manslaughter conviction. Want to finish this conversation at the station?" Torres asked.

Smith dropped his silverware on the table and looked up at the detective, suddenly concerned by his presence. "It wasn't me. I just took the rap for it because it was my lab, and my name was on the door. But I paid my debt. Six months in jail and millions in civil compensation. Going after me for my past is unfair, don't you think?" Smith redirected his glance at Claire as if to take her as a witness.

Claire lowered her eyes. She hated lies, but she believed in rehabilitation. That's what all her legal work had been: protecting the innocents against frivolous lawsuits and unfair charges. Changing one's name to start anew was practical and allowed her former clients to leave the past behind. It was often a necessary step to transition from the public eye into a normal life of anonymity. But besides what she had read in the Legal News about Karl Smith's jail time and paid damages, Claire didn't know if the man could be trusted. For starters, Smith had fired her as the show caterer without even meeting her face-to-face or offering indemnity.

"You said you changed. Is that why you failed to mention Vee's threat to go to the press about Cordelia's plagiarism? To move away from your past?" she asked.

Smith shifted uncomfortably on his chair. "I don't know what you're talking about."

"Vee Brooks knew Cordelia Jones stole her designs and passed them off as her originals. She told you about it, but you refused to do anything. To give a shout-out to the true artists or to disqualify Cordelia," Torres pressed.

"I don—"

"Stop right there. We've got the text to prove it. Unless you don't understand what *rectify it or I go to the press* means," Torres said in a menacing tone.

"You found Vee's phone?" Smith asked, surprised, his face turning red. With the cliff's many cracks and the powerful tide, finding Vee's phone would amount to a miracle. With proof of his knowledge and lack of action, Smith could be charged with copyright and trademark infringement, intellectual property theft, and unfair competition.

"How we got these texts is irrelevant. What's important is that you knew about Jones' plagiarism but didn't do a thing about it." Torres' tone was sarcastic and impatient. "You were afraid the news would ruin the show."

Smith shook his head hard. "No. To the contrary. I was hoping Vee would expose Cordelia on live TV. That would have made for better TV and publicity than a press release about her cheating. The ratings would have gone through the roof!"

Claire grimaced. Manipulative ploys in show business were frightening.

A veil of disgust crossed Torres' face. "You know what I think? I think you couldn't handle another scandal and that you were afraid to lose money on your show, so when Vee Brooks threatened to expose Cordelia Jones and your active cover-up, you decided to kill her."

"That's absurd," Smith jumped out of his seat. "I did something about it. I told Cordelia to come clean on TV. She was supposed to confess live on camera on the first day of shooting. I'm all about honest work and transparency now. My fabric lines prove it. So, if I'm not under arrest, goodbye, I have a show to put back on the rails."

Claire and Torres watched Smith exit the room, leaving his assistant behind.

"Karl's telling the truth. *Fashion Warriors* is all about honesty and transparency. The show's *Haute Nature* line promotes organic cotton and fabric manufactured with environmentally friendly materials and processes. Karl's fabrics contain no harmful dyes and are produced under sustainable, ecologically, and socially responsible conditions. I can schedule you a tour of his Tijuana factory if you wish," the assistant proposed. "We've got one leaving from Caper Cover this coming Sunday."

Claire nodded. "That'd be great! Please, sign me up."

Torres shook his head no. "I'll pass. Thanks. I don't have time for frivolous sightseeing trips. I prefer answers to my questions."

Claire inched closer to the assistant. "How bad was the rivalry between Cordelia and Vee?"

"Really bad," the assistant said, biting her nails, or what was left of them.

"Enough to lead to murder?" Claire knew that depending on the circumstances, anyone could kill, but it took a special type of person to carefully plan a murder.

"Possibly. Cordelia hated Vee. She lost a designing contract because Vee snitched on her. Cordelia had been chosen to redesign the LaVerne School uniforms. It's a fancy private school for wealthy, troubled youth. The school rescinded their twenty-thousand-dollar offer after Vee talked to the principal."

Ouch. Losing a contract meant losing an income, which must have incensed Cordelia. "Who knows about it?" Claire asked.

"Everybody does. It's not like you can keep a secret like that in this industry, especially in a small production like ours. Word spreads fast, and reputations are made or crushed in an instant. Lucky for her, Cordelia thrives on controversy. Her whole brand is about being an *outlaw badass.*"

Torres scowled. "What's sexy about that?"

"Black studs and metal spike chokers are making a comeback. They're great paired with natural prints that look like blood splatters. Cordelia called her line *the natural offender.* Just ask her. She should be in her room. She's the only one who hasn't shown up for breakfast."

* * *

The dozens of knocks on Cordelia's door got no answer, but the last pounding Torres inflicted on the wood panel brought out a couple of unhappy neighbors.

"She may be at the pool or at the spa enjoying an early morning treatment. Let's check at the front desk," Claire suggested, leading the way back to the lobby.

Torres followed her along the Wedgewood-blue corridor and down the artful elevator. "Killing someone for twenty thousand dollars? That's crazy for a TV star."

"It's not just about the money. It's about the school's network. Most of the students there are ultra-wealthy teens with amazing connections and trust-fund money they'd be willing to invest in rising designers like Cordelia." Connections were essential in any business. Knowing the right people could open golden gates to ambitious creators and could make the difference between making it big and disappearing in the sea of struggling artists.

Torres scowled. "Greed, it makes me sick. The rich getting richer and taking advantage of us all."

Claire exited the elevator, nodding. Greed was indeed the single most powerful evil motivator, which was destroying the lives of millions of people daily. It was the root of most crimes.

* * *

Small sailboats and miniature lighthouses adorned the front desk, enhancing the already strong nautical theme of the hotel. Behind it, on the light blue wall, a vintage map of Caper Cove and navigational instruments added a sense of history to the space.

A preppy-looking clerk with slick red hair and a blue argyle sweater greeted them with a smile. "Good morning. How may I help you?"

Torres flashed his badge. "We need to reach Cordelia Jones. Do you know where we can find her?"

"Ms. Jones must be sleeping. Let me check." The clerk's fingers flew over his computer keyboard. "She asked not to be bothered and suspended housekeeping all morning. She picked up one of our courtesy twelve-hour rental cars around midnight and returned before dawn this morning."

"Do you know where she went?"

"Yes, she went wildflower picking in the desert and brought thousands of wild poppies back. Marcus, our rental car manager, wasn't too happy about it because of all the dust and pollen he had to clean up from the seats. It was everywhere. It was so bad, he had to get the car detailed. You should have seen Ms. Jones." The attendant covered his mouth with one hand as he laughed. "She was really distraught like she was afraid someone would catch her, the real-life Barbie, all covered with dirt. Who knew picking desert flowers could be such a sweaty, hard-labor exercise."

"Yeah, desert dust's the worst. But flower-picking as hard labor? Tell that to the Marines at Twentynine Palms," Torres mocked, referring to the

Marine Corps Air Ground Combat Center located in the desert a few hours away.

"Do you know when she will be up or if she scheduled a beauty treatment later on by chance?" Claire asked. If Cordelia had returned from her expedition dirty and messy, the first thing she would do was clean up her appearance.

The clerk returned to his keyboard. "You're correct. She's scheduled a facial followed by a massage with Ernesto at the pool cabana at ten thirty."

"Thanks." Torres checked his watch and sighed, apparently inconvenienced by the wait.

"Why would Cordelia go flower picking, and why so early?" he asked as he settled down in one of the comfy armchairs of the lobby. It was upholstered in deep blue and white fabrics, with cushions adorned with seashells.

Claire imitated him and flopped down on the seat next to him. "It's part of her craft. In the show, each designer masters a distinct skill. Vee's was stitching; she was a fabric architect, a true genius who could make you a complete outfit without drawing a pattern. Vinyl is an expert in leather and pleather, while Cordelia is the queen of print pattern making. She created one with pressed roses and tire prints that propelled her to first place in season one."

Torres stared through the window, pensive. "You really think it's murder? I mean, c'mon. A competition about clothes can't be that bad."

"Fashion is like anything else. If there is desire, envy, and greed, criminal behavior quickly follows."

Torres snorted. "You mean women pulling each other's hair over a wedding dress on a bridal shop's sale day?"

"I'm talking about *men* killing each other over a pair of sneakers like Air Jordans or Adidas Yeezy. I can provide you with a long list of examples of people of all genders killing for fashion if you wish to know more." Fashion was a trillion-dollar industry with a nefarious side—from major crime cartels controlling illegal, counterfeit manufacturing and the underground slave labor that makes fake designer clothes to consumers exhibiting erratic behavior.

"Winning the competition is a strong motive for murder," Claire added. "There's a million-dollar cash prize, the once-in-the-lifetime opportunity to be featured in the most influential fashion magazine in the world, and the distribution contract for stores to carry the winner's brand."

Torres frowned. "What are you saying?"

"I'm saying all the contestants and the sponsors have a motive. To win the prize or withhold it because of financial duress or change of mind. Fashion can and does kill." Claire looked at the whale-shaped clock on the wall. Waiting for Cordelia to wake up suddenly felt like a waste of time. "What about driving to Pauma Valley to check where Cordelia went?"

Torres threw her a why-would-I do-that look. "Why?"

"To understand her state of mind or find out if she really went to Pauma Valley. She could have disposed of evidence, or met the killer at another location. There're multiple reasons to do it."

"Wow. First, you booked a tour to visit Karl Smith's fabric factory, and now you want to drive to Pauma Valley. You really like field trips," he said without moving an inch from his armchair.

"It could be important."

The detective stretched on his chair and yawned. "I'm not going to waste time driving when I can just wait for Jones to wake up and then question her. I've already made that mistake with Poderas. Drove all the way to San Diego to find out he was MIA. Talk about wasted gas and mileage."

"Don't you want to at least check the car's odometer or GPS to make sure Cordelia didn't lie as to her whereabouts?"

Chapter Twenty-Four

The GPS of Cordelia's rental car showed a straight path from Caper Cove to Pauma Valley without a single stop. However, Cordelia had made an odd detour to Hellhole Canyon on her way back.

Claire had snapped a picture of the itinerary with her phone when the manager showed it to Torres. Even though Torres had declared a trip to Hellhole Canyon to be too tiring or useless, Claire decided to drive there on her own. One of the things she learned as a defense lawyer was to follow all the leads. No matter how useless they seemed, one of them always led to the truth.

"Consider this little expedition a meeting with a source for your article *and* helping your best friend practice driving," Claire said, her hands on the steering wheel and her eyes on the road. She kept a steady fifty miles per hour speed along Bear Valley Road, named after the reportedly 2,220-pound Grizzly bear the town had captured in 1866.

"I've no complaints. I love road trips. I haven't seen the desert flowers in bloom for ages, *and* you're saving me from Umma. Every time I have a day off, she expects me to spend it at the spa entertaining guests," she said as she munched on a croissant. The scent of buttery pastry and warm latte filled the car. "But I don't get it. If you passed the knowledge test, why do you have to retake the road skills test? You obviously know how to drive."

"Tell that to the DMV and Detective Torres. Ugh." Since her driving license had expired and she had admitted earlier that she never drove in D.C., the DMV had required she take a road skills test. "I'm lucky though. They have an opening in two weeks."

The fields adjacent to the road teemed with flowers. Large bright patches of yellow, orange, and purple blanketed the usually arid open spaces.

Suggie gasped. "No wonder Cordelia Jones wanted to come here. We're in the middle of a super bloom or what Appa called a Botanical bonanza," she said, referring to her father, an enthusiastic gardener. "Look at all the California poppies, redwood sorrel, and tidy tips! Maybe we should scoop up some flowers too and ask Cordelia to teach us how to eco-print on silk."

Claire snorted. "She's a suspect in a murder case. We can't ask her that before she's cleared of any suspicion. But after that, why not?" Claire said. "Talking about flowers... Have you ordered your bridal bouquet yet?"

"Not yet. I'm afraid to jinx myself. You think the police will remove the yellow tape from the villa in time for the wedding?"

Only if the murder gets solved in five days, Claire thought, chewing on her cheeks. "I can't guarantee it, but I'm hopefu—"

"Turn right in one hundred feet," the navigational system's Scottish voice cut through Claire's response.

"Being interrupted by a Scottish accent sounds more sexy than rude," she laughed, picturing a kilted Highlander warrior as the man behind the voice. "Very Outlander-ish."

Suggie giggled along. "I agree. It's impossible to be angry at a sexy, exotic GPS voice telling you where to go. It's not road rage. It's road romance."

"Turn right in fifty feet," the GPS voice said. "Your destination will be on your left."

Claire slowed down, swerved at the road's bend, and parked on the shoulder instead of proceeding onto the small unpaved road.

"Why park here? The destination is thirty feet away. I'm not dressed to hike in the desert dirt, and neither are you," Suggie said, pointing at her yellow pantsuit and matching pumps.

"Something feels off." Claire stepped out of the car and into the hot air, scanning her surroundings. The April sun was unseasonably hot, and she started to regret not bringing a hat as Suggie had proposed. One set of distinctive tire treads was present on the pale, brown dirt, which meant one car had recently visited—probably Cordelia's rental.

Suggie placed her wide-brimmed hat on her head and followed Claire down the unmarked path. "What are we looking for?"

"I don't know. Anything that looks odd in the scenery. Like this." She pointed at a group of large stones that lay haphazardly on the ground.

"What, that jumble of rocks?"

"This isn't a random collection of rocks. These have been chiseled. They used to be a trail marker or monument made out of balancing stones." Claire squatted and scrutinized the stones. Once piled in a tower or a cairn, they must have formed an important navigational instrument for hikers wandering through the desert. "Why would someone destroy it?"

"Maybe a clumsy hiker bumped into it?" Suggie suggested.

"Or people got into a fight next to it," Claire said as she spotted reddish stains on some of the rocks.

"I don't get it. Why would Cordelia come here? The place looks more like a recessed shoulder than a drivable road, and there aren't any flowers around. You sure it's the right place?"

"I'm sure. Look, I think it's blood. Someone must have had a nosebleed or had been stabbed." Claire followed the crimson-brown trail to a boulder, her gut telling her she was on the right path.

"I don't like this... There's a toilet up the road. That's probably where Cordelia stopped. My car's GPS must be off... Maybe we should call the cops," Suggie said, lagging behind.

"Don't be silly, there's nothing to report...yet." Claire abruptly stopped. Something was moving on the other side of the giant rock. She could see its shadow shifting low to the ground as it emitted a small squeal.

A strong scent of rot hit Claire's nostrils as she took slow, cautious steps in the direction of the noise. She pinched her nose with her fingers and craned her neck to check on the other side of the boulder. Besides the increasing pungency, she found the cutest striped animal gnawing at a bundle of clothes. Claire didn't realize that the clothes belonged to a corpse and that the adorable animal was a skunk until the fury creature raised its tail, targeting her, threatening to spray her.

Claire gasped in horror. Her eyes wide open and locked on her newly-made enemy, she backed up slowly. Please, don't, she mentally begged. But before she could retreat behind the rock, the animal fired.

"Ahhhhh." Claire turned away and jumped behind the rock, her hands on her nose and mouth, attempting to shield herself from the noxious fog. She stumbled back as she recoiled, coughing, her eyes watery from the offensive smell.

"What's happening? Are you okay?" Suggie asked in a panicked voice as she rushed to Claire.

"Stay where you are and call 911," Claire shouted. "Tell the police we found a body."

Chapter Twenty-Five

Claire could officially add "stripping naked in the desert" to the list of things she had done. She washed herself with twelve packs of Hawaiian punch that Suggie had in her trunk and she now smelled a combination of fruit punch and death. The rising wind helped a little, but the sun was unreasonably hot, forcing Claire to shelter in the shade of a boulder. She was hoping to de-stink a little bit before climbing back into Suggie's car.

"Thanks for the scrubs," Claire changed into the purple clothing Suggie had handed her. "Is that a poop emoji?" she asked, squinting at the embroidered logo on her chest.

Suggie laughed. "Right?! Umma wanted to switch manufacturers for our employees' uniforms to save a few pennies, and this is what we got. I have a whole box of them in the trunk to return."

"Well, cheers to manufacturing mistakes and fruit punch that take away the deadly smell... or at least some of it." No amount of flavored drinks and baby wipes could completely get rid of the skunk scent.

"Our spa uniform may not be the most flattering, but periwinkle suits you," Suggie said as she tied Claire's fetid clothes to the car's back window, hoping to rid them of the stench.

"Thanks." The color had been too soft for her to wear in court, a place where Claire needed to appear ruthless in her client's defense. She always wore bolder colors and favored Navy, but now she wasn't practicing law anymore, periwinkle was definitely a color she would choose for a garment.

"What do we do now?" Suggie asked as she retreated to the cool shade and conditioned air of her Prius.

"Take as many pictures of the scene before the police get here."

"Okay, but first, how do you feel? No eye-burning or difficulty breathing? I heard that skunk spray can irritate the lungs and make you temporarily blind."

"I'm okay. My face and hands have been spared. Only my ankles and back have been sprayed. But I feel this sudden strange new connection to Pepé Le Pew," she said, recalling the animated French striped skunk from her childhood cartoons. Except that her quest wasn't love, but finding her friend's killer.

When the police and the medical examiner arrived, Claire had captured dozens of pictures with her cellphone. She had made sure to stay as far from the victim as possible, to not mess, or contaminate the crime scene, and zoomed in on certain parts of the corpse and its surroundings. She couldn't see the face of the victim since it was face-down in the dirt, but she could tell it was a man by his choice of shoes and one of his hairy hands. While Claire had played forensic photographer, Suggie had completed the first draft of her article and had chosen a "clean picture" to illustrate it. It was a snapshot of the body taken from afar and with no apparent identifying details so the family of the victim (if he had one) could be notified by the police before finding out the death of their loved one via her article.

Claire and Suggie were both patiently waiting in the shelter of the Toyota's conditioned air when Detective Torres arrived to take their statements.

"I can't believe you, of all people, found the body," he said, turning his head away to take another breath of clean, skunk-free air.

Claire shrugged, stepped out of the car, and positioned herself against the incoming wind so her newly acquired perfume wouldn't rush in Torres' face. "It's not my fault you didn't want to go. I told you the wildflower blooms would be interesting. If Cordelia got all dirty to get them, they had to be amazing, so I retraced her route."

"They're breathtaking, aren't they?" Suggie agreed, following Torres and Claire in the shade of a Joshua tree with her phone in hand to take notes.

"Right." Torres sighed. He adjusted his police-issued ranchero hat on his head and bombarded them with questions. After Claire and Suggie replied to all of them in detail, the detective closed his notebook. "Next time you've got a gut feeling, let me know. We don't need a Law and Odor unit on the police force."

"Haha," Claire forced a laugh.

The April sun beat the ground with a summer force, and the atmosphere was dry. It was no mystery how Hellhole Canyon got its name.

Torres joined the crowd of police officers processing the crime scene and stared at the body, or what remained of it, since desert scavengers, like coyotes and turkey vultures, had had a go at it.

"What can you tell us about it?" Torres asked a corpulent woman who was busy inspecting the body. The yellow striped shirt she was wearing made her look like a giant bee foraging on a Rafflesia Arnoldii, the corpse flower—a red, lumpy-looking plant smelling of decaying flesh.

"The deceased is male in his late thirties. Rigor mortis seemed to be established in the whole body. I'll say the man's been dead between six to twelve hours. He has no ID, just a paper napkin with coordinates on him," the medical examiner said without looking at the detective as she further examined the body.

Vikram Thomas assisted her, taking notes on a tablet as the woman spoke and watching closely as she pointed at different areas of the body. Every now and then, he would smile wide and bright as his eyes darted to Claire.

"The coordinates lead right here." A police officer handed Torres the bagged evidence that showed a napkin with the word Verdant Green embossed on it.

"Verdant Green? That's not far from here," Claire exclaimed as she looked at the evidence over his shoulder.

Torres pivoted to face her. "You've already given your statement. You are both free to go." He shooed them away with his hand as if they were unwanted flies on a dinner plate.

Suggie complied with the rude request and scooted back to her car, but Claire stood her ground. A flip of the wrist wasn't going to get rid of her.

"You don't understand. The lack of ID and the napkin... the victim must be a patient at Verdant Green," she said, following the detective back to the corpse. "It's a hush-hush rehab center for celebrities. Guests are usually dropped there without ID or cellphones, so they're completely cut off from the world. They want to make sure patients don't run away and have no outside influence. You could call them and ask them who's missing."

Torres ignored her and inspected the black-diamond wedding band that had been pulled from the deceased's hand. "Thank you, but I don't need you to tell me how to lead an investigation."

"Wait. I've seen that ring before." Claire swiped frantically through her phone's photo album, a sense of dread creeping over her until she found it in her "downloaded-from-texts" folder. A picture Vee had sent her of two people joining hands.

Claire gasped. The ring matched Vee's wedding ring. What were the odds that a Verdant Green resident wore the same custom wedding band? "I think I know who this is," she whispered.

Torres sighed. "How can you know? The man lost his face in the fall."

"Actually, his disfigurement wasn't caused by a fall," Vikram corrected, his eyes darting between Torres and Claire.

"Very good, Doctor Thomas," the medical examiner cheered. "What can you tell us about it?"

Vikram scrutinized the victim's visage. "It looks like he was repetitively hit by a long, thin object, which is inconsistent with a fall."

The bee-woman applauded and wiped her sweaty brow with the back of her gloved hand. "Excellent, Doctor. Soon, you'll be able to take over for me."

Claire mouthed a thank you to Vikram. "If you pull up his left sleeve, he should have the tattoo of a bear," she said.

Torres' gaze sharpened. "What type of bear? A polar or teddy bear?"

"A California grizzly bear, the same as the one on the California flag."

The medical examiner rolled up the deceased's left sleeve. "Bingo."

Torres grimaced. "Who is he?"

"It's Clay Poderas," she said. "He must have been a patient in the Verdant Green rehab center. That's why you couldn't reach him."

159

Torres straightened at the news. "Put a BOLO on Cordelia Jones immediately and bring her to the station when you find her," he told one of the officers. He pointed at the medical examiner. "I need you to return to Caper Cover to do the autopsy ASAP and confirm identity." Then, he stepped on a large rock and shouted for everyone to hear. "No one breathes a word of this until we confirm identity and notify next of kin, understood?"

Suggie giggled nervously and scurried back to her car. "Time to go home."

Claire trotted after her and jumped in the Prius, the engine already running. "What's the rush? What's going on?"

"It's too late," Suggie murmured as she put the car into gear, her forehead tense with crumpled eyebrows.

"Too late for what?"

"Too late not to tell a soul." She handed Claire her phone, which displayed the article she had just written about a nameless man found dead on the border of Caper Cove. "My article. I've already uploaded it and can't take it back."

Chapter Twenty-Six

To say that Torres didn't like Suggie's article was an understatement. Claire's ears still rang from his rant minutes after she hung up the phone. At least he got all his anger and frustration out and should have nothing more to add when he returned to their shared apartment tonight. Being roommates with a cop was certainly an adjustment. The important thing at the moment was that she was happy. She was no longer broke (though $500 hardly constituted a sustainable income, especially for one who spent all her money at the grocery store, purchasing the finest ingredients), and she welcomed her first guests. The menu: pan-seared scallops and leeks in white wine to thank Suggie for driving her around and lobster mac and cheese for Vikram for sharing his knowledge of forensic science. Plus, Niçoise salad as a first course and profiteroles for dessert.

Claire, Suggie, and Vikram were enjoying an early dinner on the terrace of her apartment, right above The Osprey, facing the ocean. A faint moon floated in the late afternoon sky like a lost buoy in a quiet sea. The briny air was filled with the tangy scents of leeks and Comté cheese and the buttery aroma of scallops and lobster—a perfect camouflage to Claire's lingering skunky smell.

"Why would Torres blame you? You haven't done a thing," Vikram hurried in her defense. He had gulped down his first serving of lobster mac and cheese and was getting seconds.

Claire glanced sideways at Suggie. "He's upset I brought a civilian to a crime scene, and that said civilian wrote about it in the newspaper."

"I'm not a civilian. I'm an investigative journalist, and journalists have First

Amendment rights. In fact, my article was picked up by the San Diego Daily. They want me to write a follow-up piece and pay me for it," she boasted, glowing with pride.

"This is fantastic, congratulations!" Claire cheered. "Are you going to do it?"

"Of course I am. Though, I'm not sure there's much more to uncover now that other journalists can't find. Maybe you can help me snoop around," Suggie suggested, winking at Claire.

"I'll see what I can do."

Though Suggie had always been on the fearful, cautious side, they had gone on a few spying expeditions as children. But finding a killer and walking the legal line was not as safe as finding out who had stolen the school's mascot and who had turned the swimming pool purple. Investigating murder, especially when drug addicts and politicians were involved, could be a risky business, from both the bad guys and the police.

"If snooping around with Suggie gets you in trouble with your roommate, you can always crash at my place," Vikram proposed. "Not sure you know, but I bought your childhood home from your dad a few years back. Sounded like a great investment. I haven't had the time to remodel everything, and your bedroom's still there."

Suggie threw Claire a knowing glance and stifled a giggle. She was lucky the terrace light was dimmed enough to mask her silly grimace.

Claire smiled, trying to chase the image of Vikram watching TV in her childhood bed from the night before. "That's very kind of you, Vic. Thank you. I'll let you know if the need arises."

"Not as long as she can pass for Pepé Le Pew," Suggie joked.

"Pepé's not that bad. I personally think Pepé's longing for love is a redeeming quality for his stench." Vikram scooted closer to Claire who was seated against the wind, far from everyone.

"Well, I'm not looking for love. Not before I get a job to support myself and get a place I can call my own. And yes, there's no way I'll ever go on a date until I get rid of my *eau de skunk*," Claire said, refilling the glasses with sparkling water. Even after a long shower and lathering herself with green apple-scented lotion, the foul fragrance still lingered around her like a cursed mist.

"About that." Vikram reached in his jacket pocket and produced a small spray bottle. "I made this for you. It's a mixture of hydrogen peroxide, sodium bicarbonate, and liquid dish soap. It changes odorous thiols into odorless acids, chemically neutralizing the skunk odor. I thought you could use it on your clothes."

"For me? Thank you!" Claire grabbed the bottle and ran back to the bathroom where her skunk-scented clothes were aerating. She could save her Yves Saint Laurent pantsuit after all!

When she exited the bathroom, Claire found her friends at the kitchen counter, staring at her murder board. She hadn't returned it to her bedroom after Torres and she had worked on it all night.

"This is really impressive," Vikram commented. It's like you predicted Cordelia's arrest."

"It was more a theory than a prediction. Anyone with the means, motive, and opportunity is a suspect. Plus, we don't know for sure that she's the killer."

"You don't think she killed Poderas?" Suggie asked.

"I have no idea. I haven't read the autopsy report. The only thing I have are the pictures I took of the scene, which suggest Cordelia's innocent," Claire said. "Vic, do you have new information to share?"

Vikram nodded, bright-eyed, staring at Claire as if happy to be the object of her full attention. "I can tell you that he died of a cocaine overdose. He had a weird needle mark at the base of the neck as if he had been stabbed by surprise."

"But if he was murdered, why disfigure him?" Suggie asked, pulling her notebook from her purse and settling at the counter.

"To slow down his identification and the investigation… or make him more appetizing to the local fauna, hoping he'd disappear fast. Being eaten away by the local turkey vultures and crows looks more natural and accidental than being dissolved with chemicals. And it can't be traced," Claire said as she added the bit of information on the board, right under Poderas' portrait.

163

"Natural decomposition or being eaten away by scavengers is indeed cleaner and yields better results, especially in this area," Vikram agreed. "Hellhole Canyon is prime territory for bobcats, coyotes, and, of course, striped skunks, all of which enjoy carrion."

"Do you know why he was there? Did his mother tell you?" Suggie asked.

Claire perched halfway on a barstool closest to the board. Her shoulders and head felt heavy, as if pulled downward by an invisible weight. An hour after they left Hellhole Canyon, Mrs. Poderas called Claire. She asked if her son was really dead like Detective Torres had told her. Claire stayed on the phone with her while she cried, trying to answer her questions about what was going on. About Jason McCarthy's custody battle, and why Cordelia Jones would want to murder her son, and who would have custody of Eva Claire, her granddaughter, now that both Clay and Vee were gone.

"Clay Poderas was in rehab at the time of Vee's death until two days ago. He was supposed to be picked up at Verdant Green, the rehab facility for the rich, by a limo service and dropped off at his house afterward. But he didn't make it all the way back. The limo driver said Poderas asked to be dropped off at Hellhole Canyon that night."

"Why?" Vikram asked, taking the seat next to hers.

"The driver didn't ask, the same way taxicabs don't question their riders about their choice of destination. But since Poderas called his mother that very evening and told her he'd be home soon, we can assume whoever he was meeting was going to be his ride. And who else can give you a ride home without phone or money?"

"A friend or a business partner," Suggie interjected, raising her arm as if she were on a TV game show.

"Yes, someone you personally know and trust. The thing is, he didn't personally know Cordelia Jones."

Suggie scribbled frenziedly in her notebook. "You think Cordelia's innocent?"

"She could be. Her getting caught returning from the crime scene seems too perfect. She's too smart to have used a rental car GPS to return to the hotel from where she supposedly murdered Poderas. Too smart to leave this kind of direct evidence behind." It wouldn't be the first time a semi-guilty party was framed for the only crime they didn't commit.

There is no honor among felons. Criminals always try to frame each other for their crimes. Stealing designs from unsuspecting students may not be murder, but it was still a crime, which would make her appear guiltier than most and the perfect suspect for both Vee's and Poderas' murders.

"Maybe she felt remorseful or stressed, or she panicked. Don't criminals always make mistakes, and that's how the police catch them?" Vikram said.

"Yes, but what's her motive?" Claire wrote *motive* and drew a question mark on the whiteboard under Cordelia's portrait.

"Maybe Poderas knew about her stealing from Vee. Maybe he was going to out her," Suggie suggested. "She's the only one we know who visited the crime scene."

"That's the problem." Claire placed her phone, screen side up, on the counter between Suggie and Vikram and opened her picture folder. "See here," she said at the zoomed-in picture of a shoeprint. "This is a men's size twelve. It was the only fresh shoeprint around Poderas' body."

Vikram frowned. "She could have brushed her own footprints off. It's messy but easy to do with the dry soil and a tree branch. Didn't you say that she returned to the hotel covered in desert dirt?"

"She could also have had an accomplice. The same person who poisoned Vee. Could be the cop who let her bypass the yellow tape at the villa," Suggie pointed out.

Claire rubbed her forehead in thought. The presence of an accomplice would explain the footprint with the nick in the sole. The same footprints had been present at the villa. "Vic, what else can you tell us about Poderas' body?"

"He had defensive wounds and scraped knuckles, like he fought. He was also dragged from the entrance pile of rocks to behind the boulder, probably to keep him hidden from the road."

Claire shook her head. "No way Cordelia could have dragged him on her own. She's what, one hundred-ten pounds tops and the guy's about two hundred?"

"Two-hundred-fifty," Vikram specified.

Claire added *250 lbs* on the board. "No way she could have dragged the body by herself."

"She looks pretty fit to me," Suggie said, "and she returned sweaty and dirty."

Vikram bobbed his head. "Yep. Women in fitness are stronger than they appear. You also looked really delicate, but you could lift me without effort. Remember, Claire, when we wrestled on the couch back in the day?"

"I don't," Claire lied, hoping Vikram would stop seeing her babysitting days as a blooming romance between the two of them. That was different, anyway. Vikram was in elementary school, weighing a maximum of seventy pounds. "Do you know if Cordelia had any marks on her and if we can go see her?"

Vikram shook his head. "They've already booked her. They were taking her mugshot when I left the office. "You think they're going to charge her with both Poderas' and Vee's murders?"

"I have no idea. I don't know what evidence they have against her." Claire could feel a headache coming on. She had come to Caper Cove to take a break, not stress out about a killer the police seemed to have already caught. No matter what her gut told her. "How about we take a break from sleuthing," she said, walking toward the refrigerator. "Who wants profiteroles?"

"Me!" Vikram rushed to the cupboard and helped her with the dessert spoons and bowls.

Claire served each of her guests three ice cream filled choux and topped them with a warm, rich chocolate sauce. She settled on one of the backed barstools and cut the pastry orb with her spoon. The crisp and golden shell revealed the creamy vanilla filling. Once in her mouth, the cool velvety texture of the ice cream paired beautifully with the chocolate drizzle. For a few seconds, time seemed to stop and the world's problems vanished at once.

"Wow, this is divine. A lawyer and a cook. Claire, a woman of justice and pleasure," Vikram said, his eyes begging—for more profiteroles or Claire's attention, no one could be sure.

Suggie laughed out loud, almost choking on her spoon. "Cheers to fancy food that's delicious and poison-free."

"Cheers to that," Claire agreed, trying hard not to blush from Vikram's longing stare.

"What are you talking about?" Vikram stretched over the counter to reach the dessert platter and served himself another serving of profiteroles. "What food's been poisoned?"

Suggie squinted at him. "Vee's sushi, what else?"

"Vee didn't die from eating poisoned sushi. She didn't eat the tetrodotoxin. She hadn't eaten anything before she died," he clarified.

Claire jumped from her seat. "What? Do you mean tetrodotoxin wasn't found in her stomach contents?"

"Exactly. Her stomach had only traces of digested oats, but no trace of tetrodotoxin. The toxin was either absorbed through the skin or via injection," he said, ladling chocolate sauce on his choux as if to drown them.

"Why wasn't it mentioned in the autopsy file?" This wasn't a minute detail. The entire investigation into Vee's death rested on that information.

"Must be a software glitch and pages got skipped during printing and digitization. We've been having issues since we've updated the system."

Suggie pulled out her notepad. "Did you find any needle marks on Vee's body?"

"Many. Mainly around her belly and thighs," he said before shoving a whole choux into his mouth.

"Vee was diabetic. Needles were part of her daily pre-meal routine," Claire explained. "Did the police test her insulin pens then?

"They didn't get any. The janitorial staff wiped the house clean yesterday. The police can't retrieve anything. Everything's been either destroyed or contaminated," he said his mouth full, lips dark with chocolate syrup.

Claire could feel anger rising in her veins. Torres had yellow-taped the private villa for a reason. They were supposed to process the scene fully but hadn't done so because they believed Vee's death was either a suicide or an accident, which didn't warrant a full combing of the house. That is, until they decided to call it a murder *after* the cleaning crew went through and, therefore, too late to properly collect evidence.

"Wasn't there any guard to stop them?" she asked Vikram.

"The officer on duty was AWOL to attend a last-minute casting call. He thought no one would dare enter the place with the police tape all around. Guess he was wrong."

Suggie leaped from her seat. "I bet it's the same officer who let Cordelia snoop in the house. We should add him to the board!"

"I think you might be right. Cordelia must have promised to cast him as a runway model for her next show. That's how a lot of people get roped into committing crimes and end up facing murder charges." Claire took a marker and added the word *guard* next to the list of suspects.

"Or maybe he's an accomplice. Maybe he wanted to make sure the janitorial staff wiped his and Cordelia's prints off their murder scene. Love can make you do anything for someone you care about." Vikram blinked, staring straight at Claire as he spoke.

Claire ignored Vikram's not-so-subtle statement. "What if I could procure you Vee's insulin pens? How fast could you test them for traces of tetrodotoxin?"

"About a day. Why, you got them?"

"I do."

"How?" Vikram asked, looking at Claire like a fish gasping for air.

"Yes, how? I'd also like to know." Torres' resonant voice boomed from the apartment entrance.

The detective removed his shoes, carelessly abandoned them by the front door, and walked toward Claire. "First, you rudely insert yourself in my investigation, then your friend writes an article against my order, and now I find out you stole evidence from a crime scene. You know that's a crime, right? You and all your friends could get arrested and charged with obstruction of justice and tampering with evidence."

Chapter Twenty-Seven

Claire hadn't expected the chief of police to be in her office at 6:30 PM on a Friday night. She hadn't planned on being seated across from Deputy Chief Miranda Ernshaw in one of the guest chairs either and feeling like an elementary school girl wrongly sent to the principal's office for chatting too much in class. But here Claire was, having to justify her "crime" to her sister's old girlfriend while her accuser-tattle teller stood in a corner.

"I've already told you. I was going to bring them to the station," Claire said of the Ziploc-ed insulin pens Torres had seized from her bedroom. She was annoyed by Torres' smug face and was upset he was wasting time. The insulin pens she had removed from the crime scene needed to be processed ASAP, but, instead, Torres reveled in having "caught her in a crime."

"Easy for you to say right after being caught red-handed!" Torres mocked, smirking.

"Let her talk." Miranda Ernshaw's voice was sharp. "Claire has proven herself instrumental in finding important leads in this case. She also has over a decade of murder-related knowledge compared to your minimal experience in the matter. We ought to listen to her."

"Thank you, Chief," Claire said, using the woman's professional title as opposed to *Miranda* to acknowledge the seriousness of the situation. "First off, I didn't tamper with or destroy evidence, nor did I obstruct justice. To the contrary. Faced with the *police's failure* to properly process the scene and the *police's refusal* to listen to my concerns and belief that a crime had been committed, I decided to collect the evidence myself to preserve it, one day after the villa was yellow-taped," she declared, gesturing at Torres every time she said the word *police*. "If I hadn't been there and safeguarded the evidence, the insulin pens would have been destroyed."

"Second, you should be thanking me instead of berating me and threatening me with criminal charges." Claire pivoted to face Torres and looked straight at him as she spoke. "If the Poderas family found out that you didn't process Vee's crime scene properly and failed to collect crucial evidence, you could be facing a negligence lawsuit for this oversight."

Torres' expression went from self-satisfied to confused. "So? Everybody makes mistakes."

Claire shook her head. "Not when it involves dirty cops."

Miranda Ernshaw scooted forward on her chair, her brow furrowed. "What are you talking about?"

Torres tilted his head backward, rolling his eyes. "C'mon. She's making things up."

"Torres, quiet!" Chief Ernshaw snapped in a commanding voice, which she softened as she addressed Claire. "Please elaborate."

"The officer you posted to guard the villa last Wednesday allowed Cordelia Jones to search the house. Who says he didn't let the cleaning crew scrub the house on purpose to get rid of the evidence?"

Miranda leaned over her desk toward Claire. "This is a serious accusation you're making here, Claire. Do you have any proof supporting your statement?"

"I do." Claire produced her phone, turned the screen toward the chief, and pressed Play on the recording. The video showed Cordelia leaving the private villa under a police officer's guidance as he warned her of the next shift's arrival.

When the recording ended, the silence was so palpable that they could hear the ticking of the wall clock.

"In case you're wondering, I followed proper protocol to collect the insulin pens. I picked them from the waste basket with a tissue, so you'll find no prints of mine on them, and I preserved them in a Ziploc bag. Also, I'm the only person who had access to them, so the chain of custody has been established and maintained," Claire pointed out.

Deputy Ernshaw's jaw was tight. "Are there any witnesses to confirm that?"

"I collected the evidence alone," Claire said, wanting to shield Suggie from troubles in the event her trespassing in the villa was considered a crime—especially since she was engaged to a soon-to-deploy Marine. His military clearance could be denied if Suggie were convicted of a crime.

Claire's answer wasn't really a lie, anyway. Suggie had been unaware Claire had retrieved and bagged the insulin pens from the bathroom waste basket at the time, and Suggie was hiding in the bedroom when Claire filmed the conversation between Cordelia and the police officer. "You won't find me on camera either. I used the beach stairs, which weren't yellow-taped, by the way, so I assumed the access and use of the area had been reopened to traffic. I realized I was wrong when I caught the officer warning Cordelia to get out of the house fast."

Okay, that last line was a lie.

Miranda was frowning hard at the video. "That's Tom Logan. I want him off the case and in my office first thing in the morning. Understood, Torres?"

"Yes, ma'am. What do we do now?"

"We've got to comb through the crime scene pictures to find one with the insulin pens to make sure they existed and were photographed by the forensic photographer before testing them. Then, send the evidence to the lab. But first, give Claire a ride back to her place. That's the least we can do for saving us a costly lawsuit. With both Poderas and his wife dead, his family's going to try to find someone to blame, and it won't be us."

"Anything else?"

"Maybe get Claire a job application so she can apply to the force or become one of our consultants." Miranda turned to Claire and smiled. "In the meantime, I'd prefer you stay on the sidelines."

"But—"

"There's no but, Claire. I mean it. We've already got two murders on our hands. I wouldn't want you to be next. Torres will let you know when you're needed."

* * *

The car ride was deadly silent but not tense. The evening sky was a mix of dark blue and radiant orange, a combination so gorgeous that it was hard not to smile. The palm trees bordering the road swayed along with a gentle breeze, turning the resentful atmosphere into a mellow moment.

Torres was driving, his mouth was a thin line of what Claire guessed could be embarrassment and regret, and hopefully a little humbling pressure. To be honest, his feelings were irrelevant. What mattered was that they were closing in on Vee's killer. She swiped quickly through her picture folder, searching for a photograph of Vee's room that showcased the insulin pens. Just in case the Caper Cove crime scene processing unit hadn't snapped the proper shot. Vee's fingerprints and the photo would be enough to confirm the evidence's provenance.

"I've got it," Claire exclaimed as she pinched out her phone screen, zooming in on a picture. Vee had texted her pictures showcasing the villa where Claire would be spending the next two weeks, including a selfie and a photo of Vee's bedroom/studio. "The selfie she sent me clearly shows insulin pens in the waste basket in the background. We can even see the prescription sticker on them. I'm sending it to Chief Ernshaw!" Claire typed on her phone and the *woosh* of sent messages sounded as Torres stopped the car along the sidewalk.

"Already? Wow. That was fast." She opened the door and was about to step out when Torres held her back by the arm.

"Look, Claire, I appreciate you preserving evidence and bringing all these facts to our attention, but it'd be nice if you could share whatever information you find with me right away and let me do my job without bumping into you at every turn."

That sounded like a half-baked apology.

"I understand, but one of my close friends was murdered, and my best friend is supposed to get married in the villa you yellow-taped. Solving this murder would not only give me and Vee's family peace, but it would also allow my BFF to get her dream wedding before her soon-to-be-husband deploys. How can I not try to find out who did this?"

Torres sighed. "All right, fine. You want to help? Be a lawyer and provide legal advice to Cordelia Jones."

"Provide legal advice to Cordelia Jones?" Claire wasn't sure she heard right. Or maybe Torres was joking. Unless…. Please, she thought, don't tell me Torres and Cordelia Jones are a thing.

Chapter Twenty-Eight

"Can't the triple Betrossen or another lawyer handle Cordelia?" Suggie asked Claire.

Both women were seated on the fancy rattan chairs of Le Citron, the small rustic bistro located right across from OhLaLa Spa, catching up on last night's events since Detective Torres had abruptly shortened their evening together. The morning light streamed through the large bay window, brightening the yellow walls. Outside, the marine layer gracefully blanketed the coastline, blending hues of soft gray and gentle blues, creating a dreamlike ambiance.

Claire took a sip of her warm, French lavender tea. "The Betrossens already work for Jason McCarthy. Representing Cordelia would be a conflict of interest for them, and there's no other criminal attorney in town," Claire explained. "There hadn't been a murder in Caper Cove for as long as people remembered, and therefore, no need for a criminal law firm specializing in murder cases. I'm the only one in town."

"So, are you going to help Cordelia?" Suggie asked as she added a cloud of milk to her steaming coffee.

"I'm still debating about it." By moving to Caper Cover, Claire had left her legal practice behind in Washington, D.C. She had no desire or inclination to go back to court, especially by potentially representing her friend's murderer. "No one should be left without legal defense, but there are many questions that need to be answered first. I told Torres I'd drop by the station right after lunch to have a preliminary meeting with Cordelia."

"Are you talking about the infamous Cordelia Jones?" The waitress, a

174

twenty-something with long jet-black hair with shaved sides, asked them as she handed them the paper menus. "That woman's really rude if you ask me. Did you know that she left Mrs. Laver in emotional tangles?"

"Mrs. Laver, the dry cleaner? What did Cordelia do?" Suggie asked, leaning toward the waitress. Town gossip was the fastest way to get the juiciest news.

"She dropped off a silk dress in terrible condition, all embedded with dirt. It was so bad, Mrs. Laver had to wash it by hand to try to salvage it. It's unbelievable how a designer could be so careless about her clothes and expect the cleaner to do the impossible."

Claire perked up on her seat. If the dirty dress was the one Cordelia wore on her trip to the flower fields, it could be an important piece of evidence. If it were ripped, it could prove that Cordelia fought with Poderas before he died. "What happened to the dress?"

"It's like new now. Mrs. Laver's a magician," the waitress said.

"Do you have a picture?" Claire was hoping to be able to see rips in the delicate dress that would suggest a fight broke out between Poderas and Cordelia. Or maybe a blood stain since Poderas had bloody knuckles when he died.

"I have better than that." The waitress retrieved her phone from her back pocket, clicked on a few icons, and showed Claire a social media post—a before and after video of Cordelia's dress dripping with mud and then sparkling clean flowing in the wind. "Ms. Jones is lucky Mrs. Laver could save it. No other laundress could have done the job."

"That's an amazing job indeed," Claire agreed. "That woman could have worked as a cleaner for the mob." The after photo showed an immaculate dress, cleaned free of any DNA evidence. It was the one Cordelia wore on the video surveillance when she left the hotel and returned dirty. It was one-of-a-kind apparel that she had designed herself during one of the Fashion Warriors challenges. It might have been dirty, but it wasn't ripped, which proved Cordelia hadn't been involved in a physical altercation with Poderas. Unless she had an accomplice, Cordelia was innocent of Poderas' murder.

"Would you like to order something to eat now, or are you still waiting for

175

your other guest?" the waitress asked.

"Still waiting, but he should be here soon," Suggie said as she checked her watch. She searched the room with her eyes until she spotted a young man at the bistro's entrance. "Here he is."

"We're having a guest? I thought this was a girlfriends' breakfast," Claire said with disappointment in her voice. After her late-night trip to the police station and the stress of the investigation, she had looked forward to a quiet time with her best friend.

"It's better than a girlfriends' breakfast," Suggie reassured Claire as she waved at the approaching boy-man. "It's a get-new-information-for-the-murder-investigation-breakfast."

"Hi, Suggie. Thanks so much for having me." The man might have been an adult, but he looked more like a young boy with his tousled blond hair, bright smile, and flip-flops. The perfect picture of a teenaged Southern California surfer.

"Hello, Mason. Please take a seat." Suggie pointed at the empty chair next to hers. "This is my friend Claire. She is a lawyer. Claire, this is Mason. He's an accounting student at the University of California San Diego. He's sent me a very interesting email, and I thought you might want to hear him out, but first, he wanted to make sure he won't get in trouble for whistleblowing on his boss."

Claire greeted him with a smile. "First off, who's your boss, and did you sign an NDA? A non-disclosure agreement?"

"Wait, you know American law?" the young man asked.

Claire sighed. She had forgotten about her accent. "Yes, I'm a criminal attorney licensed to practice law in California. I can tell you that in California, something called the California Whistleblower Protection Act protects people like you, who might have seen something wrong and decided to come forward." She would need to brush up on the particulars of the law, but she knew the law provided protection to individuals who reported illegal activities, fraud, corruption, or other wrongdoings. These protections included safeguards against termination, demotion, harassment, or other forms of retaliation.

Mason scratched his head and laughed. "Okay, good. So, my boss is the head of accounting for Poderas' campaign. His name is Jeremy Hartman, but he goes by Jerry. I haven't signed anything. I'm a volunteer. I was supposed to fold pamphlets and stuff envelopes, but when they got short-handed, and Jerry learned that I'm studying accounting, he put me on the fundraising team."

"Okay, what was your job?" Claire asked. Accounting sheets were often the first place to find criminal evidence. Financial statements could reveal various types of financial crimes or irregularities, including embezzlement, fraud, money laundering, tax evasion, and bribery or corruption. Or the suspect payment to what would later be revealed as a killer-for-hire.

"I was supposed to reach out to potential donors, you know, people who pledged to give but haven't given yet. Jerry gave me a list and I reached out to them first by email, then by phone, you know, to be more personal."

"Okay."

"So, most of them are happy to give. Poderas was a great candidate. His position on climate change, car emissions, and socialized medicine were, like, groundbreaking. That man could have changed the world. But there were a few donors that were, like, really reluctant. It was almost like Jerry gave me the wrong list of names or that they were forced to contribute somehow. Which makes no sense, right? Because Jerry wouldn't give me a list like that." He laughed.

Claire listened attentively, thinking there was sometimes a fine line between past contributor outreach and telemarketing. "What exactly made you think the list was wrong?"

"Well, usually, people make their contribution via wire transfer. It's super easy and really fast. Older people or small businesses prefer to pay by check, you know, because it's traceable. We usually get and cash them within a week. But those donors, the reluctant ones, they waited for the phone call. And when I was able to get them on the line, they were really sour, like they were getting punished. They said things like *Tell Poderas that I'm not doing it with a smile* or *Not sure if you know what you're getting into kid*. Some even swore at me." Mason shook his head as if to rid his mind of the unpleasant memories and continued talking. "At first, I didn't really get why they weren't happy trying to get a great guy elected. A guy that could make the world a better place, you know? That's what made me think hard. I think these donors were being pressured into giving."

Claire scooted her chair closer to the table. "What did you tell them when you called them?"

"We've got a set of different phrases to repeat. For people who are hard to get or slow in contributing, Clay Poderas himself insisted I tell them *If you want a happy life, don't forget to send your check*," he said, making air quotes with his fingers. "Why?"

"Sounds threatening," Suggie whispered.

Claire nodded. "Sounds like blackmail to me. Any other oddities you experienced or noted?"

"Yeah. The unhappy donors never attended Poderas' parties, which is rare for whale donors. They usually want to network or somehow profit from these events."

"Whale donors, as in his biggest contributors?" Claire asked.

"Yes, they all gave a million or more."

A million was definitely no crumbs and no pressured sales, that was blackmail in all its glory. The kind that is difficult to prove because no donor would agree to testify for fear of exposing their wrongdoing. "Do you remember their names?" Claire asked.

"I wrote them down for you." The boy-man pulled a piece of paper from his pocket and unfolded it on the table. "There's only eight here, but there might be more since I've only started volunteering for the campaign less than a month ago."

Claire scrutinized the list of names. One stood out: Karl Smith. "Is it the Karl Smith from the Fashion Warriors show?"

"Yes. You'd think he'd be happy to support his biggest star's husband, right?"

Suggie nodded enthusiastically, but remained quiet as Claire asked all the questions. She had pulled her notebook from her purse and was frantically taking notes.

CHAPTER TWENTY-EIGHT

"Do you know when Karl Smith was added as a contributor to contact?"

Mason raked his hair with his fingers and kept his hands on each side of his skull as if to better concentrate. "About a week ago, something like last Sunday or maybe Monday, a day before Vee Brooks' death, I think. I didn't see his name on the email list. He jumped straight to "donors to call." I'm the only one handling these phone calls because Jerry said I've got the perfect voice."

"You do have a smooth, assertive voice," Claire agreed. A warm, authoritative but slightly gritty voice, perfect for collecting or extorting money and reminding people that they need to pay up now.

"Do you remember when you talked to Karl Smith?"

"Sure. Two days ago. I was on lunch break and was sipping a lychee boba when he returned my call. The guy was so rude I almost choked on the drink's tapioca balls. He called me a vulture and said that he'd handle the issue with Poderas himself."

"Do you remember anything else relating to angry donors?"

"No, that's all I've got." Mason swiveled sideways on his seat to face Suggie, who was scribbling on her notepad, and looked at her with expectant eyes. "Did I help with your investigation?"

Suggie shifted on her seat, blushing. "Yes, you did. Thank you so much."

"Anytime. I think you're just great. An accountant searching for the truth. You could be a comic book hero," he added.

A light bubbling sound rose from Claire's watch, reminding her of her speech therapy appointment. Something she had completely forgotten. With the investigation taking all her time and focus, she had neglected her speaking exercises.

"I have to go," she said, rising from her chair. "Thanks again for the tea, Suggie, and to you, Mason, for all the information."

"Wait, where are you going? Your appointment with Torres isn't until this afternoon." There was pleading in Suggie's voice, as if she didn't want to be left alone with Mason.

"It is. I have speech therapy I'd completely forgotten about. You know, for my accent."

179

"Oh." A disappointed sigh left Suggie's lips. "I understand."

"Hey, it's just my opinion, but you should keep your accent. It's really nice. Accents are really like fonts for the mouth. Gives you an edge and personality," Mason said.

"I never saw it that way. Thank you, Mason. Suggie, I'll text you after my visit to the station."

* * *

The police station conference room's clock featured a sailor figurine in its center, with its arms serving as the hour and minute hands. Each number was a nautical flag. When the clock struck one, a boat horn blared, jolting Claire.

Torres shot Claire a constipated grin. "Sorry about that. That was a welcome gag gift from the office to Chief Ernshaw when she arrived. We didn't expect her to put it on the wall and keep it."

"It's fine. I'm telling you, Karl Smith is the only link between Vee Brooks' and Clay Poderas' murders. It can't be a coincidence," Claire reasserted after sharing with Torres what Mason had told her. "We should add him to the list of suspects for both murders."

Claire grabbed a sticky-note, wrote Karl Smith on it, and slapped it on the police whiteboard. It was a fancier crime board than the one she had in her bedroom. The portraits of the suspects were official DMV pictures, forensic findings had been added on bright colorful notecards, and a red string linked the victims to the suspects. From a distance, it looked more like a bright and fun craft project than a grim and complex murder investigation.

"Not so fast. What motive would he have to kill them both? Especially Brooks. He had everything to lose with her death. His show's about to flop without her as its main star."

"I don't know yet. All I know is that he wasn't that saddened by Vee's death." Yes, everyone grieves differently, but Claire sensed that Karl Smith was hiding something beyond his name change. "Maybe Vee knew something about him. Maybe she was going to tell the world about it, and he killed her to silence her. Then, he realized Vee had shared that secret with her husband, so he killed him too."

Torres took a sip from his coffee mug. "And you based that theory on the fact Smith was added to Poderas' contributor list right after Brooks' death?

"Yes. Even though Poderas might have been chagrined by his wife's death, he must have suspected foul play. With his political ambitions, blackmailing Smith was the perfect way to give a financial boost to his fundraising campaign." After years of working in D.C., surrounded by the constant ebb and flow of power dynamics, Claire knew first-hand that political candidates had frighteningly big egos and that many wouldn't hesitate to break the law if that could help their political campaigns.

"Being angry and unwilling to financially contribute to a political campaign doesn't make Smith a murderer. He has an alibi at the time of Brooks' death, and the morning Poderas died."

"That doesn't mean anything. Time of death is only an estimate. The desert temperatures can drop really low at night, and could have slowed down the rigor mortis process. Poderas could have passed a couple of hours or more before, I'm sure. Or he could have been badly hurt and died slowly after that. Which would have given Smith plenty of time to return to his hotel as if nothing happened." There were enough possible scenarios in which Karl Smith was the killer.

"What about Vee? How do you think he killed her?" Torres asked.

"Easy. You just told me that one of the insulin pens tested positive for tetrodotoxin, right?" It was the first question Claire had asked him upon meeting him that afternoon, before she even said hello. "Smith could have contaminated her insulin pen with tetrodotoxin, so she self-injected the toxin-contaminated insulin herself as she usually did before having lunch. Vee was so organized, Smith could have predicted exactly when she was going to give herself an injection. Which gave the killer a perfect alibi."

"That's an interesting theory, but you know better than me that this is pure speculation. Meanwhile, we've got a real live suspect with a serious motive and opportunity, and we've got plenty of evidence against her. Cordelia Jones killed Vee Brooks to hide her copyright infringement and protect her reputation as a creator. Karl Smith and several of the Fashion Warriors crew heard them arguing. We've got them fighting on tape. And we have irrefutable proof that she was present at Poderas' crime scene at the time of his murder. The GPS locator and the ping of her cellphone from a nearby tower confirm it."

Claire inhaled deeply, wondering how she could make Torres realize that the simplest, most obvious route wasn't always the right one. "Cordelia could have been framed. Physically, there's no way she could have fought Poderas and dragged him behind the rock. Plus, she's afraid of needles. She literally faints at the sight of them, something to do with a vasovagal reflex reaction."

"Afraid of needles, right." He laughed. "You realize that she can still sew."

"Medical needles and sewing needles are different. They don't belong to the same environment or have the same function. What Cordelia Jones suffers from is called trypanophobia, the extreme fear of medical procedures involving injections or hypodermic needles. Not sewing needles. She probably had negative life experiences or previous trauma brought on by medical needles. She almost passed out at the spa the other day when she got touch-up Botox."

"Speaking of the devil." Torres checked his watch and walked toward the door. "If you've decided to legally represent Cordelia Jones, she's waiting in her cell as we speak."

"I haven't decided yet. I'm just going to talk to her first. Maybe she'll be more willing to talk to me."

"Why, because you're both fashionistas?" Torres waved his index finger up and down, pointing at her soft gold jumpsuit, a color Claire usually wore when she conducted home visits, advising maximalist clients—people who favored loud and attention-grabbing designs with bold shapes, colors, and textures similar to Cordelia Jones' collection. Claire had made an exception to her usually quiet wardrobe. She had no clue how to make Cordelia open up, but she thought the vibrancy of her ensemble would certainly break the gray sobriety of the jail.

"Maybe. People tend to feel safer with people with whom they identify. As a female who speaks with an accent and enjoys fashion, I share more with her than you do," Claire explained. She had taken a psychology class on how to use people's biases to select a favorable jury—individuals more willing to listen and sympathize with the defendant. "Unconscious bias toward people who are of the same race, education level, economic status, and have the same values and taste influences who we trust. We subconsciously look for points of similarity in everyone we meet because similarities make us feel safer. Even if it's a fallacy."

Chapter Twenty-Nine

U nder California law, a person could be held at a police station without being charged with a crime for forty-eight hours. The idea of spending that length of time, more if arrested on a weekend, made Claire shiver. Temporary holding cells were only a few square meters in size, with just enough space for the person to stand or sit. So it didn't surprise Claire to see Cordelia Jones smile when she was brought into the roomier consultation room. It was still concrete grey, but it had a window with natural light coming through.

"You brought your girlfriend again," Cordelia told Torres as she sat confidently at the table across from the detective and Claire. Her voluminous hair had been straightened, and she wore black lipstick and thick eyeliner of the same shade—a gothic rock style that matched the jail's grim atmosphere. Though her bright orange, police-issued jumpsuit engulfed her small frame in a sea of fabric, Claire noticed the tension in Cordelia's neck and shoulders.

"Me and him? No way." Claire laughed, fully aware she hadn't said "never," which would have been a lie. By the small frown on his forehead, Torres didn't find the comment funny. Under different circumstances, Claire would have felt a bit guilty for hurting his feelings, but, at the moment, scoring trust points with Cordelia was more important than Torres' romantic ego.

"That means you don't have crappy taste. Who would want to date a cop in this day and age, right?" Cordelia snarked. The current public perception of law enforcement wasn't a favorable one. Recent highly publicized cases of police brutality and racial profiling had sparked widespread protests and discussions about police reform—controversies on which Cordelia Jones had built her platform. She gave Claire a once-over and said, "I like your style."

"Okayyy." Torres stood up and walked to the door. "I'm going to step out and let you two ladies talk about men and fashion. Ms. Jones, feel free to chat with Claire Fontaine here about anything. Including your whereabouts and the murders of Vee Brooks and Clay Poderas."

The woman flipped her wrist and gave him the finger in a dismissive wave. "You're wasting your time. I've nothing to say."

"It's fine with me," Torres added before slamming the door behind him. "The guards will take you back to your cell when you're done. And it won't be Tom Logan."

Cordelia Jones crossed her arms on her chest and shrugged. The reference to the cop who let her search the villa must have hit her hard, because her eyes darkened, and her lips flattened into a tight quivering line. She stared into the void, probably wondering whether Tom had snitched on her or was the true killer.

"We don't have to talk about the case if you don't want to. I assume a few more minutes in this spacious room is better than back in your tiny cage," Claire said, trying to establish a rapport with the woman.

Cordelia didn't reply but agreed with a subtle nod. She kept her back straight and her head high as if she was having tea with the queen. Her oversized jumpsuit was unbuttoned in the front in a risqué decolletage, and her rolled-up sleeves exposed her tattooed forearms—canvases of ever-changing temporary designs. Her skin displayed no contusions or bruises, and her manicure looked pristine. If this woman had fought and killed someone, she would bear at least a scratch. Yet, Cordelia didn't display any. And since foundation make-up is not allowed in jail, she couldn't have covered them up.

"My friends and I have watched Fashion Warriors since it first aired. We are all wondering...what's your favorite color."

"It used to be orange, but I may rethink that." Cordelia shifted on her chair, her shoulders loosening. "That's a vintage Jean-Paul Gaultier jumpsuit you're wearing, isn't it?" she asked with a chin-up nod.

"It is, but I can't take credit for picking it." As a pro bono criminal attorney, Claire had neither the time nor money to go shopping for designer clothes. "My old job gave me a new outfit every week."

"Your boss chose your clothes? They have good taste, but that's seriously F-ed up."

"Not my boss. The stylist they hired." Saying it out loud filled Claire with a little bit of embarrassment and shame. A grown-up who doesn't pick out her own clothes was laughable, but so was refusing free fancy clothes. One of the benefits of working for her prominent law firm was that HR mandated that all employees, especially the lawyers, were impeccably dressed. Projecting a professional and affluent image that aligned with their wealthy clientele's expectations and fostered rapport was an imperative part of the job.

"Wow, it takes guts to admit being dressed by someone else, especially for a French woman. What kind of job was that?" She uncrossed her arms and leaned back on her chair, balancing backward.

"I was a criminal defense attorney in Washington D.C.," she answered, mindful not to contradict Cordelia about her Frenchness in order to build trust. People tended to disbelieve her when she asserted she was a "true American," whatever that meant.

"You're here to represent me?" she asked, cocking an eyebrow.

Claire smiled. Cordelia hadn't questioned her competence as an American lawyer and assumed Claire could represent her. "No. I was hoping to convince you to talk."

"I like your directness, but that's not happening. I've already told them. I can't tell anything I know. If I do, I'll be breaking the NDA I signed, and I'll get disqualified from the Fashion Warriors finale. I can't afford to forgo a one-million-dollar prize and a feature in the top fashion magazines in the world. With Vee out of the competition, I'm guaranteed to win."

"You're still thinking about the competition? Aren't you worried about your present situation? How your sojourn in jail and potential murder charges may affect your brand and reputation?"

"Not at all. My arrest and charges are good for publicity. In fact, this oversized jumpsuit and prison slippers might inspire my next collection."

Cordelia's brand was street maximalist and edgy, a style fashion critics referred to as "a thug with a thick wallet and a golden bidet." Her bad girl/rule breaker image appealed to many, especially rebelling youth with first-world problems.

"My career depends on my fans. They would hate to see me quit. Better to go to jail as a winner than to be a safe loser." She readjusted her hair with her hands as if cameras would soon catch her likeness. "Besides, I don't mind a little drama. I'm innocent. Sooner or later, everyone's going to realize that."

"I wouldn't be so sure. The police have serious evidence against you, so I would consider sharing with them any exculpatory evidence you may have. Your Fashion Warriors NDA can't be used against you if you lead them to the killer. I would make sure of it." Non-Disclosure Agreements were common for individuals appearing on TV shows. They were in place to ensure participants did not reveal details about the show, its production, or any confidential information they might become privy to. NDAs helped prevent leaks and maintain suspense or surprise for viewers. They couldn't be used to shield someone from criminal prosecution or provide immunity from criminal liability.

Cordelia flicked invisible dust off her sleeves. "You sure about that?"

"One hundred percent certain. I worked on a case with similar facts. A wrongful death suit involving the murder of a worker in a sneaker factory. The design teams were afraid to speak on behalf of the defendant because of their NDAs."

Cordelia jerked forward, lowering the front legs of her chair back to the floor, and gazed at Claire with round eyes. "Like in the Frisbiz murder trial? You're the one who defended Frisbiz, the high-tops designer?" Cordelia asked, an ounce of admiration tainting her voice.

"I did. The case had made national news because the shoe designer, a struggling artist/rapper, had been wrongly accused by the shoe factory's top executive.

"That was an impressive defense. I'm still not sure I need a lawyer, though. I'm not like Frisbiz. No one framed me."

"What if I tell you Karl Smith was the one who sent the police on your trail? He told them about your fight with Vee and provided them with a tape of your arguing and threatening Vee with death."

Cordelia's eyes widened along with her gaping mouth. "What? He's the one who gave me the directions to Hellhole Canyon! He told me where to find all the wildflowers, that the rarest ones grew behind a rock along the road, on marker 28, next to the broken cairn."

Claire's heart skipped a beat. Cordelia was opening up to her. "Do you know why Karl Smith would want to hurt Vee?"

"I actually do." Cordelia leaned forward on the table. "Vee was about to jump ship. She wouldn't sign with Karl's brand of fabric even if she won. Please, don't tell anyone. If Karl finds out I told you, I'm as good as dead."

"I won't, you have my word. Why would Vee refuse to endorse his fabric?"

"I don't know. Am I in trouble?" Cordelia asked before chewing on her thumb.

"I'm afraid so. The police can place you with Poderas at the time of his death, and they have the tape of your violent outburst and death threat to Vee."

"It was just a passionate fight. I never wanted to kill her!" Cordelia complained, sweat beads lining her hairline.

"Convincing a jury might be hard, especially since Vee warned you to come clean about your theft." As of now, Cordelia looked like a strong suspect. The only way to exonerate her was to prove someone else was guilty.

"I guess I do need a lawyer." Cordelia's jaw quivered, her eyes welled up with tears. "Are you going to represent me?"

"I don't know." It would feel like betraying Vee if she did. But the alternative of letting the D.A. use questionable evidence to convict Cordelia, without digging deeper into Karl Smith's background and whereabouts, seemed worse. Claire couldn't not represent her if Cordelia had been framed. Though rude, selfish, and a thief, Cordelia seemed truthful at the moment. She had also been privy to confidential, NDA-protected information that might be the key to finding Vee's killer—information Claire wanted to know.

"Did you kill Vee?" Claire stared straight at Cordelia's eyes as she spoke. Body language, voice inflection, and eye contact were good determinants to pinpoint a liar.

"Of course not!" Cordelia said, taken aback by the question. She didn't look away or cover up her mouth or close her eyes—liars have a natural urge to hide from the other person's reaction. Her voice didn't go higher or have a creak in it. And her vibes—what Claire sensed about Cordelia—felt constant. Cordelia was telling the truth.

* * *

There was nothing more flashback-inducing to Claire's childhood than grilled sardines sizzling on the open flames with the rhythmic sound of crashing waves in the background. It had been Vikram's idea. The grilled fish and apple pie were the first dishes Claire had taught him to prepare when she babysat him years before. The smokey aroma laced with sugary cinnamon wafted in the evening air. The sun dipped below the horizon, casting a golden glow on the sandy shores. The temperature had dropped sharply from the high 70s of the day, but the fire pit's strong heat kept Claire and Suggie warm.

"Are you officially representing Cordelia Jones?" Vikram asked as he presented her with a plate of sardines seasoned with lemon, garlic, and paprika.

"Only until the arraignment on Monday. After that, another lawyer will take over," Claire said, scooping a piece of flaky fish with her fork.

"What makes you think she's innocent?"

"The evidence they have against her isn't airtight. She couldn't have tainted Vee's insulin with toxin. Tampering with an insulin pen or cartridge requires specialized knowledge—something she doesn't have. Nor did she stick Poderas with a needle. She suffers from trypanophobia. She literally faints at the sight of needles."

"Oh, I saw that online. She's gone viral," Suggie exclaimed.

Since Cordelia had been arrested, a barrage of videos and memes featuring Cordelia passing out flooded the internet. One of them showed Cordelia swooning at a Covid vaccination site. Another one depicted her collapsing in her high school biology class at the single sight of medical needles.

"Let's hope that'll convince the police of her innocence and force them to further scrutinize Karl Smith's background," Claire said between bites of food. Whether Claire liked it or not, social media had the potential to sway the perspective of both prosecutors and juries, influencing their opinions or biases toward a case, which would play in Cordelia's favor. Though a thief, the fashion designer wasn't the cold-blooded competitor she appeared to be. After a small talk with Claire, Cordelia had agreed to financially compensate the designers from whom she stole and promised to hire them in her future atelier if possible.

Suggie had pulled her notepad from her purse and was taking notes. "You think Karl Smith killed Vee and Poderas?"

"All I know is the man's hiding something. I'm going on a tour of his factory tomorrow. Should be as fun as it will be informative." Claire had always loved behind-the-scenes expeditions. If Vee had refused to represent Smith's fabrics, she might find some clues as to why in the factory.

Vikram loaded his plate with sardines and pesto orzo pasta and took a seat on the sand, between Claire and Suggie. "What motive would he have to kill Vee?"

"Retaliation. Vee was about to leave Fashion Warriors without promoting his fabric and clothing line. The fact he had invested a lot in the show and her image must have made him angry."

Suggie grimaced. "I don't understand. Why would Vee leave the show? That was such a great platform for her, a stepping stone to stardom."

Claire nodded. "That's what I want to find out. Vee had mentioned needing my legal advice and was supposed to explain everything to me once I arrived at the villa. Something she never got the chance to do. The fabric samples from the folder might clue us in the right direction."

"You really think it's safe to visit his factory if Smith is the killer? What if he has the local Mexican police in his pocket and has figured out you're after him?" Vikram asked.

"Vic's right. It could be dangerous."

Claire shrugged dismissively. "Smith doesn't know I suspect him. Plus,

I'll be in a tour group. He can't kill an entire group of forty people and get away with it, believe me. Thank you for worrying about my safety, though. It's very sweet. I'll text you both throughout my visit if you want."

Suggie bobbed her head enthusiastically. "I would really like that."

"What about you, Vic, anything new about the case?" Claire set her empty plate aside and grabbed a slice of apple pie. She could smell the subtle fragrance of cardamon and ginger Vikram added to the traditional recipe.

"Sort of," he said. "The tetrodotoxin from Vee Brooks' insulin pen is the same as the one that killed her. One peculiarity about it is that it didn't contain any salt residue as you would expect coming from a saltwater fish. The tetrodotoxin that killed Vee Brooks had been purified."

Purified? Claire thought. Purification of venom meant separating the toxic components of the venom from other substances present in the venomous secretion.

"Why would the killer process the toxin?" Suggie asked.

"The only reason to do this is to experiment with it, to remove any variables," Claire explained. "The toxin must have been readied for scientific research and testing purposes, which means it came from a lab… The killer isn't an amateur poison handler!"

"Any of the suspects work in a lab?" Vic asked.

"At least one. Smith is a chemist. He used to own a pharmaceutical lab a long time ago, but he isn't allowed to manufacture medicine in the US anymore, so he switched to making fabric dyes. Not sure if he's ever worked with tetrodotoxin, though."

"What about Mexico? Is he allowed to manufacture medicine there?" Suggie asked, switching back and forth between her pen and her fork.

"I've no idea. Operating a pharmaceutical laboratory typically requires a license or regulatory approval from the appropriate governing body in the country where the lab is set. I'm not familiar with Mexican requirements and regulations and whether or not Smith fulfilled them. But he sounds more suspect by the second." Claire took a quick sip of water and resumed her spoken rumination. "If Smith has a textile lab that fabricates organic colors from plants and naturally occurring bacteria, he could very well continue his pharmaceutical research on the side."

Suggie dropped her plate to the side and swiveled in the sand to face Claire. "You think his textile lab could be a cover, and he's experimenting on tetrodotoxin instead? One of Daniel's friends from basic training is enrolled in a tetrodotoxin medical trial at the VA hospital. He'd been severely wounded in Afghanistan and jokes about how a blowfish can ease his pain."

"I think his textile lab is legit. His shows and clothing line depend on his textiles and dyes, but he could have an illicit pharmaceutical lab on the side. Drug development is highly profitable."

"It would be one of the most profitable drugs on the market," Vikram exclaimed. "Snake venom is already used to treat cancer, heart attacks, and Parkinson's disease. I can only imagine how lucrative a tetrodotoxin, non-opioid drug would be. It could treat millions of pain sufferers without the addictive side of drugs."

"And Smith sure looks like a man who really loves money." His haute-couture wardrobe alone was worth a brand-new luxury car, Claire thought.

"He does have an expensive lifestyle. When he visited the spa the other day, he got the platinum package with all the extras. He spent more in one day than I make in a month. Umma was thrilled. She loves spendy clients."

"One more reason for me to visit the factory. I hope we get to tour the lab."

Chapter Thirty

Claire was curled up in the blue womb chair by her bedroom window, recalling the day Aurora had let her raid her closet in search of a perfect outfit for the middle school dance. Claire had picked a white sequined dress that Aurora adjusted to Claire's size by crossing the straps in the back. That day, Claire had felt like a princess. Now, it was Suggie's turn to feel special as she pulled her wedding dress out of the bag that Claire had safely kept in her closet. This was going to be the only dress fitting Suggie would have before sending it to the dry cleaners and maybe the tailor if it needed alterations. And the fitting needed to be kept secret. Nobody could know the gown had been snatched from a yellow-taped house. Not the groom nor Suggie's mother, and certainly not Claire's roommate.

"I knew I should have held off on the apple pie," Suggie groaned as she slipped her wedding dress past her waist, gently pulling on the fabric.

"What are you talking about? The dress fits you beautifully." Vee had made the gown from Suggie's measurements—numbers Mrs. Oh, Suggie's perfectionist mother, had taken herself.

"You think?" Suggie tiptoed to the bedroom's full-length mirror and paused. "You're right. The waist must be stretch lace. It's so comfortable."

"And it's gorgeous." Claire snapped a picture of Suggie to capture the moment. Her best friend radiated joy. She was the picture of the perfect bride, with a velvety blue sky filling the window in the background. The ivory gown featured a fitted lace bodice with a sweetheart neckline and a full skirt made of multiple layers of silk organza. It was a perfect blend of classic elegance and modern sophistication. "You're dazzling."

"I am." Suggie twirled in place and laughed, her eyes welling up with tears. A thin gold thread had been sewn in the veil, making the fabric sparkle under the room's crystal chandelier. "I'm so grateful to you and Vee for this gift. I'm sorry I won't get to thank her in person," she said, sniffling.

"I'm sorry, too. She would have loved to see you." Claire dabbed her eyes with her sleeves. "So, straight to the cleaners?"

"Straight to the cleaners. No need for alterations," Suggie agreed as she shot a last glance at her reflection in the mirror.

Claire helped her with the side zipper and delicately laid the dress on the bed, admiring the artistry that went into the making of the dress—from the careful stitching and the delicate lace appliqué to the row of decorative buttons that extended down the entire length of the dress. Vee had incorporated all the elements to satisfy the traditional "something old, something new, something borrowed and something blue" in one single gown and had sewn a Tiffany-blue ribbon in the lining of the dress.

"Wait…. There's a bead sewn in the pocket… Is that the cherry blossom bead from our twin friendship bracelets?" Suggie asked, perplexed as she stared at the pink flower-shaped bead.

"Yes. It's for the *old and borrowed* requirement." They had made the bracelets together when they were twelve, the summer before Claire left Caper Cove for New York. Claire had worn hers every year through middle and high school. "I'll need it back after the wedding, though."

"Oh my god, Claire, this is so thoughtful." Suggie wrapped her arms around Claire and squeezed her in a tight hug. "You really want to make me cry."

Claire hugged her back. "Isn't that what best friends are for?"

As they delicately folded the dress into a box, Claire noticed a bulge in the hem of the skirt. The fabric creaked as she pressed it between her thumb and index finger.

"That's odd. It's like there is a piece of paper lodged underneath, and the stitching looks unfinished." Claire examined the area closer and pulled on a loose thread. As the string unraveled, a rolled paper note fell to the ground.

Suggie picked it up and unfolded it. Inside, a handwritten nine-digit code accompanied the words "check lab result." "What does that mean?"

"Your guess is as good as mine."

"We should call Torres," Suggie suggested.

"To tell him what? That we removed your wedding dress from the villa so he can pick it up and keep it as evidence until the end of the investigation?" Claire wanted to believe that the case would be solved fast, but if it weren't, Suggie would be left without a reception hall and wedding gown.

"You're right. We don't even know what the so-called results are about. They might have nothing to do with her murder."

"Let's find out." Claire was now confident that Vee had left the gown in the blue room for Claire to find as well as to preserve the written code. After a rough childhood and a stint in juvenile hall, Vee didn't know who to trust. That's the reason why she hid some important information that only Claire could find: the hem of a dress Claire had commissioned for Suggie.

They checked online by entering the nine-digit number into the search engine, but their inquiry yielded nothing. They searched for a list of labs, but there were thousands to choose from.

"Do you recall seeing any package or letter in Vee's room?" Claire started perusing through her phone photos, hoping to find some indication as to which lab Vee might have used.

"This is useless," Suggie moaned. "She wouldn't have left proof of the lab in the open like that if the results were private."

Lowering her shoulders in defeat, Claire held her head with both hands and scratched her skull. "You're right," she said, about to give up. Vee wouldn't have left information about the lab result in the open unless she were alone. Which she was for a whole week before the Fashion Warriors crew joined her.

Claire closed her album and flicked through her text messages as a realization crossed her mind. "Vee sent me selfies of herself and pictures of her studio days before my arrival. Maybe there is something on them."

"There it is!' Claire shouted as she stared at a picture of the room Vee occupied in the private villa. The yellow walls with racks of clothes and rolls of fabrics in the background. In the foreground, the worktable with a sewing machine, scissors, and a rainbow of spools of threads, and next to them a manilla envelope. Claire zoomed in on it. It was addressed to *BioVeri Lab* in San Diego.

"I've got the lab's name and address." Claire highlighted the envelope writing, clicked on copy, and pasted the words in the internet search box. A few seconds later, the lab's website jumped on the screen.

BioVeri Testing Laboratories
Offering High Quality and Testing Standards Worldwide — Dedicated to Textiles for over 60 years.

Suggie looked over Claire's shoulder and gasped. "Why would she contact a textile testing lab?"

"That's what we're going to find out." Claire clicked on GET YOUR RESULTS from the navigation menu and entered the nine-digit number in the blank space marked CODE. Then she pressed ENTER.

A message appeared:

Sample Still Being Processed. Please Check Again Later.
PS: We Will Not Provide Results Over The Phone.
Do Contact Us Via Email If You Forgot Your Code.

"Darn. We were so close," Suggie moaned.

"Yes, but we are farther than before. Look!" She pointed at a line of writing on the screen. Four new words had appeared to the right of the code she had entered: *Fabric sample – toxicity test.*

Claire leaned back on her desk chair, enjoying the eureka moment. "Vee was checking Karl Smith's fabric for toxicity! That must be the reason why she didn't want to endorse his fabric or his brand. She must have found out that his claim that his fabric was organic and consciously sourced was a lie."

"But, how could she have figured it out?"

"It could be anything. Maybe a whistleblower told her, or she found proof that the dyes weren't locally sourced but imported from countries with lax safety standards....Wait...." Claire sat upright in her chair. "The series of letters and numbers Vee had texted herself could be a tracking number! They could be proof of synthetic dyes from China!" Shipping codes and tracking number formats could vary greatly between countries due to differences in postal systems and carrier preferences. Each had its own format for tracking numbers, and these formats could differ based on their systems and operational requirements. That's why Claire hadn't realized what that code was until now.

"What are you going to do? Tell Torres?"

"Not yet. Until we have the results, this is all speculation. Right now, I'm going to sleep. The factory tour bus is leaving early in the morning."

Suggie regarded her with worried eyes. "You think you're going to find something on Karl Smith there?"

"If there's something to find, believe me, I'll find it. Even if I have to comb through the factory's dumpsters."

* * *

The trip to the Mexican border took only forty minutes, but the bus had suddenly slowed down to a snail's pace. Lines of vehicles stretched for miles at the San Ysidro Port of Entry. Spread over ten lanes, a diverse array of cars, trucks, and buses representing a mix of tourists, commuters, and commercial vehicles waited to undergo immigration and customs inspections before entering Mexico.

The tour guide, a white woman in her mid-forties with a blond messy bun atop her head, was strafing the passengers with facts about the town of Tijuana. Like how the Caesar salad had been invented there in the 1920s, by an Italian chef, and how Tijuana had emerged as the medical device manufacturing capital of North America in the 21st century.

"The line to submit your immigration forms is expected to be long. San Ysidro Port of Entry is considered one of the busiest land border crossings in the world," the guide said, switching to a more serious tone. "Nonetheless, make sure to have your passports and tourist cards ready. Border agents will board the bus and ask for your documentation."

The woman seated in front of her, a blond Latina with a multi-color knit top and skirt and a Cardi B tattoo, stood up and stretched. "Good thing we're in a fancy bus with an onboard bathroom. I won't have to hold it until we're in Mexico."

Claire nodded in agreement. That was a good thing indeed. The long-haul passenger bus featured spacious, luxury upholstered seats with thick padding. They were plenty comfortable, and Claire didn't mind staying seated another hour, especially since she could stretch her legs on the empty seat next to her.

She pulled her phone from her bag and checked whether the fabric toxicity test results were available on the *BioVeri Lab* website. She entered the nine-digit code and hit ENTER.

The results filled the screen at once.

Fabric sample name: KS fabric

Toxicity: POSITIVE for malachite green (MG) dye; Azo dye.

Claire's fingers strummed quickly on her phone keyboard and entered *Malachite green* in the search engine. The KS in the fabric name had to mean Karl Smith. She thought as she skimmed through the long list of results.

Then she dialed Suggie's number.

The phone didn't have the time to ring once before Suggie picked up. "Is everything alright? Did you make it to the factory? Do you need help?"

"Everything's fine. I'm still on the bus, so I can't say much. We're about to cross the border," she whispered into the phone as the tour guide explained loudly the statistics of San Ysidro as a Port of Entry.

"I just wanted to tell you. The lab results are in. The fabric Vee tested is positive for a dangerous chemical compound called Malachite green."

"Like the pretty green stone?"

"Yes, except that this one isn't a stone but an illegal synthetic dye that's been banned in Europe and the US for its carcinogenic and teratogenic effects."

"So, not the natural, organic, toxic-free dye Karl Smith claimed his fabrics to be."

"Exactly. Which gives him a very strong motive to…you know."

"A motive to kill Vee."

"Exactly." Smith must have wanted to prevent Vee from reporting him to the authorities. He wasn't manufacturing safe, organic textiles. He was producing cancer-causing textiles! By using cheap, dangerous dyes instead of the natural, handmade pigments and selling his clothing line at a higher price, he was maximizing his sales profits while risking people's lives.

"Maybe I should tell him about it. See how he reacts," Claire added.

"Who, Smith? You can't do that! Just call Torres and tell him everything you know. With all the evidence you have, they'll be closing in on an arrest, and this whole thing will be over."

"I can't tell Torres yet. I don't want him to raise the alarm. I can't risk you-know-who destroying the evidence before I find more about his research." If Smith knew they suspected him, he wouldn't hesitate to burn down his factory to dispose of any toxin or chemical dye he possessed.

"You mean Karl's pharmaceutical lab?"

"Yes. I need to find out if he's storing the toxin there. It's the only way to link him to … you know," Claire said, looking over her shoulders to make sure no one eavesdropped on her conversation.

"To link him to Vee's and Poderas' deaths?" Suggie's voice sounded both interested, but concerned.

"Exactly. That's why I still think it's a good idea to talk to him. The factory tour includes a visit to his office."

The call dropped before Claire could hear Suggie's contradictory reply, and a grunt of disapproval rose from the crowd.

"What's happening? My phone stopped working!" someone groaned.

"Mine too," another whined.

Standing next to the driver, facing the passengers, the tour guide stopped her speech on Tijuana's culture and history. "Do not panic. This is completely normal," she said. "As it was explained in the email you received to confirm your tour reservation, American carriers require you to obtain an international plan to use your phone while in Mexico. But I can assure you, you do not need it. First, phones aren't allowed in the factory due to trade secrets and manufacturing matters, so you'll have to leave your bags on the bus while we tour the facility. Second, we're almost there and should be back within American carrier cellphone range in about three to four hours. So take these internet-free moments as an opportunity to disconnect from the internet and get to know your fellow passengers. Third, my phone works and is available to all. Emergencies only, of course," she specified.

Claire's phone screen flashed: Welcome to Mexico. Do you wish to switch to an International Plan? International rates apply. She hit the YES option, internally cheering for the reliability of her phone company. An extra $5 wasn't too bad for a day in Mexico, just in case she would need her phone, and she had just enough on her debit card to cover the expense.

"Does anyone have any questions?" the guide continued.

"Actually, yes." A heavy-set white, middle-aged man with compression socks and a beer gut stood up. "Why does the owner of a successful show like Fashion Warriors have a factory in Mexico? Why not keep the factory jobs in America for American workers?"

The woman seated next to him was tugging down on his sleeve in a vain attempt at getting him to sit down. Her pale face was turning beet-red.

"We get this question a lot, so no need to feel embarrassed," the guide said. "Textile manufacturing is a business like any other whose goal is to satisfy customer demand and make a profit. American customers want low-priced items, which is impossible to produce if workers were paid American wages." Then she went on to talk about Mexican low labor costs, tax breaks, well-developed textile industries, and a skilled Mexican workforce, which seemed to put half of the passengers to sleep while fascinating the other half.

Claire wanted to add that some of the reasons Karl Smith had set his factory in Mexico was probably because the Mexican government hadn't explicitly listed Malachite green as a banned or illegal substance. So Smith could easily import and use it without breaking the law.

Her phone blinked with a message: *Your international plan has been activated. Welcome to Mexico.*

Claire sighed in relief and immediately texted Suggie to reassure her that the conversation drop wasn't something to worry about.

Finally, the bus moved, passed through immigration, and started the climb up Camino a la Fábrica, the hill leading to the factory. The road was lined with artisan booths showcasing a variety of local crafts, souvenirs, and culinary specialties on one side. On the other, horseback riding clubs allow tourists to explore the scenic landscapes of Mexico while riding well-trained horses.

"Caballeros!" a young woman in a pink jumpsuit and blue hair rejoiced. "How romantic it would be to ride to the beach in the sunset. We must so do this!"

"Can we stop for souvenirs?" another passenger asked.

"We will stop there on the way out to grab a few souvenirs and have lunch. The Fashion Warriors factory has a small store a little higher on the hill. But I'm sorry to say, we won't have time for horseback riding. The bus follows a very strict schedule and will leave at 1:00 PM sharp," the guide explained. "However, if you wish to spend extra time in Tijuana, feel free to do so. There are plenty of taxis and rideshares that can take you through town and back to the US. If you decide to do so, make sure to take your bags and passports with you when you step off the bus. The factory has a few lockers that you can use since phones aren't allowed in the facility."

"Do you want to join us on a horseback riding tour afterward, if it doesn't rain," the woman across the aisle from Claire asked. "My friend and I are going. We can split the taxi back to the US afterward."

"I wish I could, but I can't," Claire said with longing in her voice. She and Suggie had attended many horseback riding camps along the border when they were children, times she recalled as some of her most memorable summers. "Thank you for the offer, though."

"No worries. Let us know if you change your mind."

* * *

Fifteen minutes later, the passengers walked through the Fashion Warriors textile factory gate. Claire lagged behind. Her phone was ringing in her pocket, and she had to return to the empty bus to take the call. The picture of

Mr. Darcy from the recent Pride and Prejudice movie brightened the screen. Suggie had uploaded the picture into Claire's contact list so she would smile whenever Torres called.

"Hello?" Claire blocked her free ear with her hand as farmers on loud four-wheeled bikes pulled trailers through the neighboring field.

"I got a frantic call from Suggie about you being in danger, followed by a nevermind. What's going on?" The detective seemed genuinely concerned, which Claire found sweet. She had felt some electricity between them and knew Torres was the "hero type," but she was convinced he would be happier watching her make a mistake with an "I-told-you-so" than calling her concerned.

"Nothing. Our call just got dropped, and she probably panicked. Suggie's a worrywart."

"You're not investigating the case, are you?" His tone had shifted from caring to authoritative.

"Why would you ask that?" she asked, trying to stall, knowing it wasn't the time or place to tell a lie. She was in a foreign country about to visit the factory of a criminal and needed Torres on her side in the event things took a turn for the worse.

"Because I'm starting to know you. Suggie quickly mentioned Karl Smith and illegal dyes. Anything you might want to share with me?"

Darn, Suggie. "Sure. I was going to call you about that."

Claire explained to him in detail about the testing code in Suggie's wedding dress, the lab results, and how Vee had refused to endorse Karl Smith's fabrics and clothing line. "The fabric Smith's manufacturing isn't the organic and responsibly sourced textiles they're supposed to be. Smith's cutting corners by using cheap synthetic dyes to increase profits. Vee found out about it and was going to expose him."

Though Torres lectured her about the dress, he did it quickly and directed his focus on Karl Smith. "You're telling me the list of letters and numbers Brooks texted herself is possibly proof Smith bought Azo dye from China and shipped it to Mexico?" he asked.

"Yes. the customs paperwork should confirm whether the package included Malachite green and other Azo dyes or not." Claire squinted and strained her ear as the four-wheeler ATVs were getting loud.

"Anything else?" Torres' voice was faint.

"Did you check Verdant Green's outgoing call?" she asked.

"They don't have a landline and are off the grid."

"That's a lie. Though there's no national requirement to have a working phone, at least one worker must have had one. Most working businesses need a working phone, landline, cell, or satellite to be able to operate a health facility. It's a question of insurance and liability."

"So?"

"Poderas claimed he couldn't be reached about his wife's passing because of the rehab center's complete off-grid isolation, but he was lying. He probably heard the news but needed a day to collect himself and decided to profit from his wife's death to help his campaign. Then he must have called Smith to blackmail him into contributing to his campaign and to meet him at Hellhole Canyon."

A long pause broke the conversation, making Claire wonder whether the call had dropped, until Torres finally spoke. "How does Cordelia fit into that?"

"She's innocent. Smith's the one who told Cordelia to go to Hellhole Canyon as a favor to find the best flowers. Cordelia was framed."

Torres snorted at the end of the line. "That's a stretch."

"No, it's not. I'm going to prove it to you. Probably by the end of the day."

In the background, the farmers' quad bikes were roaring as they shouted instructions to a group of workers, making it nearly impossible for Claire to hear Torres.

"Where are you...? Are you in Mexico, at Smith's factory?"

"I've got to go," she said.

"Claire, stay away."

Chapter Thirty-One

The factory was located a few miles from the border. From its large-windowed walls, looking north, one could see the tall steel fencing of the Mexican-US border wall. Inside, the air buzzed with the rhythmic clatter and hum of machinery and smelled of bleach, oil, and heat.

"The factory's divided into sections dedicated to specific stages of the textile manufacturing process. Each section is represented by a different color," the guide explained as she took the group through the raw material area where large bales of raw cotton were sorted.

"It's crazy that the factory's open and working today," someone noted. "Isn't Sunday usually considered a rest day in Mexico?"

"It usually is, but there are exceptions. Textile factories like this one may operate on Sundays when they are engaged in continuous production and when there is a high demand for their products. Fashion Warriors fabrics have been in high demand since the show aired two years ago. We can barely keep up with orders from the Smith fashion line since it aired last season, and we aren't ready to stop."

I wouldn't bet on that, Claire thought as she followed the red floor line like everyone who preceded her. She scanned every hallway, room, and wall recess to find a sign for Smith's secret lab, if it existed.

The guide led the visitors through the spinning section, where massive machines transformed the fibers into yarn, and the weaving section, where enormous looms interlaced the yarns to create intricate patterns.

"And this is the dying and printing section, where the fabrics for the Fashion Warriors show are made and given their vibrant colors and unique patterns," the guide continued as she ushered them into a bright room where the floor line had turned blue. "Some dyeing processes require elevated temperatures, while others require room temperature or cold dyeing methods. As you can see here, we follow traditional dyeing techniques like vat dyeing or reactive dyeing which involve hot water or steam and help the dye molecules penetrate the fabric fibers effectively."

The sounds of circulating liquids, rhythmic thumping of printing cylinders, and ventilation systems competed with each other, dimming out the guide's voice.

Claire wiped her sweaty brow with the back of her hand and waited to exit the room before asking a question. "Where does the dye come from?"

The guide stepped on a green floor line and smiled. "It's created right here, in our lab." She pointed forward and gestured for the visitors to follow her. "We hand-pick the highest quality ingredients for our natural pigments; that's why you'll see a collection of plants, flowers, fruits, or even insects known for their rich pigments."

"Insects?" an elderly man with a black toupée asked with a grimace and a tone of disgust.

"Yes, the cochineal is an insect that lives on cactus pads and produces a bright red substance called carminic acid. Carminic acid is an excellent textile dye that gives our fabrics beautiful reds and purples," the guide replied with a smile, unfazed.

Claire shuddered. The idea of wearing fabric dyed from the crushed bodies of thousands of insects took the glamour out of fashion.

"What about the other pigments?" the Cardi B. tattooed girl asked.

"Yes, where do they come from?" Claire said, hoping the guide would mention importation. If the woman named a specific importer, she would be able to establish a direct link between Smith and illegal dyes.

"Some are grown right here, in the state of Baja California, and brought in via horse. All in an effort to support the local economy while leaving the smallest carbon footprint possible."

"Love this. So old school," a design student with pink-streaked cornrows shouted. "Do you offer internships?"

"Not at the moment, but I'll notify Mr. Smith of your interest. Also, feel free to write your questions at the end of the customer survey you'll receive via email at the end of the day."

Claire trailed along with the group in a state of hyper vigilance, trying to find the proof of a pharmaceutical lab. She was about to give up and started to rethink her theory on Smith's involvement when she noticed a white lab coat hanging from one of the windows in the opposite wing. A blue light emanated from the outside window. It was a shimmering glow that only a pool or an aquarium could produce.

"What's on the other side?" she asked, pointing at the window.

The guide directed Claire away from the glass. "Administrative offices, mainly. As you might have noticed, a painted floor line links all the sections of the textile factory. The color varies. The floor line helps guide VIP guests and tour groups like ours. Since the administrative offices are off limits to the public, the line is nonexistent."

"We have the same thing at the hospital where I work," a short, corpulent fortyish woman exclaimed. "A color for each specialty on each floor, so the visitors won't get lost."

"Really smart indeed," Claire agreed, as satisfaction filled her. There was definitely water in that building, and she could sense that it had more to do with pufferfish in a tank than with an indoor pool.

The tour concluded with a visit to the maceration-distillation-solvent extraction lab, a mouthful of a name, where natural colorants were extracted from raw materials. On the way out, each visitor got a fabric swatch from the dye application area as a memento of their visit. Claire made sure to get a green one.

"I'm really sorry, but Karl Smith won't be able to join us today. He might try to make an appearance as our bus leaves after our visit to the street vendors along the road, but it's no guarantee." The guide retraced her steps along the red floor line back to the entrance. "For the ones who desire to remain behind in Tijuana, remember to grab your bags. For everyone else, stay with the group. The bus will leave at 1:00 PM with or without you. In case you miss the bus, you can still call for a taxi from the factory phone.

Worst case scenario, you can walk the few miles to the border."

As the visitors moved along, chatting about color trends and designs, Claire broke away from the group and hid in the bathroom. From the lavatory's small window, she watched the group exit the factory gates. Then, with nimble steps and a heart-racing against her ribcage, she dashed down the unmarked corridor, guided by her intuition. At the end of the white, interminable hallway was a double door.

* * *

Except for the water tanks filled with pufferfish lining an entire wall, the pharmaceutical lab looked like any other research laboratory. The space reminded Claire of the cutting-edge research and development lab of the National Institutes of Health, where one of her friends worked. Claire hurried through it, searching for the vials of purified tetrodotoxin.

"Here you are!" She whisper-shouted, finding a set of tubes marked TTX in a wall cabinet. She grabbed five of them with the hem of her sleeve to not compromise any fingerprints. She made sure they were tightly sealed and placed them in a Ziploc bag before tucking them in her bra. Then she rushed down the unmarked floor, retracing her steps back to the visitors' entrance. If the tetrodotoxin samples she seized proved to be the same analog as the toxin that killed Vee, it would irrefutably prove the direct link between Smith and Vee's death.

On the other side of the large factory window, stormy grey clouds had invaded the sky, dimming the day's natural light. The rain began to fall, pitter-pattering on the roof. Claire still had to run down the endless blue and red floor lines through the building when her watch beeped one o'clock.

The bus! Claire bit her lips, hoping the guide's punctuality as to the departure time had just been a warning to scare the wandering tourists. But when Claire reached the exit, the bus was gone. In its place was Karl Smith. The man was trotting back to the entrance with hunched shoulders as if his posture could protect him from the drizzle.

"Who are you?" he asked, tapping his feet on the entrance tile to rid his shoes of the wet dirt.

She retrieved her phone and her purse from the visitor's locker, relieved he didn't remember her. Since she wasn't her true thirty-five but seventy years old in Smith's misogynistic book, she wasn't surprised the man had forgotten her face. Past a certain age, whichever it is, women become invisible to men like Smith.

"A visitor who spent too much time in the bathroom and missed her bus, it seems." She smiled as she exited the building, hoping the tubular bulges in her bra wouldn't betray her.

Smith frowned. "Wait a minute. I recognize you. "He grasped her by the arm. "You were with the cop who asked me questions about Vee and Cordelia."

Claire forced a giant grin. "Yes, obsessive fan here, guilty as charged. Pulling strings with the police to get as close to the Fashion Warriors crew as I can," she said since she couldn't deny who she was. She jerked her arm free and stepped outside as she adjusted her crossbody purse over her shoulder.

She thought about running down the hill after the bus when a mark in the sand stopped her. It was a set of footprints with a little symbol in the heel—the same half-moon pattern found at Vee's and Poderas' crime scenes. She bent forward to take a look at them, holding her bra with both hands to keep the toxin tubes in place, and glanced back at Karl Smith's shoes.

"What is it?" His eyes darted between the footprints, his shoes, and Claire's face. His puzzled expression shifted into a scowl as if a realization hit him. "What were you truly doing here," he asked in a menacing growl, his upper lip curling.

"Nothing. Just trying to digest an unfortunate breakfast, I guess," she said, trying to ignore the clenching of his fists and the tightening of his jaw. Loping, she tried to put as much distance as possible between Smith and her. "I've got to catch the bus."

"You aren't going anywhere," he shouted as he rushed toward her.

Claire started to run in the direction of the street vendors. She dove into the crowd of artisans closing their booths as raindrops plummeted around her. If that man killed two people to cover up his use of illegal dyes, Claire could easily imagine what her fate would be if he caught up with her. She knew too much—the illegal dyes and the murders—for him to let her go. She needed to reach the border before him to be safe.

Though her physical therapist had made her run on a treadmill every day, Claire wasn't sure she could outrun an angered, desperate man whose life was about to crumble. Desperation could fuel unexpected endurance and strength in people.

"Alguien vio a la gringa?" Smith yelled for the vendors' attention. Claire wasn't fluent but she knew enough Spanish to know that Smith was asking for their help in finding her. "Le dare mucho dinero al que me traiga la gringa."

Claire sprinted to the closest stable. She emptied her wallet, $235 plus coins, in the ranchero's hand and jumped on the first saddled rental horse she saw. "Vuelvo en tres horas prometo," she promised to return in three hours.

She gently squeezed the middle of the horse's ribcage with the calves of her legs to cue it to move forward and sent it into a gallop through the rain. She headed northeast toward the San Ysidro port of entry, praying that Smith didn't know how to ride a horse. She needed to reach the border and call the American authorities before Smith caught up with her.

When she looked over her shoulders, Smith was retreating to the factory. She pulled gently on the reins to slow the animal down to a trot and continued straight toward the border, relieved that he had given up the chase. But her relief was short-lived because, minutes later, Smith was barreling toward her aboard a farmer's ATV.

Chapter Thirty-Two

No matter how forward she leaned or how slightly she raised her body from the saddle, Claire's horse couldn't pound the earth any faster. Eluding a fast-approaching all-terrain vehicle was impossible. The thirty-miles-per-hour of equestrian power couldn't compete against the fifty to ninety miles per hour of mechanical power. Luckily, the horse could jump over ditches and cactus clusters while Smith had to drive around them. But there weren't that many obstacles among the chaparral vegetation to slow the motorized vehicle down.

With one hand on the saddle to keep her balance, Claire opened her phone and called Torres. But instead of Torres' voice, a woman answered as if his calls had been redirected.

"Caper Cove Police Station. How can I help you?"

"Detective Torres, please. It's urgent."

"Hold on, I'll transfer to the right language line," she said. Then, after a beep and a click, a warm voice addressed her. "Estación de Caper Cove, cómo puedo ayudarlo?"

"What? No, I don't speak Spanish. No hablo Español. I need to talk to Detective Torres. Necesito hablar con Detective Torres," Claire said between breaths. Speaking on a phone while riding a horse was harder than people thought.

"Please hold."

"I can't hold. Can you ping my location and tell Torres about my call, please? It's a matter of life and death."

Dust billowed behind the speeding ATV as it was catching up with Claire, its engine roaring like thunder.

Thinking fast, Claire opened her video call app and dialed Suggie. Whether her friend answered or not, she could always record a video message. At the beep, Claire explained what was happening, all while balancing on the horse. The secret pharmaceutical lab, the tetrodotoxin vials, and Smith's half-moon mark in his shoeprint.

"Karl Smith's chasing me. He's trying to kill me," she said, facing the camera, capturing the fast-approaching ATV in the background until the vehicle closed the distance between them.

The four-wheeled bike passed her and skidded to a halt in front of the horse, kicking up a mix of dust and mud. Frightened, the animal reared up, jerking Claire off balance and her phone out of her hand. Her electronic device tumbled through the air before hitting a rock with a cracking sound. Claire's heart sank as she regained control of the horse, coaxing it back onto all fours.

"Give me back what you stole, and I'll let you go," Smith said, blocking the way east. His ice-blue eyes stared at her through lethal slits, and he pointed a gun at her.

Claire sneered. As if, after fifteen years of criminal law practice, she could still believe the word of a serial murderer. Ha!

"I don't know what you're talking about," she said, trying to stall, calculating her way out of the situation. In front of her and to the right, the border's tall steel fencing wall and the port of entry sentry reminded her that she wasn't very far. That she was close to being safe if she found a way to get past Smith and his gun.

She scanned the arid landscape for a way out. From years of working in D.C. surrounded by felons, she had learned how to use her environment to her advantage. A garbage lid could become a shield, and a heeled shoe a lethal weapon if needed. But here, the chaparral land and its tangled shrubs left her confused and powerless. There was nothing sharp and pointy besides the cacti. If only…. That's when she saw it. A spread of short Cholla cacti blanketed the ground behind a wall of tumbleweeds. If only she could lead Smith's vehicle into it, the cacti thorns would puncture Smith's tires all at once.

"Give me your purse," Smith shouted as he disembarked his ATV.

Lightning struck, shaking the ground, morphing the light rain into a downpour and rattling the horse.

"Okay, no need to shoot." Claire pulled her crossbody purse over her shoulder and held it by its strap as she pretended to hand it out to Smith. When he came close enough, she swung her purse against the gun as hard as she could. Then she galloped away in the direction of the Cholla cacti ground cover.

Claire didn't need to turn around to know that the gun hit the ground. She heard the cling of metal hit the rocky dirt along with the multiple expletives Smith shouted.

It took no time for Smith to rev his ATV engine and aim straight for Claire. As she had expected, Smith was too blinded by anger to notice her horse's long jump over the cacti's barbed spines and sharp segmented stems. Once Smith drove over them, his quad bike's wheels flattened, bringing the ATV to a stop.

Though a sixty-year-old man with skin-tight pants couldn't outrace her horse to the border, Claire didn't slow down until she arrived within walking distance of the border facilities.

With the rain still pounding on her head and shoulders, Claire dismounted the horse and walked down the pedestrian path with the animal in tow until she reached a border agent.

"Necessito ayuda. A man tried to kill me," she said. "Necesito hablar can la policia."

The border agent looked at her up and down. "Are you hurt?"

"No, I'm alright. I just need to talk to an American agent. I lost my phone and passport," she said, shivering. Now that the threat of death had vanished, her body became suddenly aware of the sharp wind and the cold.

"Hold on. The agent spoke a few words into his two-way radio and turned back to her. "Is that your horse?"

"No. I rented it from a ranchero on Camino a la Fábrica. I was trying to escape from the man who was chasing me," she said, trying to control the chattering of her teeth.

A few minutes later, a woman with a raincoat, with a *veterinaria* patch took the reins from Claire. "We'll take care of it and return it to its owner."

Claire nodded, let go of the horse, and followed the border agent to a building straddling the border. There, she was led to a grey interview room where she gave her name, address and was asked to wait for an American agent.

The room wasn't as cold as outside, but it wasn't warm either, and her soaking wet clothes dripped water, forming puddles on the floor. A young woman with a black ponytail brought her a towel, mopped up the wet grey linoleum, and left without a word.

Shortly after, two U.S. Customs and Border Protection officers finally came. They were clad in dark blue uniforms with *CBP* patches on their left shoulders and gold badges on their chests. One had a pornstache—a thick, bushy mustache that extended beyond the upper lip and covered the width of his mouth. The other had the crooked nose of a boxer and the large eyes of a doe.

"What's your name and the reason for crossing the border," Mustache asked in a firm tone.

"I'm just returning home. I left this morning for a visit to the Fashion Warriors factory but was attacked on my way back."

"What's your address?" he continued asking without acknowledging the words of her attack.

"1001 Ocean Lane in Caper Cove, California," Claire replied, a little surprised by their stern demeanor and lack of reaction.

"How long have you lived there?"

"Five days. It's my dad's place. I used to live in Washington, D.C. before that, but I grew up in Caper Cove."

Mustache crossed his arms and leaned over the table, separating him from Claire. "And you're sure you're an American?"

"Yes, I'm sure. Born and raised in the US," Claire insisted, realizing that her accent was again getting in the way of her credibility.

The CBP officers exchanged a glance and snorted. "She said she's

American. I really wonder where her accent came from," Mustache mocked.

Tension shot through Claire's forehead. "I'm telling you. I am an American. I can give you my social security number."

"Nah, anybody can get one." Mustache swatted his hand as though shooing away a pesky mosquito. "And what do you do in America, Ms. Fontaine?"

"I am an attorney." She decided to forgo the lengthy explanation of her leaving the law behind to become a private chef to keep it simple and believable.

"Sure, why not? And I'm Santa Claus." The agents laughed. "Okay, follow us." Mustache pulled her by the arm and guided her down a sterile corridor at the end of which was a door marked *Detention*.

"I'm serious. I'm not lying," Claire exclaimed, wanting to free herself from the man's hold, refusing to relive the unpleasant airport incident of five days before. She took a deep breath, telling herself that anger would not solve anything. "Call Caper Cove police station and ask for Detective Torres. He'll vouch for me."

"Yeah, right, Missy Attorney." Mustache pushed open a door and locked Claire in a cell already filled with people. "Just a piece of advice: next time you want to impersonate an American citizen, work on your accent."

* * *

Her call for help, requests to see a supervisor, and demands to get her phone call to contact her family were left unanswered.

"This is unbelievable!" Claire mumbled as she settled in the corner of the overcrowded cell. She checked her smart watch, and its battery was at a low five percent. Since it was connected to her lost cellphone and didn't have a separate cellular plan, she couldn't make outside calls, but it could link to Wi-Fi or someone's hotspot. Filled with hope, Claire pushed on the watch's crown, scrolled down to SETTING, and turned the Wi-Fi on.

Bingo, she thought. She scrolled further down to FIND PEOPLE, clicked on SHARE MY LOCATION, and sent a 911 message to Torres and Suggie just before her watch screen went blank.

Minutes stretched into hours without a word from the outside. The only positive to being locked down was practicing her Spanish with her fellow cellmates—asylum seekers from Honduras, El Salvador, Guatemala, and Mexico, a Norwegian with an expired visa, and an American student caught trying to smuggle drugs into the US. When 6:00 PM struck, Claire was still stuck in an overcrowded cell. A border agent opened the cell and asked everyone to form a line, except for the student.

"We're taking you to a detention facility where you'll be processed and spend the night," the agent said.

"Wait! You can't do that. I didn't have my phone call," Claire protested.

"You probably did and forgot," the agent said.

"I didn't forget. As an American, I cannot be detained without knowing the charges against me, and I am allowed a phone call. And if an undocumented immigrant is detained by immigration authorities in the United States, they generally have the right to contact their consulate or embassy as soon as possible," Claire stated with her most confident voice. "The phone's right there, on the wall."

The agent reached for the baton secured in his belt holster and smirked. "You'll get to make your phone call at the detention center. Right now, you're all getting onto the bus."

This is not happening, Claire thought. Her head heavy and eyes to the ground, Claire followed the other detainees into a single line out of the building. Stupid, stupid accent.

"Hands up and legs spread," a woman commanded. "I'm gonna pat you down."

"Wait. What?" Claire raised her head, panicking. "I need to declare something. I've got vials of tetrodotoxin on me."

The gloved woman frowned. "Teto-what?"

"Tetrodotoxin. It's a potent poison I collected as part of an investigation," she said, her jaw clenched with regrets, realizing she should have declared it earlier or hidden it before crossing the border. Without Torres or Caper Cove officials by her side, the border agents would assume she was a terrorist of some kind.

"A poison?" The border agent jumped back and pulled her weapon. "Do not move."

Before Claire could blink, a dozen agents surrounded her, their guns pointed at her. "Get on your knees," someone shouted.

The evening sky was dark with storm and night, but Claire couldn't see the stars. The sentry flood lights were directed straight at her, blinding her.

Her hands high above her head, Claire complied and lowered herself to the ground. "I'm not dangerous. Call Detective Torres from Caper Cove. He'll explain everything."

The hurried footsteps of backup agents arriving in droves slapped the asphalt. The air buzzed with questions. The words *terrorism* and *chemical weapons* floated in the air.

"We don't care about your local cop. The only thing you're going to see is a federal marshal and the inside of a federal prison.

Chapter Thirty-Three

"Claire Fontaine? Is that you?" Though the voice wasn't familiar, Claire knew that voice, but she couldn't place it. She couldn't see where it came from because she was facing the asphalt, kneeling on the ground, in the line of fire of several border agents.

"Yes, Claire Fontaine, attorney at Beaumont, Farrell, and Volk," she shouted over the pouring rain, hoping her work title would make the armed agents think twice before shooting her.

"It's me, Auggie McGraw. Remember me?" The masculine voice got closer, and a set of shoes appeared beside her.

Her hands still up in the air, Claire turned her head slowly sideways toward the voice. Her gaze shifted upward, beginning with a glance at the shoes, then tracing along the short legs, girthy torso, and finally meeting the rounded face of the CBP agent who had held her at the airport five days earlier.

"C'mon guys, put your guns down. I know the lady. I made the same mistake last week," Agent McGraw shouted, shaking his head. "She's a true American. Criminal attorney from Washington D.C. and all. If you don't stop this shit, you're all going to lose your jobs."

Claire listened to the sound of people holstering their guns but remained on the ground. "Could you call the Caper Cove police, please? Deputy Chief Ernshaw or Detective Torres will explain the situation," she stuttered. Her jaw quivered from either the cold or the fear of being shot.

"There's a Detective Torres already in the building. He's been inquiring about you, and I thought I'd check *the cage*."

Claire lifted her head, filled with hope, holding back a sob of relief.

"Detective Torres is here?"

"Yes. He's put an APB out on you," Auggie McGraw said, pulling her up to her feet.

"Claire?" Torres' voice cut through the storm, his silhouette running toward her. "Are you alright?"

Claire had never been so happy to see the detective's face, but she didn't tell him. She just rushed into his arms, burying her face within the fold of his sweater. "I am now."

* * *

After hours spent at the border to untangle the nightmarish mess in which she found herself, Claire had decided to spend the next day in bed. Nothing bad would happen if she stayed inside, sheltered from the world by her soft comforter. In the safety of her room, no one would question her Americanness and try to deport her to God knows where. Though, she wouldn't have objected to a forced trip to France if that's where the border agents intended to ship her. The French Riviera was supposed to be lovely this time of the year.

The window was open. The wind filled her bedroom with briny ocean air and played with the gold curtains. The sound of the waves lapping the shore was soothing, and the buzz of The Osprey customers would soon rise to her apartment.

Suggie was seated cross-legged on the bed next to her, the way they did during their sleepovers when they were twelve years old, when they stayed up late and woke up early to talk about their imagined futures and boys.

"Did they charge you with anything?" Suggie asked. She had brought Claire a sweet potato latte and a bear claw that was bigger than a human hand. The velvety drink and buttery Danish were Claire's childhood favorite cures against the blues, and it seemed to be working. The filling had spilled out of the pastry as it cooked, and Claire picked at the caramelized almond paste that webbed the claw.

"Nothing." Claire sighed, recalling the past night's ordeal, and smiled at the fact it was now in the past. One day, she would laugh at the situation, she told herself. Being chased through the desert while carrying tubes of toxin in her bra would be a great story to share at parties. The horse had been returned to its owner, who vouched for Claire's generous rental payment, and Claire's declaration of the tetrodotoxin she carried before being searched couldn't be considered smuggling.

"Karl Smith didn't accuse me of breaking and entering, because in doing so, he would have to confess that the toxin was his and that he was experimenting with it in an illegal lab. He even denied chasing me or seeing me, making everyone believe I was crazy or on something. I had to go through a psych eval and a drug test to be released." Claire bit into the sweet, flaky pastry instead of letting anger rein her in. "The negative results sort of shamed them, which is a small but satisfying victory for me."

"Thank goodness for Auggie McGraw!"

"I never thought I would say this, but I owe him. Without him, I don't know what would have happened to me." She shivered at the thought. She had heard horror stories of undocumented migrants disappearing within the immigration detention system. Depending on how powerful or long Karl Smith's reach had been, she could have gone missing for good. "What about Cordelia? Do you have any news?"

"Not sure—"

"We released her," Torres' resonant voice boomed from outside the bedroom, interrupting Claire. "May I come in?"

Claire shifted in her bed, quickly combed through her hair with her fingers, and straightened her pajama top under Suggie's amused gaze. "Yes, come in. I want to hear everything you have regarding the investigation."

Torres stepped into the bedroom slowly, carrying a blooming blue hyacinth bulb in a small vase. "I thought this might cheer you up after yesterday's nightmare." He set the flower on the desk and stood tall in front of her bed. "You were right. Karl Smith's involved."

Whether it was because Torres admitted she was right or the fact he brought her a gift, Claire found him particularly attractive that morning. His fitted shirt outlined the lines of his muscular arms and chest, his smile

219

seemed brighter, and he trailed the scent of green apple body wash.

"We arrested Smith for Poderas' murder," the detective continued. "As you suspected, Poderas placed a phone call from Verdant Green's emergency phone. According to one of the orderlies, he was babbling about campaign money and his wife's accident. Since Verdant Green keeps a recording of all the emergency phone conversations for a week's time, we've got Poderas on tape blackmailing Smith, demanding a million dollars in campaign contributions for his silence."

Suggie pulled her notebook from her purse and waved her pen at Torres. "Okay if I take notes?"

"Be my guest. We'll be holding a press conference tomorrow morning. Feel free to enjoy these few hours of exclusivity."

Claire smiled at Torres' generous gesture. "How can you prove Smith killed Poderas?" she asked. The D.A. couldn't convict with a motive alone. The prosecution needed to establish the actus reus, prove that Smith committed the act that caused Clay Poderas' death.

"Poderas used his driver's cell. The driver overheard him arranging a meeting at Hellhole Canyon the night he was released. We traced the call back to Smith's phone. That same night, Smith got a hotel courtesy car. He didn't use the built-in GPS, but the car's odometer recorded the trip's length. The exact round trip to Hellhole Canyon and back to the Agatha hotel. His phone also pinged at a cellphone tower nearby at 5:30 am the following morning."

"What about Vee? Will Smith be charged for her murder, too?"

"I'm not sure. The D.A. said the evidence is only circumstantial."

Suggie frowned. "Circumstantial? What about the toxin and the shoeprint at the scene?"

"We can't prove the tetrodotoxin comes from Smith's factory. The vials were free of fingerprints, and no American judge would issue a warrant to search a place outside of their jurisdiction. And even if we could prove provenance, the fact that Vee visited the factory the day before—"

"Is enough to cast a reasonable doubt as to whether Vee killed herself or not," Claire said, finishing Torres' sentence. She gulped her sweet potato latte and sunk into her bed, pouting. Her Tijuana ordeal was for nothing. Talk about a worthless field trip, she thought.

"I'm really sorry." Torres sat at the edge of the bed, by Claire's feet, and placed a hand on her legs. "The only good news I can give you is that we removed the yellow tape from the house. You're now free to move back in if you wish. The owner confirmed the rental has been paid till the end of the month, and your name is on the occupant list."

Suggie sat up straight on the bed, tipping over Claire's empty mug. Her eyes widened, and her mouth fell agape in a mixture of disbelief and joy. "For real?"

Claire cracked half a smile. She was happy for Suggie. Her best friend would have her dream wedding after all and Claire herself would have the opportunity to show off her culinary skills to the Caper Cove community by catering it, which would garner her new clients. But her heart was heavy. How could she celebrate when Karl Smith wouldn't be held accountable for Vee's murder?

Suggie jumped off the bed. "I'm sorry, Claire, but do you mind if I go? I want to confirm my hair and make-up appointment and the wedding invites and send my article to *The San Diego Daily* before noon."

"You're writing for *The San Diego Daily*?"

"Yes. They've vetted me as one of their freelancers. I got the news yesterday. I didn't tell you because of all you went through."

"Oh, Suggie, this is wonderful! I'm so proud of you. Of course, go! Thanks for breakfast."

"Thanks for understanding. You're the best!" Suggie kissed Claire on the cheek, waved at Torres, and dashed through the door. "Call me if you need anything," her voice trailed off as she left.

Claire shifted on her bed, feeling almost naked in her pajamas now that she was alone with Torres. Relax, he's just a roommate, she told herself. A very good-looking, sexy roommate.

"You want me to leave your boudoir, my lady?" Torres asked, curtsying awkwardly with a smirk.

"No, it's fine," she laughed. "Where did you learn to curtsy like that?"

"By watching Jane Austen movies with my mother and sisters," he said. "You may not believe it, but they used to call me little Darcy."

Reserved, aloof, prideful, and distant, that was about right. "I believe it. How many sisters do you have?"

"Three. The oldest, Maria, is about to have a baby. I'm going to be an uncle."

Claire scooted to the empty side of the bed to make room for Torres. "Congratulations. About babies... what's going to happen to Vee's little girl?"

"The judge rejected McCarthy's paternity request and granted the grandmother temporary custody. Poderas is still considered the baby's father," Torres said as he perched at the edge of the bed. "In fact, Poderas rejected McCarthy's offer to pay him to have his name removed from the birth certificate. Poderas might have turned his wife's death into a financial opportunity, but the man was unwilling to sell his child's paternity, whether he was the biological father or not. He truly loved that kid."

Claire's lips turned into a wistful smile. "There's always a little good even in the most terrible of people, I guess." Though trying to turn the loss of his wife into a money-making machine was akin to making lemonade with lemons, Claire couldn't accept the fact Clay Poderas had been willing to keep the name of his wife's killer a secret to boost his electoral chances.

"You're going to stay in bed all day?" Torres asked.

"That's the plan." Besides a speech therapy appointment she couldn't miss, she was thinking of sulking and binging on romantic thrillers all day. "Why? You know of a paid catering opportunity?"

"I have better than that. The DMV has a last-minute cancellation for their driving test. I thought you might want to jump in. I can give you a ride if you'd like."

Claire sat upright in bed. "What time's the test?"

Torres glanced at his watch. "In an hour."

Chapter Thirty-Four

Today is going to be good, Claire repeated to herself, leaving the DMV with her driving license in hand. Now, she needed to find a job and buy herself a mode of transportation. Though Caper Cove was pedestrian-friendly, no one could survive in California without a car, especially someone who wanted to manage a successful catering business. Claire would need a vehicle with a trunk to carry the groceries or cooked dishes to wherever she catered.

She walked from the DMV to the beach and strolled along the shore, wondering how she would pay for Suggie's catering. She had pre-ordered the oysters, scallops, and sea bass, and her bills were coming due, and she still needed to shop for the side dishes' ingredients. Her cooking gig with the Fashion Warriors show was supposed to cover her food expenses, but now that the show's owner was in jail and her job was officially canceled, Claire was completely broke. She not only had to shamefully borrow $100 from Torres to pay for her driving test and DMV fees, she would also have to ask her dad for money or come clean to Suggie. Most of all, she wasn't in a cooking mood and doubted she would ever be in a festive state of mind as long as Smith wasn't held accountable for Vee's death.

The ebbing tide had uncovered thousands of tiny clams and attracted the local sandpipers and seagulls to the shoreline. The birds picked at the sand, ignoring Claire's passage. The stormy clouds were long gone, and a mid-April sun was gently warming the land. Off the coast, sailboats glided on the water's surface, their billowing sails resembling bright butterflies.

"Hey, Frenchie. I heard about your stunt at the border. I wished I'd been there to film it," Dylan Fletcher greeted her as he approached, his drone controller in hand. "You alright?"

"I'm fine, thank you for asking," she replied, wishing the police station clerk was a little more discreet when it came to people's personal dealings. "I just got in a lot of trouble for nothing."

"I read in the Caper Cove Whisper about Karl Smith and the tetro-thingy tubes you can't use against him. That really sucks." Dylan glanced at her, still keeping an eye on his drone, and smiled. "You think you'd be willing to reenact the scene for me or let me interview you for my documentary?"

"I'll pass on the reenactment, but I'll do a Q&A." Between her firm's explosion and the border kerfuffle, Claire had had enough action for a lifetime, but the interview, if broadcast, could bring her catering clients. "I'll need to approve the questions first."

Claire tracked the drone with her eyes as the device hovered over hill properties where many wealthy vacationers, including celebrities, retreated for some peace and quiet far from the crowds. "Aren't you entering a no-fly zone right now?"

"Sort of, but I won't get in trouble. I'm keeping this for my private collection, so no one will find out." He pushed his thumbs on the control sticks, making the drone dive away from the cliff. "You aren't going to rat me out, right?"

"Don't worry, I won't, but I have to ask you something. Did you fly your drone over Golden Peak last Tuesday, by chance? In the morning between 10 AM and noon." Maybe his drone had captured Vee right before she fell, Claire thought. Maybe the recording would show whether or not she was alone or what prompted her to fall.

Dylan simpered. "Probably. I've been filming every morning for the past fifteen days for a timelapse promotional video I'm doing for the Caper Cove Tourism Bureau." The young man manipulated his controller a little longer and landed his drone on the sand in front of Claire. "You want to buy me a beer while I go through my videos?"

Claire's heart skipped a beat as hope rushed through her. "I can buy you a beer, sure. I can also add a serving of tacos if you give me a copy of the video, if you have it," she proposed, extending her hand.

"Deal." He shook on it.

* * *

Though her tab at The Osprey was climbing steadily, Claire added a dessert to Dylan's order before calling Torres. Dylan Fletcher's drone had caught Karl Smith's premeditating Vee's murder on tape, and Claire had the video proof on her cellphone.

"I'm so sorry that happened to your friend. That's so F-ed up. I hope you catch the guy," Dylan said as he sipped his drink.

"I'm going to make sure of it." Claire wiped her eyes with a paper napkin and dialed Torres' number.

Unlike the night before, the detective picked up right away. "What's wrong? Is everything alright?"

"I'm fine. I just wanted to let you know that I have the irrefutable evidence that Karl Smith is responsible for Vee's death," she whispered over the phone, her voice filled with a mix of anger and sorrow.

"What is it?"

"A video of Vee's murder." Claire swallowed hard, trying to clear her throat from the grief tightening her neck. "Can you make sure Chief Ernshaw and the D.A. are there?" Claire couldn't wait for such an evil man to be charged with her friend's murder, and she didn't want to have to repeat herself. Then she texted Suggie.

CLAIRE: <Can you pick me up at The Osprey right away? I have a scoop for you. I need to go to the police to bring them the proof that Karl Smith did it.>

SUGGIE: <On my way>

* * *

As promised, Chief Ernshaw and the District Attorney were waiting in the police station conference room with Torres. Vikram was also in attendance, probably as a forensic expert familiar with the case. The room was equipped with a state-of-the-art smart board prominently displayed on the wall. After a quick introduction, Claire connected her phone to the police Wi-Fi and airdropped the video right onto the screen.

"This is an aerial view of Caper Cove from a drone," she explained as the video showed a bird's-eye view of the shore and the village, travelling slowly toward Golden Peak.

"Here." Claire paused the video and zoomed in on the image of the three-hundred-step staircase linking the beach to the private villa. She zoomed in further until the screen showed the bay window of 179 Golden View. The picture was so crisp and detailed that they could clearly see the furniture inside the villa, more particularly the inside of Vee Brooks' room and the person inside.

"That close-up is crazy clear. Who's inside?" Torres asked.

"Hold on," Claire zoomed in to the maximum. When she pushed Play, the video resumed, showing Karl Smith pulling an insulin pen from his pocket and placing it on top of Vee's insulin supply bag.

"Everybody knew Vee's insulin injection schedule because the show's filming hours and meal breaks paralleled it," Claire explained. "Smith knew that every lunch break, Vee would first give herself an insulin injection and proceed to eat lunch. It was like a predictable, well-oiled clock, and Smith used that to his advantage. He tainted Vee's insulin with tetrodotoxin, knowing she would be injecting herself at 12:30 PM sharp."

"Why didn't Vee go with the film crew?" The prosecutor asked, his eyes riveted to the screen that showed Karl Smith grabbing Vee's sparkling phone and setting it at the cliff's very edge.

"Vee wasn't the most social of creatures. Unlike the film crew, she preferred to stay in, and that day, she was waiting for me. She had ordered sushi like she always did on the first day of filming. Sort of a superstitious tradition, the same way people wear the same lucky tie when they go for an interview."

"Could she have been saved if someone had arrived earlier?" The prosecutor asked again, calculating the evilness of Smith's act, probably mentally drafting the argument he would use in the case.

Claire shook her head, her eyes welling up with tears. "I thought about that a lot."

Vikram placed a comforting hand on her shoulder. "With the amount of toxin in the syringe, there was no way we could have saved her. The toxin affected her nervous system as soon as she injected herself."

Silence settled in the room as everyone watched Vee desperately searching for her phone and stumbling outside.

"Because there was no one there to help and no landline to call, the only thing Vee had to save herself was to call 911. What she didn't know was that Smith had moved her phone from her desk to the cliff's edge, knowing she would be looking for it," Claire resumed, her voice faltering. "That's why Smith called her from the restaurant, at 12:31 PM, one minute after she always injected herself. While pretending to call to ask her if she wanted something else for lunch, he ensured the phone ring would catch Vee's attention. Since it was the only way she could get help, Vee was forced to get to the cliff's edge to get her phone." Claire's voice faded as tears filled her eyes and her throat. She turned away from the screen, unable to watch her friend fall to her death again.

"What's your take on this, Dr. Thomas?" the D.A. asked.

"There's no cure for tetrodotoxin poisoning. The toxin works extremely fast, weakening and paralyzing the muscles. As you saw, Ms. Brooks started shaking right after the injection."

"What about you, Detective Torres? What can you tell us about the condition of the terrain?"

"After the past days of rain, the cliff was extremely unstable. It's no surprise the rim collapsed under Brooks when she tried to reach her phone. The video clearly showed Smith placing Brooks' phone at the edge of the precipice and later Vee plunging to her death because of it."

"What about the text?" the prosecutor added, questioning them about every piece of evidence to make sure his case was airtight.

Claire stopped the video. "Smith must have gotten into Vee's phone earlier that day. Her lock was her daughter's birthday, so easy to guess. He must have scheduled the goodbye text to be sent to everyone on the Fashion

Warriors crew. So when the text went out, they were all in the restaurant, and it appeared Vee killed herself by jumping to her death."

The D.A. rubbed his chin between his thumb and forefinger. "There may be privacy issues here with the use of a drone by a third party over private property."

Claire shook her head. "There won't be. As an official resident on the villa's rental contract, I gave my permission to Dylan Fletcher to fly over and film the property."

* * *

Later that same afternoon, a Tijuana judge issued an "orden de cateo," a search warrant of Smith's textile factory. The Mexican police found tubes of tetrodotoxin, which they handed to Detective Torres. The tetrodotoxin samples were a perfect match with the toxin that killed Vee.

The next morning, Karl Smith was officially charged with the first-degree murders of Vee Brooks and Clay Poderas, along with many other charges, including obstruction of justice and knowingly selling or distributing fabrics contaminated with illegal carcinogenic dyes.

Chapter Thirty-Five

L ater that day, Claire moved to the private villa. Catering Suggie's wedding in less than five days required an early set up of the kitchen. Claire also needed a quiet place to retreat and fulfill her duties as executor of Vee's estate. The next days would be a juggling act of grocery shopping to fill an empty pantry, meal planning, clearing Vee's room, and carrying out her executorial duties. It felt strange settling into an empty mansion. It was so quiet in comparison to D.C.'s urban life with the constant sound of car horns or the beach apartment with the warm chatter of The Osprey customers below.

"You sure you want to be alone? I don't mind spending the night with you," Suggie proposed as she followed Claire through the empty house. "It would be like old times when we had sleepovers all summer."

"Yes, I'm sure. Enjoy Daniel's presence before he deploys. After that, we'll have as many sleepovers as we want."

The blue room welcomed her into its azurean décor. Claire collapsed on the bed and scanned the room, her throat tight. Vee had picked that room on purpose: the blueish-white walls were soothing, the lush green private garden outside the window was invigorating, and the blue theme represented freedom. All the elements Claire had needed to recover after the D.C. tragedy and the perfect place to regroup and think.

"It's great. The room has its own fancy wood hangers," Suggie said as she transferred Claire's clothes from the luggage to the closet. "How long are you going to stay here?"

"Two weeks. That's the length of the lease. After that, I'm probably returning to my dad's."

"That'll make him so happy. He loves to have you near him, and I think Torres does, too," Suggie said. She gaped at Claire with a playful duck face, her eyelids fluttering as if enamored.

"That's exactly why I can't stay there. I love my dad, but it's weird having to share a bathroom with a strangerish man." Torres was far from a stranger now, but he wasn't family yet. Claire didn't want, one day, to forget to lock the door and for Torres to find her seated on the bathroom throne reading a fashion magazine. Plus, familiarity was said to breed contempt.

"A sexy, strangerish man."

"It doesn't matter how handsome and smart Ben is, or how many sparks I feel when I see him. Romantic connections with roommates are like minefields."

"So you *do* feel a spark," Suggie teased.

"That's not the point. I need my privacy and my independence." Vee's death had stirred up haunting, painful memories of her sister's disappearance, which Claire had spent years denying. Though years of avoidance had offered temporary relief, her craving for truth was now catching up with her. And she was ravenous. She wouldn't let another loved one's or friend's death/disappearance go left unresolved and was better investigating alone without the input or the nosiness of her roommate-cop.

"Okay. Okay." Suggie laughed. "Returning to your wardrobe, don't you own anything that doesn't have a designer label? You could make money just by selling a few pieces online."

Claire nodded. Her law firm's employee benefits had been more than generous, and with all the clothes she owned, Claire was sartorially set for her lifetime, sparing her the need to buy any new clothes. But now, Claire needed to face her new life and the harsh reality of job hunting.

"Of course I do. See?" Claire pulled a worn college t-shirt out of her bag and waved it in front of Suggie before shoving it into a drawer.

Once the luggage was empty and all the clothes were neatly folded in a dresser or hung in the closet, Claire hugged Suggie as thanks for her help.

"Why don't you pick an outfit from my wardrobe? Anything you like, it's yours." Except for the few extra pounds Claire had gained during her "chocolate and beignets" recovery, Claire and Suggie had always been about the same size.

"Are you serious? I can't. You're already catering my wedding. I can't take advantage of you like that."

"Fine. I'm going to pick it myself." Claire sorted through her haute couture wardrobe, appreciating the unique personality and memory embedded in each garment—what she wore during which legal case, in whose company, or at which specific meeting or gala.

Suggie was laughing. "Don't waste your time. I'll never take the clothes off your back."

At the end of the clothes rack was an unfamiliar thick black garment bag with Claire's name on it.

"What's that? It isn't mine," Claire pulled the heavy clothes bag out of the closet and laid it on the bed. She assumed it was Vee's secret collection, a set of outfits so unique, Vee had to keep it hidden from fashion spies. "Vee must have written my name on the bag to mislead the curious."

"Let's check." Suggie rushed to Claire's side and helped her unzip the plastic carrier.

Instead of a new collection, Claire found six gowns in the bag. Five of them were the winning dresses that had earned Vee first place in the second season of Fashion Warriors and a place in the Fashion Warriors All-Stars finale. The sixth one was brand new. It was a gorgeous organza dress whose layers of varying blues were reminiscent of a cloud.

"That's my dream dress," Claire whispered as emotions stole her voice. A golden crown had been embroidered on the right sleeve, and the gown had pockets. In one of them, Claire found a note and an envelope full of one hundred dollar bills. Plenty to pay all the contractors and the food for the wedding.

"That's at least five grand," Suggie said, glancing at the envelope's contents with her accountant's eyes. "What does the note say?"

With trembling hands, Claire brought the note close to her teary eyes.

"You were there for me when I only had ghosts by my side. Now it's my turn to take care of you. (1) Do with the dresses whatever you please, wear them, sell them, or burn them. They are all yours. (2) The envelope is for the legal fees I never paid you. Use it to jump-start your catering business or to find your sister. If you think she's out there, I believe you. (3) The crown on the dress is to remind you what you once said to me: on the darkest days, when you feel inadequate, unloved, and unworthy, remember you mean the world to me and straighten your crown."

* * *

Claire spent the next two days handling Vee's estate. She closed Vee's bank account and transferred the funds to a trust she opened for Eva Claire, Vee's daughter. Her late friend didn't have much besides the clothes she made and a sketchbook of designs. Claire contracted with a publisher for the sketchbook to be turned into a book. The proceeds of its sale would go toward the trust fund to provide for Eva Claire's care and education. She also handed Vee's wardrobe to a clearing house to be sold at auction the following week, to benefit San Diego Blooms, according to Vee's testamentary wishes. The news of Vee's death had rocked the fashion and reality TV worlds, and everyone seemed to be wanting a piece of Vee's creations. Claire kept Vee's favorite pieces of clothing aside for Eva Claire, so the three-month-old baby would get to wear some of her late mother's designs when she came of age.

Claire concluded her executor duties by holding a bonfire memorial for Vee, the evening of her friend's funeral. She had rented the outside patio of The Osprey, took over the giant fire pit, and set up a buffet—a sample of Vee's favorite dishes from sushi, mini-quiches, and smoked salmon canapés to mini-hot dogs and pizza bites.

Claire had invited Nina Rock, the youth counselor, and the youth group Vee had sponsored—two dozen teenagers dressed up in handcrafted suits and gowns that turned the beach into a runway show, just like Vee would have wanted. The Fashion Warriors crew was also in attendance, including Vinyl, the participant who had disappeared on the other side of the border.

"I was gone for a day, and when I returned, the show's canceled, and I'm having dinner on the beach," Vinyl said as he piled up his plate with food to vertiginous heights.

"Max Vinyl Berkley?" Torres grabbed him by the sleeve and walked him away from the buffet before he toppled his plate. "I don't know what you ingested, but you may be a little high. You disappeared for eight days. Your family's really worried. You should give them a call."

The yellow sun slid below the horizon, streaking the sky in pink and orange hues. A gentle breeze carried a sense of serenity through the air as it played with the bonfire's flickering flames. One of the guests was playing the ukulele, and Suggie was taking pictures and interviewing people for an article—a short profile on Vee for a fashion magazine.

"Thank you for everything you did," Mrs. Poderas said. The grandmother was holding Vee's baby who was stretching her pudgy little arms toward Claire. "You mind holding her?"

"I'd love to." Claire picked up the babbling infant and cradled her against her chest, feeling the little heart beating fast against her. Vee's memory would live through her beautiful daughter.

Mrs. Poderas pulled a folded sheet of paper from her large purse and handed it to Claire. "I'm not sure if you're interested, but just in case you are. This is a list of fashion collectors interested in Vee's dresses. I wanted to let you know. Then, she pulled out her smartphone and took a few pictures of Claire with the baby.

"We're going to go. It's getting late and a bit chilly for Eva Claire, but I wanted to make sure to have a few pictures of you and the memorial. I will text you the one of you and Eva Claire," Mrs. Poderas said as she carefully and softly took the baby from Claire's arms. "Ready to leave Auntie Claire?" she asked the baby.

Claire kissed the babbling baby and secured her in the car seat stroller Mrs. Poderas had brought with her. "Can I walk you out?"

"No need. My chauffeur is waiting for us in the parking lot." The older woman enveloped Claire in a long, tight embrace only mothers know how to give. "Please, stay in touch."

"I will," Claire promised with a heavy heart as she watched the woman and the baby disappear into the twilight.

As the night grew darker, the number of guests dwindled along with the fire until there were none. The stars blinked brightly in the unclouded sky, promising a radiant next day. The rhythmic ebb and flow of the waves lapping on the shore sounded like a lullaby.

"Hey, stranger," Torres said, leaving the medley of laughter and clinking of glasses coming from The Osprey behind. He smiled, his eyes and teeth sparkling with the distant glow of moonlight. "The apartment misses you."

Claire laughed, secretly wanting to whisper that she missed the apartment too. "I'll be back soon after Suggie's wedding."

"Your dad can't stop talking about his daughter, the great chef, and the upcoming wedding. He's making the entire police force salivate with details of the menu. He says that he wants to hire you, but you declined?"

"He doesn't need me. He wants to give me a job out of pity." Between the free rent and the open tab at The Osprey, Claire had accepted enough of his help. She didn't want her return to Caper Cove to be as a dependent. "I want a job unrelated to my dad."

"About that... Chief Ernshaw wondered if you'd be interested in becoming a police consultant from time to time. You know, to help with the more demanding cases. Not that we expect to have any more murders in town."

"I appreciate the offer, but if I can choose, I'd prefer cooking. It's quieter and has a more controlled environment."

"Of course. No pressure. Just something to think about," he said, typing on his phone. "I've just texted you the form to fill out in case you change your mind."

Claire checked her beeping watch. "Got it! I have to go now. With only two and a half days to cater a wedding, I need all the sleep I can get."

"Do you need a hand?" Torres proposed.

Claire giggled. "For what, tucking me in?"

Torres looked at her with tender eyes and a gentle smile. "I mean, for the wedding. I'm pretty good in the kitchen, and I'm overdue for some time off. I would be happy to help."

Claire paused. She chewed on her lips as she considered the offer. "I do need strong arms to carry cases of oysters and champagne, and I wouldn't reject a willing sous-chef," she said. She had recovered from the explosion, but still needed to take it easy, especially after her Tijuana trip. "Can you drop by the villa tomorrow morning at nine?

"I sure can," he said with a wide grin.

"One more thing," she said, hesitating. "Would you like to be my plus one at the wedding?"

Torres grinned. "I'd love to. Is that a date?"

"Let's not put a label on it."

"So it's a date."

Chapter Thirty-Six

Suggie and Daniel's wedding day was like a fairy tale. The bride and the groom exchanged their vows on the green lawn overlooking the ocean. The parcel of dirt surrounding the beach staircase landing had been fenced off, and blooming daffodils were blanketing the grounds in bursts of yellow. As Vee used to say, "Find joy and celebrate where sorrow once stood so good karma can fill the world."

The florist had transformed the infinity pool into a lotus pond and a violinist performed choreographed songs of the couple's favorite music albums. Floral displays guided the guests to the reception area inside where tulips of vivid shades of pink, orange, and red had turned the ballroom into a rainbow of colors.

"This was so perfect. The French-Korean fusion dishes and the whole dinner… I don't know how I could ever repay you," Suggie said, pulling Claire to the dance floor.

"This is what best friends are for," Claire replied, following the beat of the music.

Remarkably, throughout the entire time she was on her feet catering the wedding and up to now, her back hadn't troubled her at all. She felt a sense of physical contentment. Returning home, cooking for the ones you love seemed to work wonders for her well-being.

"Distinguished guests, may I remind you that this is the second to the last dance," the DJ warned. "So grab your loved one or secret crush and enjoy."

"Oh, I better find Daniel, *my husband*. I so love that word. *My husband*." Suggie giggled as she trotted away to retrieve the groom.

"Will my famous daughter give me the honor of this dance?" Frank Fontaine asked as he grabbed Claire by the hand. He had traded his turquoise surfing shorts, matching T-shirt, and flip-flops for a Navy blue suit and closed-toe shoes, prompting comments of admiration and amusement from the wedding crowd.

"Dad, of course, you can have this dance. For the record, I'm not famous, just trendy."

"Tomayto, tomahto. I heard that you are turning down jobs now. Is that true?"

Claire laughed. "Yes, it is. But that's because I can't hold down two catering jobs at once or clone myself."

Suggie's blog, the Caper Cove Whisper, had exploded in popularity. The covering of her wedding preparation with flashbacks to Vee Brooks' story and Claire's investigation went viral. The Southern California Tribune picked up the story and asked Suggie to write a profile on Claire, an article her friend titled "CLAIRE FONTAINE, THE FRENCH CHEF AND SLEUTH WHO SOLVED THE CASE."

"I've received so many job offers, I'm booked for the entire year." Strangely enough, Claire's French accent and sleuthing skills had increased her popularity in town. She was scheduled for week-end-long murder mystery dinners, and hotels wanted her to hold weekly cooking classes.

"The newspaper has been calling you the French chef. Are you okay with that?"

"Right now, yes. It's not something I can change anyway. It's only by owning our struggles and embracing what makes us unique that we grow, isn't it? That's what mom used to say."

"Your mom was right. Is that why you stopped your speech therapy and started French lessons with Roxy?" Frank asked with paternalistic concern in his voice.

"I haven't completely stopped speech therapy. I just put my sessions on hold for a little while." Though she wanted to sound like her old self, her accent had given her a different perspective on the world, and Claire wanted to dig deeper into that—what it meant to be an American with a Foreign

Accent Syndrome and proving to the world that one doesn't need a standard American accent to be a true American.

"If I sound French, might as well embrace the whole French chef personality," she joked, withholding the fact that becoming French might be the perfect way to "relocate and stay low" as the FBI had suggested she do after her law firm bombing. "Isn't life about reinventing yourself when an opportunity presents itself?"

"Cheers to that!" her father said, waltzing her around the floor. "Do you have any new projects in mind?"

"Just catering, Dad," she lied, knowing her father would never understand her digging into their past to find out what happened to her sister. "Just catering."

"Excuse me, Frank, but I'd like to ask Claire for this last dance," Torres said, cutting in on the pair as the tender melody of a slow dance emanated from the speakers. He extended his open palm to Claire. "Would you give me the honor of the last dance of the night, Mademoiselle?"

Claire smiled, put her hand in his, and let him guide her. "With pleasure, Monsieur," she replied in French.

Acknowledgements

Special thanks to Verena Rose and Shawn Reilly Simmons of Level Best Books for believing in my story, and to Deborah Well. My heartfelt gratitude to the Pitch Wars mentees class of 2015 for their support and camaraderie through the writing journey, especially Alison Miller, critique partner extraordinaire; to Jonathan Maberry and his Writers Coffeehouse meetings, for stressing that writing is as much a business as it is an art; to Kate Jackson for her guidance in the world of published mystery writers; to Gretchen McNeil for inspiring me as a writer and fashionista; Dennis Crosby for his literary memes; and Mairi Kilaine for her friendship. With love and thank you to my sons, Aiden and Neil, for their unwavering belief in me, and to my husband, Tony, for reading all my manuscripts.

About the Author

Elle Jauffret is a French-born American lawyer, former criminal attorney for the California Attorney General's office, and culinary enthusiast. She holds a Master of Laws from Université Côte d'Azur Law School (France) and a Juris Doctorate from the George Washington University Law School (USA). She is an avid consumer of mystery and adventure stories in all forms, especially escape rooms. She is a member of Mystery Writers of America, Sisters In Crime, and International Thriller Writers. She lives in Southern California with her family. You can find her at https://ellejauffret.com or on social media @ellejauffret.

SOCIAL MEDIA HANDLES:
  https://www.instagram.com/ellejauffret/
  https://www.facebook.com/elle.jauffret
  https://www.threads.net/@ellejauffret

AUTHOR WEBSITE:
  https://ellejauffret.com

Printed in the USA
CPSIA information can be obtained
at www.ICGtesting.com
LVHW090753011124
795258LV00001B/1

9 781685 127510